CONJURING TIBET

CHARLOTTE PAINTER

CONJURING TIBET

MERCURY HOUSE
SAN FRANCISCO

Published in the United States of America by Mercury House, San Francisco, California, a nonprofit publishing company devoted to the free exchange of ideas and guided by a dedication to literary values.

United States Constitution, First Amendment: Congress shall make no law respecting an establishment of religion, or prohibiting the free exercise thereof; or abridging the freedom of speech, or of the press; or the right of the people peaceably to assemble, and to petition the Government for a redress of grievances.

Printed on recycled, acid-free paper and manufactured in the United States of America.

Designed by Thomas Christensen.

Cover images (clockwise from top left): "Standing Maitreya" (9th–10th c., Museum of Art, New York); 19th c. engraving; Woman making a temple offering, from Barbara J. Scot, *The Violet Shyness of Their Eyes* (Corvallis: Calyx Books, 1993); Unnamed peak in the Makalu massif, from Daniel Taylor-Ide, *Something Hidden Behind the Ranges* (San Francisco: Mercury House, 1995).

Library of Congress Cataloguing-in-Publication Data:
Painter, Charlotte.
Conjuring Tibet : a novel / by Charlotte Painter.
p. cm.
ISBN 1-56279-095-1 (alk. paper)
1. Americans—Travel—Tibet—Fiction. I. Title.
PS3566.A346C66 1996
813′.54—DC20 96-42526
CIP

9 8 7 6 5 4 3 2 1
FIRST EDITION

For my son,
Thomas Voorhees

NOTE

This book is based on a diary and fiction notes I kept while on a visit to Tibet just before the Tiananmen Square massacre. Long before the advent of Communism in China, the thirteenth Dalai Lama said this to England's consular representative in Tibet, Sir Charles Bell: "The Chinese way is to say or do something mild at first, then to wait a bit, and if it passes without objection, to say or do something stronger. If this is objected to, they reply that what they said or did had been misinterpreted and really meant nothing." This national trait persists, widely evident now in China's diplomacy and shifty stance on human rights.

The facts of the Cultural Revolution launched by Chairman Mao Tse-tung in the Sixties have come out—the Red Guard's torture and imprisonment of dissidents and intellectuals and suspected anti-Communists, and the systematic destruction of cultural and religious art and monastaries, which was especially devastating in Tibet. Though the Chinese still forbid Tibetans to travel outside China, many manage to escape continuing oppression by fleeing into India, where the fourteenth Dalai Lama has created a constitutional democracy for more than 100,000 refugees.

Charles Bell understood that Tibet remained remote from world affairs because of a leaning toward spiritual development, which might not lead to material progress. The country's riches—gold, forests, strategic territory—remained unexploited until China grew powerful enough to claim them. That move precipitated an agonizing awakening for the Tibetan people, whose high deserts and mountainous terrain had kept them in isolation even from one another. As Tibetans awoke to the modern world, they also came to the realization that they had something to offer it. More than five million Westerners now follow some form of Buddhist practice.

There is a global meaning in a term from Tibetan philosophy, "dependent arisings," which signifies the interrelatedness of all beings in a mutual dependency. The Dalai Lama's work is directed toward that realization among nations as well as in the spiritual lives of individuals. Although he remains a man without a country, his life stands as a reminder to the world of how inadequate our grasp is of the mystery that the Chinese ancients called the mandate of heaven.

In taking my journey, I think I was looking for a path through the imagination, which Einstein said is better than knowledge, to a ground where no boundaries hinder the mind. I anticipated experience of one of the last far places on earth untainted by the debris of tourism, of vast snowdrifts beneath brilliant cloudless blue, of silences broken by the creaking of snow that precedes avalanche, of mantra intoned from a cliff-side cave, of mysterious scat left by unseen hairy creatures, of the unexpected encounter with a rare bird arising mirage-like from a desert plateau. As I think of the many writings about Tibet, from European colonials and adventurers, mountain trekkers, religious seekers, and even Tibetans who know the country well, I sense that same desire—to conjure a place where one may find some proof of rare qualities in oneself or enter a spell in which some insight occurs, in a reign of peace, a feast of the soul.

The Dalai Lama may be counting on that universal hope in his "five-point" proposal to the world that Tibet be released from Chinese dominance and made into a nuclear-free zone for the study of peace and ecology, for everyone must have a Tibet, whether we call it Shangri-lá or Shambhala or Bali H'ai or Camelot.

I owe a debt to many people for advice about Tibetan doctrine, though they might prefer not to be named by one who has taken such liberties with it as I have here. Errors of fact and theology are entirely my own, but I would like to express my appreciation of the Tibetans who have so generously helped me. I'm grateful, too, to my insightful readers, Nell Altizer, Josephine Carson, Mary Jane Moffat, and Frances Mayes, and to my dedicated editor, Thomas Christensen.

—C. P.

Given the gulf between being and knowing,
man has no choice but to make and believe
in some fiction or other

—Chinua Achebe

CONJURING TIBET

I

1959. The Tibetan woman struggled until they reached the narrow suspension bridge. Then above the swift river her body went still. The two Chinese soldiers turned her back to them as they bound her hands behind her. They didn't want to look at her face. She was a young woman, but her face was not young, was too terrible to look at, ferocious, crazed, and her hair rose above it in a tangled corona of black. They had stripped her, and could see chill mounds rising on her flesh as she stood naked on the river bank.

This took place on a bitterly cold, cloudy day in a remote desert in Kham. One of the men bent down to bind the woman's ankles, slender ankles for a Tibetan's. The rope slapped against the sand where her feet dug in. They had beaten her on the legs earlier, but she had stopped bleeding; in fact, the men felt edgy because they could no longer see any trace of the whip on her calves. Next they lifted her. One seized her shoulders, the other her ankles, and they ran with her onto the shaky bridge. They held her facedown over the rushing water.

Ever since they were stationed there eight years ago, she had jeered at the soldiers and spat in their eyes. She had hexed them into strange suicides and sent tigers to attack them. She had even called up ghosts of ancestors the Chinese had exorcised from their minds by self-criticism. She was insane—their commanding officer had decided that. They wouldn't look at her face, and so they did not see its fiery concentration. They simply flung her into the agitated water, then turned and walked back to the horses they had taken from her ranch.

As they were mounting, they heard shouts from a settlement across the river. A number of Tibetans were hurrying down to the riverbank. The soldiers smirked at one another, for they knew the woman could never be rescued. The current would have already taken her half a mile downstream. Anyone trying to get to her would drown in that surging water. It was over for the witch.

The soldiers angled the horses toward the bank, to enjoy the futile effort of the natives. The Tibetans had waded waist deep into the water, were crying, reaching out their hands. All at once their voices rose in something like a cheer. The soldiers looked down then, and they saw the woman. She was not drowned but had rotated face up, her arms and feet still tied. Chill mounds formed now on their own flesh under their khaki uniforms. Even at that distance they could see her eyes, as brilliantly lit as if a shaft of sunlight had parted the clouds to illumine them. She rode the wild river, her hair spread out behind her head like spikes of cast iron. She lay calmly, floating toward her people. She was floating *upstream.*

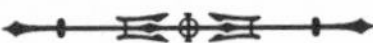

In May of 1989, more than thirty years after that incident, I went to Tibet to visit the woman with power over river currents. I accompanied a young nephew of hers, who had not returned to Tibet since infancy.

We were making the trip on behalf of the woman's brother. Tibetans are loyal. The brother, who had become a refugee in 1959 after the Chinese occupied his country, and who was now a US citizen widely respected as a lama and meditation master, still supported several villages in his homeland where he was remembered with fierce devotion. The only way he knew to get money to his people was hand-to-hand. He meant to bring funds he had raised for them, in a return after long exile. But his plans underwent a sudden change when he learned that even after so long a time the Chinese intended to kill him. And so, instead, he was sending his nephew, Lama Mingme, and asked me to go along.

Mingme is not a real name, but the Tibetan equivalent of No-name. I'll call his uncle "C"—C. for Chinese, or indeed my own first initial. This is the mode used by some Asian teachers to suggest the unimportance of personal identity; Krishnamurti, for example, was often called "K," and Gurdjieff "G." That is not usual the Tibetan way; followers show respect by stringing out long titles, such as His Eminence The Venerable Lama Tulku Rinpoche So-and-So; hierarchy is very much built into the Tibetan mind and heart. But the initial suits my purposes of anonymity for this tale.

In the Hong Kong airport, as Lama Mingme watched for our luggage on the chute, I glanced among the crowd of placards held aloft for incoming passengers, looking for the young woman who would be going with us as Chinese translator. We would fly together into Chengdu, the capital of Sichuan province, and from there go westward overland into Tibet.

Lama Mingme quickly spotted my pack and grasped it with shaking hands, giving me a heart-faced grin, as if to say, "See?" He had wrapped around the handle a white crumpled rag, a scrap of *khata.* That is the silk scarf Tibetans give one another as a respectful greeting, rather like a Hawaiian lei but offered on the open palms, head bowed. I had several others folded away inside my bag. Straightening his clothing, a yellow shirt under maroon robes, he said, "I told you we find easy at this end with *khata.* No problem." I took the tremor in Lama Mingme's hands for nervous excitement. All his wiry, eager frame seemed to tremble.

A sign with his name on it appeared, a small and slender young woman with black shoulder-length hair waving it above her head. This was Dorje, a Hong Kong student of Buddhism. Hers was also an adopted Tibetan name. When we joined her on the other side of the gate, she took my bag and efficiently herded us into a taxi. I told her the name of the hotel where I had made a reservation.

Nothing would do but that we stay in her family's apartment. "Like all one family," she insisted, giving the driver her address. We headed into the city's stifling heat, and up the slopes of Hong Kong's skyscraping hillside.

Dorje, twenty-five maybe, piquant and curious in her broken English, was astonishingly wised up and direct. Almost at once in the cab she wormed out of Lama Mingme that he was no older than she, that Lama was a common Nepalese surname he had assumed when he took out his Nepalese passport. He was not a real lama, had not undertaken the three- to six-year retreat necessary to qualify; his title was an honorific given him because he managed a meditation center in the US. Realizing he was no further advanced in Buddhist studies than herself, she asked, "What I am to call you?" He conceded she should drop the "Lama."

"You think we meet the Khandro in Tibet?" Dorje asked. Mingme said he hoped so. The Khandro was "C's" sister, the woman who could float upcurrent. The notebook I carried with me, aside from notes for a novel and other jottings, held stories of a number of Tibetan women as well as of the Khandro. She was regarded by her people as a seer; *Khandro* is *dakini* in Sanskrit. The word literally means "sky dancer," one whose powers of mind extend to the skies. The first time I heard it, *Khandro* sounded like *conjure* to my untutored ear, and so that was how I thought of her, as a conjure woman. Tibetan women supposedly have greater status than women anywhere else in Asia. In some parts of Tibet a female only child is considered the root of the family and manages its affairs when the parents die, and so the Khandro runs the monastery property where she lives.

"Khandro very magic. Chinese tried execute her," Lama Mingme grinned. "She bend bullets."

"I know the story," I said. I had a version of it written in the notebook I carried with me. "It gets better every time I hear it."

Sizing me up from that remark, Dorje said, "You not real Buddhist," to which I had to say, "True." Then I added, "But not unreal either." At that she gave a high, rippling laugh.

The sanity of the Buddha's philosophy drew me, but my suspicion of the participation mystique has kept me away from the consolations of all religion. My imagination is taken by the tensions of a woman like the Khandro just because she shows a strong ego. Logic can explain away her magic in the river as the luck of a reverse current, but a woman pressing with all her will against the tide, the trend of things, even against logic—that's individualism, not a trait greatly admired in Asia.

Dorje wanted to know next: "How old you?"

I replied somewhat evasively, "Old enough to have a son as old as you."

Again she laughed and asked, "Not afraid of trip?" When I shook my head, she pursued her inquiries, "Why you want go? What your son think of trip?"

Three conditions keep us on the wheel of life according to the tenets of Dorje's faith: desire, aversion, and ignorance. Ignorance is the most difficult of these to identify for oneself—a vast, unmeasured quagmire where doubt lies adrift with the seven deadly sins. I was a doubting pilgrim, ignorant of my own purposes. I knew that we needn't actually go anywhere to be pilgrims, that the pilgrim spirit arises through awareness of the brevity of life, is impelled by its mystery.

I didn't answer Dorje at once, seeing again my son's forgiving gaze as he brought up the subject of my mother, who was ill. He was working as a technician in a hospital near her nursing home. Would he have to see my mother through her death in my absence?

That common American disorder, the denial of death, was denied to me early in life, widowed first at twenty-eight, then again shortly after my second marriage at thirty-six. And for many years now my mother has suffered from a lingering illness that will eventually bring her to death. It was no wonder I was drawn to Tibetan philosophy, which teaches the acceptance of death as a transitional part of life. Simone Weil, that severe saint and mentor for disbelievers, who even after her conversion to Catholicism refused baptism, wrote that in early youth she realized the human task was to adopt a right attitude toward the problems of this world rather than to wonder about God's existence. However, she also held a belief, which I share, that the moment of death was the center and object of life ... "an instant of pure truth, naked, certain, and eternal ..."

I can imagine my mother's death, already on its inevitable course, but can I imagine my own, as Tibetan teachings advise? A plane crash, a failure of heart? Visitors sometimes do not return from Tibet, sometimes die of altitude sickness or of falls into a watery chasm or an abyss of snow. Was I racing my mother to death's door?

Probably Lama Mingme also wondered why I had agreed to come along. *Why, why, why?*—the question of adolescence. My experience in life had not brought me wisdom, but at least I knew that *how* was a more appropriate question for maturity. How to live the rest of it in the right way, how to die.

I told Dorje my son was a little puzzled about my trip. My restless travels had been more than a puzzle in his life, for when he was small I had often left him with my mother. Behind his forbearing look lay a history of my intermittent childhood absence from him.

Dorje explained the feng shui of Hong Kong as we ascended its peak. "Five dragon lines run down from the peak, positive currents in underground water. All carry good chi, follow direction of magnetic fields. Lines meet in central business district. Is why Hong Kong so auspicious for money." The secret of Hong Kong's marketing success revealed!

Dorje's family, however, has evidently not prospered in this city where money is king. We entered a slum, as Dorje explained to us how very expensive their apartment was. From the downslant of the street we could see straight to the ocean under a cloudy, cindery sky. Our cab pulled up in a narrow alleyway, darkened by highrise buildings on all sides. Dorje led us into the dim hallway and pointed the way to her door on the first floor. Beside the door a bouquet of wilted roses lay on a piece of cardboard, along with several crumbled cookies and a burnt-out candle. Seeing I took notice of these objects, Dorje said, "My mother in Canton visit her sister now, but she always leave offering for household guardians."

She led us into the shabby railroad apartment. "My mother pray to local deities when I growing up. I never believe in them, so have no faith. Then about five years ago, Chenrezi come to me in a dream. I never hear of him before, but he promise me, 'I will take care of you.'" A very nice promise for Chenrezi, the Buddha of Compassion, is said to live incarnate in each successive Dalai Lama. "Few days after my dream, I find center of Tibetan studies here, and they have a big painting of Chenrezi at the altar. Just like my dream." Nearly every devotee has a magical entry story.

Dorje wore a pendant disk with an image of Chenrezi on it, and she turned the disk to show me the picture of her guru on the other side. She told us it was he who gave her the Tibetan name Dorje Lhamo, which means Thunderbolt Goddess. The "thunderbolt," or *dorje,* is represented by a brass scepter always found on Tibetan altars.

"Now I take care of lamas when they come," she said. Taking care of lamas can be a time-consuming business, as every dharma teacher in the world goes through Hong Kong and needs housing and a booking agent. She showed us to the room that we would share. The "lama room," as she called it, was actually a tiny space usually occupied by children, who had been displaced for our stay. The right-angled child beds obliged me to try to sleep with Lama Mingme's feet nudging my pillow.

Most of the night, I lay awake, again doubting the purpose of this trip for myself. Kierkergard: *"Do not make yourself important by doubt."* Can doubt, which I find somewhat paralyzing, really have such power?

Finally, I went into the living room, where its altar, improvised on a Western-style highboy, held plastic carnations at one end and at the other end geyser water in a begrimed bottle. Above the seemingly random clutter—from a pile of nut shells, to the *dorje* and bell, to a bottle of Diorissimo perfume—were tacked faded photos of Buddhas, pages cut from a calendar, and many aging color pictures of deities clipped from magazines. High-backed chairs lined the wall, as if used for family services before the altar. It was not yet dawn, but as buildings rose just at the windows, the room would probably be dark all day. I sat in one of the chairs against the wall.

The face of "C's" wife appeared before me in the darkened room, an American friend, a writer and journalist. She had been married to "C" for some years. Like ministers and rabbis, Tibetan lamas may marry if not under monk's vows. She had encouraged me come on the journey with Mingme, knowing that I was an avid traveler and that I was on leave from my teaching job at the university during the spring semester. I envisioned her lovely patrician features, not quite undermined by the tight knot in which she wore her long blond hair. The knot reflected dedication—devout Tibetans never cut their hair—but I had always thought of her restraint of vanity as submission to a patriarchal system. In the darkness of Dorje's living room, I replayed her stance of a true believer.

"This journey could help you heal the mystery of your faith," she had said. She meant the absence of faith, which may also be a mystery. "I think it has to do with some past-life breach. Tibetans believe that if someone makes a break with faith it becomes very hard to reestablish it in a later life. You could be trying to purify some karmic breach, and that is why you are willing to help us. It's mysterious. You remain outside of everything. You're caught in a spiritual drought, and so you never enjoy any of the riches, any of the benefits, that come from real faith." I had no answer for this stinging analysis, for even if I did not believe in such things as a "karmic breach" and found all jargon irksome, I knew she was right about the "drought." Something was missing from my life that the world could not satisfy. "The Khandro could help you," she said. She was trying to see my going as a generosity, from which I might garner some spiritual reward. All I could imagine, however, was that an American passport might be useful during the risky travel. Cynical, of course, but I didn't see my role as cynical. I would not have come along if I did not at least aspire to what Buddhists call a Bodhicitta wish for an open, generous heart, even though I knew I had not achieved it.

Then there was my notebook.

The notebook I carried with me held childhood memories of Tibetan women, now old, who had endured *thamzing,* self-struggle sessions, a brainwashing that is Communism's modernization of Chinese water torture. These women now live as refugees all over the world: one runs a shop in Kathmandu, another cleans houses in Vancouver, another is an aide in a nursing home in Northern California. I had gathered their stories in the last year or so, some thirty years after Tibet fell to the Chinese. When we talked one woman said, "You are getting me back to thoughts I buried long ago!" A strange happiness filled her, awakened by the remembrance of old sorrows. I wasn't sure why I wanted to write down the stories, but I felt intimately connected to them, not as a journalist might feel, or even as a fiction writer. Perhaps it was their firsthand knowledge of death for which I felt an affinity. They had learned not only from their tradition, with its death teachings, but also from Chinese terror, which had provided deadly proof to them of life's one certainty—change.

What the women had told me strengthened my dissatisfaction with many indulgences of modern life. I was writing of people forcibly detached, cut off, coerced into homelessness and great inner resourcefulness. I thought such experience had some bearing on my "spiritual drought."

A shaft of light shone on the window of the next building, signaling daylight outside. Soon Dorje and Lama Mingme were up. He wanted to join the throngs of shoppers in the muggy Hong Kong streets, to buy a camera and altimeter, as well as Levis to wear in China.

Dorje's sly sense of the fun in things came through again. She held her fingers over her lips in a parody of the old Chinese woman's way of hiding the mouth from view, and said, "Lama robes not popular there."

2

Chengdu, Sichuan province. Young men throng together outside the JinJiang Hotel, white shirted, impeding the bicycle traffic of hundreds of earnest blue-shirted workers. Khaki-shirted police, restless, armed with pistols and rifles, look on as the students raise banners at the hotel entrance near vendors of art, animal horns, and medicinal innards. The young men unfurl a bolt of white cloth, slashed with heavy black ideograms, and fix it onto long poles they have brought to the hotel entrance. I think of something the Dalai Lama's brother Thubten Jigme Norbu wrote: "The only truth worth anything to anyone is the truth in which he believes with his heart as well as his mind, and toward which he strives with his body." In the May sun, the faces of these students are beaded with sweat, foreheads creased with fierce intent, their stance defiant. Heart, mind, and body …

Earlier, inside the hotel, three college women approached me, asking if they might practice their English. But when I asked them what they thought of the students demonstrating in the streets, they tittered and covered their mouths, their conversational range quickly exhausted. Three Little Girls from School, needing only fans. "Why are no women marching?" I pressed them. "Politics for men," one replied. This, in today's China? Where a woman inspected my passport at airport customs, another registered me at the hotel, where women are working everywhere, and of course are demonstrating in Tiananmen Square in Beijing. Have these young women forgotten what their mothers endured? Agnes

Smedley, the American journalist of China's Revolution, who helped teach their mothers and grannies to throw off the old oppression, had led me to expect better, but she had also foreseen how Communism could stifle their complicated stretch to consciousness. I told Mingme about them. He said, "Spies are everywhere! Pretend always to know nothing."

It is very warm for May. Beside the broad and muddy Nanhe, a channel of the great Min River that runs past the hotel, I sit on a bench with my notebook and watch these ardent students. They wear black armbands on their white shirtsleeves, mourning for the democracy they have never known.

Last night I awoke at 3 AM—a sharp rap at the door. Then, looking about at the darkness, I remembered my recurring auditory dream. I used to imagine a noise from the street had seeped into my dream narrative and awakened me. But the dream continued in many forms, sometimes a loud, angry banging, sometimes the cool Avon doorbell, sometimes a scratching like ghostly fingers at a windowpane. When I answer the door in my dream, only darkness, a slight wind. Nobody there. But last night, something *was* going on outside, singing. I recognized the *Internationale.* My room overlooked the hotel's unlit courtyard, and I went out onto our balcony. I could not see the singers. The music—strong male voices—worked in the darkness to create an eerie sense of displaced time. I felt transported to the thirties, to the Revolution. A swell of excitement, of rushing, momentous events ... *The Internationale shall be the human race* ... A crowd cheer rose in the night air as the song ended. I dressed and went downstairs, but a guard at the lofty lobby entrance refused to let me pass into the street. The singing had stopped. Beyond the door, at the outside gates, no one there. In the bar all the hotel personnel were gathered, murmuring, glaring apprehensively at me, the only guest in the lobby. Nosy white-faced foreigner. They refused to let me go into the street. Gates locked, was all they would say.

The world already knew of students who filled Tiananmen Square in

Beijing, but the Sichuan zealots hadn't found their way to the TV screen. Before we left home, I had heard eyewitness accounts of demonstrations in Lhasa. A number of monks and nuns were shot and killed in the streets; hundreds were imprisoned. Every March, on the anniversary of the Chinese takeover, Tibetans in Lhasa face the often fatal consequences of demonstrating for independence. Travelers report killings each year, but little news of these events reaches the US press, for the Chinese allow no camera crews from anywhere into Tibet. There is a trickle of information from visitors and fugitive Tibetans who cross into Nepal and India. Since March this year the government has chosen to forgo tourist business in Lhasa to prevent witness of police violence, for the student strike in Beijing has also sharpened the government's concern about what foreigners might see in Tibet.

Today Lama Mingme and Dorje are running around talking with officials, begging for a travel permit; we have no plan to go as far as Lhasa, but the demonstrations may outlaw travel anywhere in Tibet. If he can't get a permit, we'll go outlaw anyway, he says.

As I watch the students, I scribble in my notebook. A writer is forever dwelling on the past, has to. Even to a journalist in the thick of it, something has already happened, been witnessed. Scribble over notes, revision, re-vise. I pore over my collection of stories. Fierce slogans from the crowd, shouted into an already high level of general noise, split the pages. Past and present fold into one another.

In the fifties the wife of the Communist general stationed in Lhasa had created an organization meant to promote understanding of the New Order, the Patriotic Women's Association. In the early years of occupation, it offered constant training sessions in Chinese Mind. But as a Party mechanism, the PWA eventually backfired. Never before had the women of Tibet been organized for anything except picnics and mahjongg. Suddenly they had a political focus of their own.

Some of Chimey Norbu's memories: "The women started the demonstrations in Lhasa against the Chinese. I was still a child, but my oldest sister was with them." Chimey lives in California now, has a young daughter. Her memory yields only impressions, but she will pass them on to her daughter, and her daughter's daughter ...

The house was filled with unusual sounds—banging, flapping, whispering. Chimey's aunts were in the house, their voices murmuring in the dining room. None of their usual laughter and mirth. Their fear sank into her, became hers. Her sister Pema, age nineteen, was speaking. What had come over her sister, always so shy, so quiet? Now her voice rose above the whispers. She was saying, "Go, right away." Go where? She said: "All India should know what is happening to us. Before you get to the mouth, you have to pass the nose." Chimey knew this saying—Ani-là had explained it. You had to do things in the right order. One of the aunts said, "It's too late, maybe too late." But they left, they went wherever Pema sent them. Hurrying to India? Such a long way away. Much later Chimey would know about consulates, that there was an Indian consulate there in Lhasa not in sympathy with the Chinese invaders.

Next-day impressions: A sleeve reached over the flowers painted on Chimey's bed, her mother's sleeve. She dressed Chimey quickly, pulling on her felt shoes, an embroidered blouse, and sleeveless brown pinafore. Where was Ani-là who usually did this? Why were her mother's hands trembling, her smile eaten up by a strange cloud?

This is only days after Losar New Year's celebrations. Firecrackers went off like omens, and everybody laughed at the fear they caused. Just days before, the young Dalai Lama, only sixteen, had passed his final examinations in fierce debate, earning Tibet's highest degree of Geshe. He knew how to debate, flinging his arms wide in bold gestures; he knew how to joke, make a mockery of his opponents, turn them into cracked barley. This is how holy men fight, her father had explained this. How proud the people were that the Dalai was both handsome *and* intelligent!

They walk the Barkor marketplace. Chimey's mother is looking for something, not saying what. Sandbags lining the streets, barbed wire strung from roof to roof. Chimey stares about. She only goes into the Barkor to shop with Ani-là walking past the butcher stalls of hanging meat, corpses Ani-là called them, the steaming "mo-mo" stand where they would snack, with warm dumpling juices running down Chimey's round cheeks. None of the "mo-mo" places is open. Her mother grasps her hand, walking along briskly with her aunt. Crowds of women, maybe hundreds of women, are headed up toward the Potala, another half mile. Many Chinese soldiers follow them, carrying sticks and rifles. There is a crowd gathering on the Potala steps, more and more women are massing there. The soldiers are watching them. The solders have formed a line around the steps. Some of them have rifles on their shoulders. Chimey can see other children she knows there, young girls, old women too. She sees playmates and their grandmothers with them. Then suddenly her mother cries out, points toward the steps. Who is it? Her sister! Yes, Pema is calling to the other women there, shouting in a loud voice, her hand raised, her hand in a fist against the blue sky. Is that the way the Dalai Lama raised his arms in debate? Her mother calls out to Pema: "No, No!" But her sister doesn't hear. Women's voices are chanting. "Tibet is independent. China out! Free Tibet!" Her mother runs toward the steps. Her aunt holds Chimey back so she can't run to her mother. Her aunt clasps her up against her paneled apron, presses her face against the colored silk stripes, but Chimey can turn her head to see a soldier striding after her mother, then passing her.

Chimey's aunt tries to cover her eyes, but through her fingers Chimey sees a soldier raising a stick, hitting, hitting Pema on the face. Her sister falls down, and the soldier goes on hitting her. Her mother's scream reaches her next. She has never heard her mother scream before, but she knows the sound comes from her mother. The soldiers grab Pema and tie her hands behind her back. Even her aunt, as she grasps Chimey in her arms, is shouting now as the women rush up the Potala steps toward her sister. Screams fill the air; several women fall under blows from the soldiers. Chimey, looking up, sees this, the sky bright blue, the steps, the women between sky and steps, falling, hands stretched out, their long skirts, their striped aprons crumpling. Her aunt's hands still press her head against her breast, but she sees them, the women of Lhasa falling, falling on the Potala steps.

Yet no shots were fired in this violence. That would come later. The Chinese released Chimey's mother, but they took her sister to prison. It was weeks before her mother was allowed to see her. By then the Dalai

Lama and many of his people had gone from Lhasa. All their friends and neighbors became fugitives, escaped across the borders of Nepal and India.

Her mother and aunt talking about the visit to the prison: "A filthy bandage over half of her face," Chimey heard her mother say. Then—"pulled it off ... It was hanging out." Her mother gripping her fists to her eyes, crying, "I can't stand it any longer!" "What was hanging out?" Chimey asked her mother. "What was hanging out?" She could hear her own voice go small with fear. But Auntie led her outside to Ani-là.

Chimey's sister, blinded, has never been released and may no longer be alive.

I look up from my bench at the hotel entrance, at a rise in activity there. Shouts and confusion. A policeman's khaki arm thrusts out against the white shirt of a demonstrator. Other students press in angrily. Police surround the students, disperse them, create a barrier with sticks held between their hands. The students move back but stand together, their faces flushed, fierce. This is an overlay of what Chimey saw in Lhasa.

Just then several taxis and a bus drive through the hotel entrance, separating police and students, serving to distance them from one another's anger.

How much easier it is to define threats to freedom than to defiine freedom itself! I may burn myself out with banners on the Washington steps, or even burn myself up there to protest a war, but still the question—have I freed myself or anyone else? Self-immolation is the sign of a disordered mind to Westerners unable or unwilling to make an association to the sacrifice of Christ. To the Buddhist it is a martyr's offering of the body to create awareness of the ignorance that war represents, to show the powerful how illusory clashing egos are; it is the act of a saint engaged in seeking the freedom of all beings. Chimey's sister Pema is seen by her people as a saint.

My collection of stories is part of Ordinary Mind. "Cut it," say the lamas. Not denial but self-surgery of the mind. Cut all negative attachments as they flicker into your consciousness. Never mind that they may return. No dwelling upon error, as Christian Scientists put it. The Dalai Lama would not allow photographs of Tibet's desecration in his memoir, *My Tibet*—no bombed-out monasteries, no raped and tortured nuns, no blood of murdered monks flowing in the Jokhang Temple. Enlightened beings, even those following their path, affirm a View to the nature of suffering, its cause and its cessation, and believe impartially that all things, pleasure and pain, are impermanent phenomena, subject to change on the turning wheel, and moreover are part of a mutual, limitless interdependency, samsara and nirvana together. This, in my limited understanding, is called the View.

However, practitioners do not avert their gaze from the suffering of others. The trick of it is not to dwell, or fixate, as photographs of destruction might encourage one to do. A woman lama I know went into the market of Singapore where live animals awaited slaughter to pray for them, and also asked a disciple to take her to see *The Killing Fields,* for Cambodia's suffering, she said, reminded her of the agony of Tibet.

I glimpse Mingme and Dorje headed toward the hotel entrance and wave to them. Mingme is wearing his skinny jeans purchased in Hong Kong, and Dorje the print blouse that I lent her this morning when I realized she hadn't brought a change of clothing, perhaps didn't have one. She is not your typical materialistic Hong Kong resident. They sit beside me, discouraged, and report: No permits, no travel in Tibet allowed. No flights to Lhasa. No entry at all. "Is okay," Mingme affirms. "Will be okay, I know that."

I call their attention to the demonstrating students, to whom they have paid no notice. I tell them of something Hannah Arendt said, that the first step in total domination of a people is to make justice appear hopelessly out of reach. "China hasn't succeeded in destroying the sense of justice in these students," I say. Mingme and Dorje shake their heads, not drawn in. Empty phenomena, they seem to think, another turn of the wheel of desire and aversion—"bitter ocean," in Chinese.

"Mingme, this may be happening in Lhasa too." That registers, and he shakes his head, but still says nothing. This is Ordinary Mind. Where little girls from school will come to meet with rude awakenings, where women who acquire power may be flung into the flood or struck down in the streets, where young men may sacrifice themselves in the clash of ignorant armies. Cut it. Do not dwell there. Return to the View.

3

In the streets of Chengdu, no children, no beggars. Beside the taxi stand on a cloth spread on the sidewalk, two tiger claws are up for sale, and a monkey's hand. "For wind balance," Lama Mingme explains. A young Tibetan woman, barefoot, sidles up as we get into the cab, to tempt us furtively with something hidden in a grubby handkerchief—a tiny frog. Solid gold, she says, but Dorje shakes her head skeptically. "Maybe dipped," she tells me.

In the taxi Dorje asks Mingme, "Why you always so nervous, Mingme?" I had often noticed his shakes, but had wrongly assumed them to reflect anxiety and eagerness to discharge his commission.

Now he tells Dorje that as a boy when his family were refugees in India he once had a very high fever and had been given a blood transfusion that affected his nerves. Or perhaps it was the high fever that caused damage. It wasn't easy for any Tibetan to adapt to the heat of the Indian climate and the low altitude. Many children as well as adults died from the change, even though as a group Tibetan refugees have adapted successfully in India.

The taxi barges us slowly through an ever-flowing canal of bicycles, thousands of them, impeded often by slogan-chanting students. The drab conformity of the clothing is oppressive, the same faded dark blue cotton jackets everywhere. The air the people breathe is noxious; from the unrestrained exhalations of buses, trucks, and factories a smoky cloud hangs over Chengdu, once considered a beautiful city. Cyclists who go through red lights are punished with public humiliation. Upbraided by police at intersections and forced to wear red headbands, they stand in repentant shame, late for school or work. It looks like a joke, but it isn't.

Mingme brings out an unusual *mala,* the Tibetan rosary, made of crystal beads, to pray as we ride. Dorje takes the *mala,* showier than ordinary beads of wood or seed, to examine the clear, rounded spheres, counts them—one hundred and eight—and reluctantly returns it. Clearly she covets it.

Mingme has fallen for forthright Dorje, or so I imagine by the pressure of his hand against hers as she returns the *mala* to him. Last night she did not come to the bedroom she shares with me in our suite but stayed out in the living room where Mingme has been sleeping. Later, she told me they had talked long into the night, then practiced meditation.

The taxi finally pulls up at a Buddhist monastery, open for tourism. The three of us buy baked sweet potatoes from a vendor outside and wander into the dusty sacred precincts, eating them. Mingme, mistaking an offering box for a trash container, tosses his sweet potato skin into it. That is too much for Dorje. She collapses against my shoulder in ridiculing laughter. We point him in the direction of the actual trash receptacle, a large ceramic Chinese dragon, and he retrieves the skin and drops it into the dragon's mouth. Then he points out to us that trash is falling from the rear end of the dragon, from its bottom. This strikes us all as hilarious.

Lama Mingme takes a photograph of the dragon, with the camera he purchased in Hong Kong, then snaps others of the interior cement courtyard, smudged and strewn with litter. To the rear of the courtyard an ancient monk sits beside an offering plate, guarding an altar so dimly lit we can scarcely see. A gilt Buddha of Compassion statue flickers in candlelight. Chenrezi, or in Sanskrit the not-so-easy-to-say *Avalokitesvara,* a lotus resting in his hand.

Dorje stands before the statue and slips her pendant disk of the same deity inside her blouse. This is so that the disk will not strike the floor as she prostrates herself three times, body facedown, arms extended full length before the altar, nose on the floor. This is how you genuflect in Tibet. No wimpy kneebend at a pew—the whole body is flung into this reverence, even upon a floor smeared with dirt and candlewax. Dorje has made 100,000 of these prostrations, as part of her preparation for a three-year retreat. Many more than Mingme has done in his lifetime, she confided to me.

They sit before a statue of the goddess Tara to do some mantra practice. To Tibetans, Mother love is unstained by self-interest. Although Tibetans admit some Western mothers may go wrong, nearly every person alive at some time, to some degree, has experienced that mysterious selfless love. Tibetans have made it doctrine; like Catholics, they know that Mother love has a religious source. The believer strives to extend it to everyone else alive.

The practice calls upon a Tibetan strain of fantasy. As Dorje and Mingme pray, their minds are engaged in a visualization of Tara, creating the goddess in explicit detail from her bare extended foot to the beads of her necklace. The vast array of Tibetan dieties have roles in many rites of visualization, which I think of as cultural creative acts. There are no novels in Tibet, only these religious fantasies, and teaching tales. The fictions we in the West create must seem to them like distortions of ego.

I find a bench in the courtyard, open my notebook, and scan some of my ego distortions, notes for a novel. In my own strain of fantasy, Tibetan magic and mind power are plotting for political liberation. What if the inner secrets of Tibetan magic actually had some temporal power? That is of course the question doubters always put out—if your magic is real, show me. Jesus raised the dead, after all; let's see you unshackle prisoners, free the world....

THE GOLDEN ROAD

Time: Soon after the present;
Place: the Yak and Yeti Hotel, Kathmandu, Nepal.

The monk opened the door to the small conference room. Even though he was disguised in maroon layman's robes and a fur hat, there was an immediate scrape of chairs. Years ago, he had fled the Chinese into exile from Tibet in a similar disguise, and now it evoked good-humored smiles among those present in the room. Their standing up obliged him to stoop to avoid towering over them, as he was more than six feet tall. Actually, because of an inbred humility he had a lifelong habit, of more than fifty years, of hunching his shoulders. He removed his hat and strode immediately to the oldest person there, a very small, aged nun of Eastern European origin, with mischievous eyes. He pulled out a chair for her, then signaled the others to sit.

The charge in the room, which seemed to extend out through the window to the blue and white ice of lofty Mt. Everest, really originated in the mountain itself, he thought with an inner smile. The mountain—source of energy, bliss, and zeal—qualities keenly needed for the work ahead of them.

He seated himself beside the nun, folding his robes around him, and smiled. Only then did the others in the party take chairs at the table: the American video director, her Tibetan assistant, and the British coordinator.

In strongly accented English, the only tongue common to all present, in a voice made deeply resonant by lifelong mantra intonation, he murmured to the nun: "Mother, I've bought you a nice straw hat. You must go in disguise, too."

"What—give up my habit?" Her wizened face was gnomic; her heavy eyebrows disappeared under by the blue and white sari stretched across her forehead and folded about the length of her tiny form.

The monk was familiar with the universal power of small women, but this woman was utterly compelling. Her strength was like the mountain's, irresistible to all who drew near. Yet he enjoyed the privilege of teasing her. "Such an attachment!" Again laughter. "Your habit is too much a giveaway."

Then the monk turned to the coordinator, an attorney with Amnesty International. He beamed and said, "Well, we're all present." The attorney smoothed his silver sideburns, which gleamed with reflected hues of the mountainside.

"Only five of us?" asked the nun.

The coordinator said that the completion of their operation would rely upon a great many others. "But only you four will go into Tibet."

He opened his briefcase and carefully distributed maps as if they were stemware filled with a specially aged sherry. Although a turncoat colonial who left the foreign service a decade before, the man had an inbred superior sensibility of the sceptered isle. But his appearance undermined the inner man. For years now in his work seeking amnesty for political prisoners, he had reflected upon the nature of torture, of the bodies of men and women torn, mutilated, deprived of identity. He had sought, through thousands of letters, to try to move others to identify with the experience of a body in pain. He knew he labored against the trend of objectification of human life, that the torturers had the upper hand. For this reason he had decided to ask the help of the monk, whose faith insisted upon the unity of all beings and called for a ripening of the compassionate heart. The attorney had masterminded an extraordinary expedition, and now two of the greatest benevolent spirits of the modern world would participate in a journey designed to elevate world consciousness.

The monk was speaking to the team. He said that from now on he wished to be called "A" and provided each person with a new name. The nun would now be known only as "Mother." The wiry young Tibetan cameraman, who wore a monk's robe, would be known as "Youngden." The coordinator would be called "B," he said, adding humorously, "for 'Brit.' And in thinking of my name," he said with a smile for Youngden, "remember the Tibetan letter for *A*, on which you have so often meditated." Youngden grinned, for he knew the letter *A* well.

"Is gateway to imagination," he said.

The monk replied, "And it is the imagination that makes all transformation come about."

He turned to the video director, whom he had recognized at once. With her dark hair haloed by light from the great mountain, she underwent a transformation in his mind, and he saw her as a young novice in his own order in an earlier life, saw that she had spent several years in a retreat cave. Frequently when young people were possessed of especially strong dedication, their past lives would appear to him. Born in New Jersey, educated at Berkeley, and now working for the BBC, this young woman carried the burden of an almost voluptuous beauty, half-white, half–Chinese-American. From her shoulder-length hair to her slender, sandaled feet, she sent out an aura of seductiveness imprinted early in this karma by her small-time Chinese-Mafia father during her childhood Mandarin lessons. "A" could see that like other Catholics-turned-Buddhist, she was devout but worldly, and still trying to overcome, probably through sexual impulses, the denial of the nunnery caves. In that life she had suffered from bouts of depression and had once even tried suicide by anorexia, refusing to drink her barley broth, a self-denial from which she had been rescued by visions of Tara bringing her a drink of milk, which went down her throat so warmly that she grew ravenous and ran outside her cave to eat nettles. He could see all this.

She presented valid credentials from the BBC, and a well-counterfeited People's Republic passport as well as forged video credentials from Beijing's military authority.

He smiled as he looked them over and said, "For our expedition, you'll be called 'Bodhi'—for Bodhisattva."

She pressed the palms of her hands together at her chest in a *namaste* greeting; her laugh was contained but seductive. "I hope I won't suffer from inflated self-esteem, 'A,'" she said. "May I ask—does 'A' stand for your Sanskrit name?"

His reply was merely to press his forefinger against his lips with a smile of conspiracy.

The briefing session went smoothly. Beijing had lifted its on-again–off-again ban on flights into Lhasa from Kathmandu. "B," who would be coordinating the work of the many other participants, distributed their schedules. "A" and "Mother" would fly to Chengdu, then proceed by jeep, partly because "B" believed their incognitos would be too easily blown on a direct flight into Lhasa. They would take with them the video equipment disallowed on current flights into Lhasa, in the expectation that overland it would not be detected and confiscated. The video team would fly directly to Lhasa, then proceed to take still photography of designated sites near their rendezvous point until "A" and "Mother" arrived with the equipment.

Clearly Bodhi knew her business and was a risk taker. "A" had no doubt her footage would overreach other BBC coverage when the moment of action arrived. As the only English-language news service that had shown any determination to cover Tibetan news, the BBC would now scoop other networks worldwide. He said to her, "You'll find that when you travel with Youngden his qualities really come out."

Bodhi well knew that the word *qualities* without a modifier left room for ambiguity. The qualities most apparent to her in Youngden were shyness and anxiety. She also knew that this was Tibetan usage; "qualities" are virtues developed through meditation practice.

They pored over the map of Tibet. As "A" pointed to their destination, "Mother's" white-shrouded head bent closer to the map, her forehead crinkling upward. "You needn't answer this, but I have to ask." She stretched a lean forefinger to trace the line of their route. "This is very far north. Do we pass through Shambhala? I always liked the sound of Shambhala. It must be like Paradise. Will you show us where it is?"

The question sent a bolt of expectation through the group. The others looked up at "A," quietly alert. They all knew that the great mystic kingdom was suppoed to be in a northerly direction, but none had dared bring it up. Could "A" be taking them there as part of this mission?

"A" bowed his head to "Mother," glanced at the other tense faces, then burst out laughing, greatly amused. He said, "Once an American journalist asked me the exact location of Shambhala. I told him that if you go in a straight line to the north you pass over the North Pole and come out in America, so perhaps America is Shambhala!"

The others smiled at the joke, but were somewhat downcast. Secretly everyone wanted Shambhala on the itinerary. However, one could never be too sure of anything with "A"; he was as unpredictable as any saint. He hadn't actually answered the question.

"Mother" said, "Keep us out of America. I heard that in California the nuns wear blue jeans."

"A" smiled at this. She was a radical, always disputing church doctrine. She would have priests marry to keep them out of trouble, as she put it, and she would have women priests as well, and yet she had this attachment to her robes. "A straw hat and black skirt and blouse will provide a necessary cover for you," he said. He felt a strong love of this great woman; every crease of her face aroused a tenderness in him for all beings. "A" imagined her bringing to their mission the same force she brought to her missions of mercy in Hong Kong, lifting first this homeless being, then that one, from the gutter. He imagined her brushing away the dust of the street from a still-breathing body, offering comfort and love before the rescued being entered the transition of death. Fearless woman.

"B" reported on the work and readiness of all participants from Kathmandu to Delhi, to Brazil, South Africa, Geneva, London, New York, and San Francisco. He had anticipated inevitable foul-ups in Nepalese satellite communications, and had coopted standby service from Norway. Timing was everything.

There was a pause. Clearly, everyone was waiting for "A" to make some closing statement. He obliged, offering a simple mantra everyone knew and repeated.

Then, abruptly, he spoke more fully. "There is no doubt we have come to the Kali Yuga, the Age of Darkness, the worst of times predicted by all the Buddhas. We have been told that in the Kali Yuga change must come about with some drama, perhaps even cataclysm. Remember that the Ten Incentives tell us to seek the antidote to the predominance of evil. That is our mission. If the world is to survive as the spiritual improving ground for beings we have always believed it to be, then this task of ours must be accomplished now with our most skillful means. Spiritual means was the tool I learned as a boy, and to which I am still dedicated, but all my life, often against my will, I have been obliged to make political acts. It is as if some mysterious force demands it of me. This brilliant plan of "B's" has persuaded me once again to take part in what will be seen as a political act. It involves us in scheming and concocting, which my spiritual side would like to see come to a final end. I believe, however, that what we do on this mission will serve to bring the two paths, the political and spiritual, into closer harmony for this distressed world. The message of our action must be clear and unequivocal. The Kali Yuga is not a time for subtlety. There must be no mistaking salt for honey. A final battle for the souls of men has long been foreseen, in which enlightenment prevails to usher in a golden era. I believe that we can show the world its own suffering—which can awaken the imagination, as it once awoke the Buddha who defined suffering for us. It is my great hope that the world is ready to awaken to its golden prospects." He folded his hands with a gentle smile. "May our actions benefit all beings."

As they carefully synchronized their watches, "A" added, "A great Russian poet Anna Akhmatova wrote, 'Our clocks are all striking the hour of courage.' *Tashi delek.*"

With smiles and *namastes,* the group adjourned.

Within a day after the briefing, "A" and "Mother" were stashing the duffel bags containing the video equipment inside their hired jeep in Chengdu. Bodhi and her assistant Youngden were flying straight into Lhasa, to prepare for the rendezvous. And "B" was flying West, to coordinate an operation on which the sun well might never set …

As we leave the monastery and wait for a cab near the ongoing stream of bicycles, Dorje presents us with a news note. Her mother and aunt have arrived in Chengdu from Canton, on vacation, she says. Curious coincidence. She hasn't mentioned their plans to travel here before. She wants them to come along with us into Tibet. "Like one family," she says.

A warning bell sounds in my mind. Was this preplanned? Wouldn't two more Chinese women put a crimp in our visit to Tibetans, who have no reason to trust Chinese? I say, "It's a hard trip. Not a vacation."

Dorje is used to having her way. "They like adventure, like you."

Cheerful Mingme doesn't share my misgivings. "Sure they welcome," he says. I wonder if Dorje wants her family along to discourage Mingme's designs. But didn't she stay in the outer room all last night? What does it mean?

Dorje sizes up my resistance. "They brave, also like you," she says.

Knowing I see through this flattery, she adds a put-down clincher. "Young, too. Mum only fifty." There is a slyness in Dorje's face now. Finally, Dorje sees I am not exactly a pushover, and expresses some underlying fears: "I don't like Mum and Auntie travel alone. In China terrible things happen. People grab women, cut out their eyes and organs and sell them."

I can't suppress my skeptical look. I say, "We may be stopped at any time ourselves, by police, fined, jailed—who knows what?"

"Better they with me if any trouble," Dorje insists.

"And we don't know if there'll be room, or if we can even get a driver."

Lama Mingme brushes this aside. "We getting jeep. Lot of room in jeep."

Baffled by his enthusiasm, I wonder if I really saw him place unnecessary pressure on her hand in the taxi. Maybe he and Dorje *did* meditate all night long? Perhaps his desire to please her is at this point stronger than his desire. Perhaps I am supposed to distract the relatives to enable their romance. Perhaps I am of a past generation.

"You not used to Chinese way of all one family," Dorje observes to me in a small understatement. "You sort of—detached." That touches a nerve, reminds me of "C's" wife and her parting analysis. My longtime widowhood had reinforced an innate detachment that I thought first sprang from being an only child. Yet I know it is a quality not necessarily shared by other only children; my son, for instance, doesn't have that detachment at all, is outgoing and affectionate, and seldom prey to ambivalence.

"Never mind," Mingme tells her. "We make room." All one family comes naturally to him. I think of the fiction notes I just read in my notebook, the figure of the "Mother." Fiction is so often tinged with prophecy; although I had in mind someone of global stature, rather than Dorje's Chinese mum, how often is life as large as we imagine?

Once Joseph Campbell admitted that when a young woman insisted to him that she wanted to make a hero's quest herself, he told a male colleague he knew the time had come for him to retire. Good thinking, bull's-eye! Greek mythos must have a place in the psyche of anyone born to Western civilization, but the woman who prefers to go on the road like Ulysses rather than to weave like Penelope is still not a welcome sight. Claiming the hero's journey isn't easy yet for a woman of any age. I relent—sure, let Mum and Auntie come along.

Suddenly Lama Mingme darts into the street, arms in the air, shouting, "My friend, my friend!" He is chasing after a tall, maroon-skirted lama, a man of considerable height and dignity. What can this comedy mean? Dorje's fingertips go to her smiling lips again, as she watches Mingme wade through the bicycle stream. He hasn't told us he has a friend in Chengdu. Perhaps he can help us find the way.

4

My doubts assert themselves again. Is this risky errand really necessary? Mingme and Dorje talk anxiously about money changing. How to get the most money for our money, how to change the funds for the Khandro from traveler's checks into People's rather than Tourists' currency. Whether to use the black-market agents lurking about the hotel. Whether to go outlaw all the way. They decide to go to the Tibetan Hotel to look for someone who might help. I wonder if money is so important that the three of us—now five—should risk our necks. Already sick of China's self-oppression, I fantasize a quick flight south to never-colonized Thailand for R & R, a bask in the veil of smiles in Chingmai. Instead, I decide to go to the American Consulate, conveniently located in our hotel, to see about cutting all this short. Lama Mingme would not like my speaking to an American official, but I have the arrogance of citizenship he lacks.

An American diplomat, a good-looking black man, asks to see my passport, shakes my hand. His head inclines toward me as he glances at a watchful consulate employee, male, Chinese. *Spies are everywhere!* I let my voice sink to a whisper. Weren't there certain international agreements, I ask, that would make the transfer of money as possible here as anywhere else in the world?

At that he places his body as a shield between that watchful employee and myself, shows me into a private office, and shuts the door. My sandals sink into a Chinese carpet as he offers me a green leather chair opposite his gleaming mahogany desk. I wonder about the life in China of this solid foreign-service officer, so careful to protect me from guarded Chengdu eyes. Chinese women on campuses have caused riots, news stories say, by talking to, maybe even dating, African students here. Racism in China is not limited to national minorities like Tibetans and Mongols. Is this black American more closely watched than other diplomats?

The Bank of China, he says, cannot be relied upon to make delivery of money sent to Tibetans. "We cannot send it ourselves for you, nor could we collect it from the bank. You could wire it; then, if after a certain time it did not arrive, we could communicate with officials. Make them uncomfortable with inquiries." The Chinese could stall, he continues, say they were unable to locate the wire and so on, meanwhile collecting interest on the funds. I think, Enough! We are on the fast path, and cannot regress. As I leave, the same covert gaze follows me out.

My visit to the consulate alarmed Lama Mingme, cautioned by Tibetan refugees in America not to mention our destination to anyone, or even to speak his own language. I reassured him I hadn't revealed where we were going or the nature of our mission. Besides, he himself is irrepressible. He constantly approaches strangers in the hotel bar, exotics from Nepal and perhaps Tibet wearing elaborate robes and colorful tribal hats, to have lengthy conversations in his only fluent tongue. "They my people, some very high," he says.

Finally, help arrives. "So lucky I find him," says Lama Mingme. He is the lama Mingme chased through the traffic after our visit to the Buddhist temple. "Is okay now. I know will be okay." Mingme explains that his friend is a reincarnate lama, a *tulku,* of considerable reputation, a writer of books. I will call him "P" for the sake of obscuration. "P" for Projection, and for Philosophy, Politics, Passion—quite a cluster of *P*s surround this lama.

He arrives at the hotel bearing a box of delicious pastries for us.

With an aquiline, Mayan-like profile and a leanness uncommon in Tibetans, he mingles an unusual air of sophistication with good humor. Perhaps he is my own age, though probably a decade younger—the cultural revolution was an aging experience. His hair is unshaven, constrained in a knot, indicating that he is not a monk, as monks' heads are shaven.

Dorje speaks to him in Mandarin, translating his offer of help. I wish that I might have a conversation with this man, an exchange of ideas about a number of things. Philosophical: What of doubt? Passion: What of the emotional students in the streets? Political: What of a reported reprocessing plant for American batteries in Chengdu, contaminating workers with mercury poison? However, we can only munch Pastries.

The next day "P" comes to the hotel to discuss with Dorje a plan for changing money, but she and Mingme are out. He signals he would like to use the bathroom. Of course, I say, pointing him toward the clean towels. Then I hear water running in the shower. For a long time. Why not?—a bathroom would be a rarity in his life, I imagine.

I pick up my journal and flip through it, stopping at an entry about Mingme's uncle "C":

Tulku. Tibetan tool of succession, like a Dukedom of the mind. The genius of the *tulku* system is in the instinct for recognizing the exceptional child. A *tulku* chooses the body into which he will next incarnate, to be "found" after birth by Wisdom Holders, i.e., men (always) with special insight about lineage. So it was also in the Manger of Bethlehem. *Tulkus* are sometimes gifted children of commoners, like the present Dalai Lama, and are carefully trained. A few *tulku* children have been born of Western believer-parents. The system might offer the world a democratic tool—give talent its birthright, train it from infancy in responsible concern for others, and only then elect it to office. But how could the West choose its trainers? Imagine an Electoral College as an academy of Wisdom Holders!

"C's" followers believe him not only a *tulku* but a Bodhisattva, which means he must always place service to others above his own self-interest. Bodhisattvas face the biggest double bind of their faith, for they must decide after death between resting in the Pureland of the Buddha and returning to earth to work tirelessly for other beings. The choice, however, is preordained, for true Bodhisattvas are rather like the 100 last just men in the Jewish tradition and the saints of Sufism.

The Bodhisattva cannot rest, must always defer to an innate need for every sentient being to attain enlightenment. Tough line of work, being a Bodhisattva.

I feel myself closer to the hungry ghosts. "C" talked about them once on a campus where I was teaching. They have small mouths, practically no esophagus, and huge stomachs, he said, which make it impossible for them to satisfy their ravenous hunger. Immediately I remembered my roommate after college, a free-spirited actress who called herself "Ghostie" and left notes around our apartment with cartoon drawings of herself that I too identified with and that looked somewhat the way hungry ghosts sound. They must wander in perpetual starvation filled always with an unmet desire, never nourished, throughout their term of existence. And where are they? I asked "C," remembering my roommate and sensing an uneasy affinity for these ghosts. They live in the Realm of the Hungry Ghosts, one of the six realms of being, he said. I asked, "Not here among us?" He only laughed, and said, "Could be." This he often says when confronted with metaphysical paradox.

Later, when I rented a studio in the Berkeley hills, the owner invited "C" to give lectures in the house. He sat in her living room on a cushioned throne above a large group of people gathered on the carpet at his feet. I tried but could not sit still either for the meditation, which made me uptight, or the teachings, which were long and repetitive, despite the interesting, mythic stories "C" told. There was no dialogue; this learning was a one-way street, transmission from the holder of undisputable knowledge to the aspirant. I had taught seminars with disputatious college students too long to put up with this. I would steal away up the stairway to my studio to write. Taking refuge in art may not be as old as taking refuge in the Buddha, but Goethe, among others, recommended it. I crept away from the lama out of deference to Goethe's view. Ten minutes of listening to mantra made me remember how much I love Mozart.

Yet somehow I felt troubled by my resistance to what I liked to call "gu-ruse," and so when he was off the pedestal at meals I talk with him, and his good humor undermined my besetting sin of irony. Once I tried to explain that I was too culture-locked for his path, that the visualization techniques he taught only made me restless, made me want to scream and weep.

"C" said, "In Tibet we have contraries, people do things different way. Opposite." *Contrary* was also a term out of my southern past—my family called me contrary. But Southern families have little tolerance for the contrary, an ornery being, disrespectful of tradition, a wanderer or bum.

The Tibetan contrary may be more like the Cheyenne who sits on his pony backward, who if asked to do one thing does the opposite, who fights alone, not with others, and who is revered for spiritual skills. Believers make much of such cultural diffusion. Tibetan sand mandalas are used like the ephemeral Hopi sand paintings, as spiritual protections. In both cultures the sand is eventually dispersed and returned to the elements. The Hopi prophecy that men in Red Hats will come to deliver the world also dovetails with the name of the oldest Buddhist sect in Tibet, the Red Hat order, which in turn holds to Shakyamuni Buddha's prophecy that 2500 years after his death his doctrine would spread "in the country of the red-faced people."

"Is okay to be contrary," "C" told me.

"We question authority," I said, and he laughed engagingly.

The knowledgeable traveler Bruce Chatwin wrote that his whole life had been a search for the miraculous but that at the first faint flavor of the uncanny he turned rational and scientific. I, too. Given my fascination with the invisible world and my unwashable brain, I should probably have been a microbiologist.

The shower finally stops, and "P" emerges. The first thing I notice when he comes out is that he has shod himself in some of the plastic maroon slippers provided daily by the hotel maid; they match the color of his robes. With a quite sensual sigh, he stretches out, tall and lean, on my bed. He lies on one side, with his head propped upon his hand, his other hand extended along his raised hip. This is a dying Buddha posture, famed in statuary, Buddha in *parinirvana.* I find myself wondering if the Buddha knew how sexy his dying posture was, with its languorous half-odalisque. Probably he did, having given so much attention in his life to both sex and death.

"It's *all* about sex, you know," a Tibetan scholar once told me, rather sweepingly, only half-joking. He spoke eloquently of the classical art depicting Yab-Yum, literally mother and father, male and female in union, and of the Tantric way to enlightenment, centered in a meditation that engages the imagination in sublime, transforming activity that may or may not involve the earthly body. Even the most common of mantras, *om mani padme hum,* represents ecstatic tantric union of lingam and yoni, the jewel in the lotus. Tantra, which originated in India, found a ready acceptance in polyandrous Tibet. Padma Sambava, who brought Buddhism to Tibet from India, demonstrated with who-knows-how-many-partners the power of consort practice over the elements, changing fire to water for example. American Buddhists of my acquaintance have even married for the purpose of pursuing tantric practice, so strong is their passion—for enlightenment.

On my bed, "P," smiling, scrutinizes me—am I imagining it?—openly appraising my body. I am dressed scantily on this warm day, in a sheer print dress, my feet in barefoot sandals, where his glance comes, most unexpectedly, to rest. I close my notebook, folding a pencil inside it.

What is this strange stirring I feel? I have to acknowledge to myself a rising something or other. His poise is not a little bit disturbing. Is this a test?

From where he lies "P" can glimpse the students below who are carrying new protest banners in front of the hotel. Their voices come up to us; they are shouting the Mandarin equivalent of, I think, "Down with Deng!" "P" sits up and lifts a fist overhead, mocking them. Then he lifts the other, mocking the police who are calling out for the students to desist. A clown; this is crazy wisdom.

Stories abound about crazy wisdom among yogis, who, in common belief, cannot be held to ordinary standards of morality. In one such story an itinerant sage, or *mahasiddhi,* Virupa, went to a town and got drunk in the inn, borrowing a lot of money for his bender. After a while people started wanting their money back, and he told them that at noon the next day he would pay up. They waited. It remained morning for three and a half days! Worried, the people consulted their local sage, who advised them to tell the monk, "Never mind, you don't have to pay us back." At that, the monk released the sun, and a few minutes before noon, pay-up time, to stay on the safe side he disappeared from the town.

"P" lies back, a reclining Buddha again. He signals to my notebook, and so I show it to him, try to explain that like himself I write books. He sits up and pantomimes a Tibetan text, flipping its unbound pages, which are like oblong flash cards printed with woodblocks. Comically, he mumbles a parody of mantra chanting. His hands are long and slender, with graceful tapered fingers. I am charmed by his ironies, of course, as he stretches back comfortably, cleanly, on my bed, his red robes folded loosely about the length of his legs.

Suddenly, his gaze penetrates my body. Desire crosses the room on a maroon swath. I have already translated my attraction to him as wanting to have a conversation. Now I realize that I am merely deflecting excitement. Such a depressing tendency! I am not of course trained in the Tantric arts, as he must be. Acquaintances have married for Tantra, true, but others have been less constrained and taken what comes from traveling wisdom. What to do? If this is a test, or an opportunity, I am not meeting it. My habit of reserve clashes with my inner flickerings.

This series of responses is not lost upon "P" of course. He can see that my transitory charge at his signal is routed. Too bad, but I'm not to learn this lama's inner secrets.

"P," who wouldn't have to be a mind-reading adept to read me, rises from the bed. He gives an ever so gentle shrug and goes to retrieve his shoes from the bathroom.

Later, when he is waiting for us downstairs, Dorje inspects the bathroom, aghast. "The lama had a bath," I sigh.

"But every towel soaked. And the floor flooded!" She eyes me with humorous suspicion.

But then in a taxicab she also glimpses "P's" wayward desires. As we ride to the bank with him, he sits in front next to the Chinese woman driver, who is young and very pretty. We notice that he asks where she lives, even obtains an address. He strokes the skin of her forearm with his long fingers as he leaves the cab. She turns her head to gaze out her window, her lips curving slightly.

"A different kind of lama," Dorje murmurs to me thoughtfully. "Worldly kind of lama."

I lift my eyes heavenward. "Definitely not a monk," I say.

Dorje's fingers go to her lips to shield her merry smile.

The bank is closed. A holiday. "P" says he will come again the next day, and leaves us to run for a bus, his feet sleuthing out.

The next day "P" decides he will change the money himself, tells us he will go to a neighborhood away from the hotels where officials watch the lurking black marketeers. Dorje accompanies him but I stay behind, thinking police would be more likely to notice a Westerner in a black market exchange.

I walk to the bridge beside the river near the hotel and watch the students. There is a rise in excitement, a march in the streets. The large banners have been taken down from the hotel. The swell of demonstrators has increased. Hundreds of young men throng together, following the banners. Suddenly they are running, to keep up with someone being driven in an open car. One of the students pauses breathlessly beside me, and I ask in English if he can tell me what is going on. He appears to understand my question, but answers in Chinese, as joyful a flow of words as I have heard since I arrived. He speaks with the abandon of an idealist in action, his face flushed, his white shirt unbuttoned halfway down his chest. Somehow, I understand him. The force of his desire rushes wildly in his blood, transforms him, makes me understand him. We connect in a way that "P" and I could not. Our desires may reduce us, but how they also elevate us, admit creative power only dimly imagined before! How wonderful, to have such freedom in China, he seems to say. One of the well-known Beijing demonstrators has come to Chengdu. Everything will change! He rushes away to follow his friends to a meeting place in the square, where their leaders will urge them to seek their heart's desire, to take the strong decisive action that will change everything. That will bring them to their cruel destiny.

I remember Chimey's sister on the Potala steps, and think that I will never forget this young man's face.

When Dorje returns, she tells me that "P" had simply gone into the middle of a crowded street and changed the money with a black marketeer he didn't even know. "My heart still pounding," she says. "But 'P' totally cool. Just like always," she says. This is the quality admired by men who defend Don Juan's lechery as an integral part of a revolutionary hero's makeup. Fearless Action! Results! Grace under pressure!

"A complete yogi," Dorje says.

Crazy Wisdom can get away with anything—if you can stop the sun in its tracks.

Dorje says, "We have driver now, coming tomorrow. Tibetan driver. Called Mr. Fu."

"Chinese name," I observe. *Fu,* I recall from the *I Ching,* can mean turning point, or return.

At bedtime I write in my notebook, submerged in my fiction notes, in which a Chinese army officer sits in a remote desert office. He has lost all his hair; his bald head shines like a dome. I try to look into it like a crystal ball, as if I possess the gift of prophecy. The head of—yes, a commander of a military police company stationed at a secret Chinese outpost somewhere near the Gobi desert, whose job is deadly, both to himself and others. He is working with nuclear waste. The commander is miserably unhappy in his post. Drifting into my crystal ball is the young woman, the video producer Bodhi, so named by the sainted monk of my imaginary expedition. The commander doesn't know her yet, as he is stuck in his remote station. She will eventually be interviewing him for the clandestine video. Now she is just arriving in Lhasa in the company of her assistant, Youngden.

THE GOLDEN ROAD

When they checked into the Lhasa Holiday Inn, Bodhi thought she was going to have to teach Youngden everything in the few days before the final rendezvous. He was so nervous! The first thing she had to do was to try to calm him down. She was not surprised that he was Tibetan, had even expected that her assistant would have to be at least disguised as a Tibetan, but this person—so skinny and nervous—really she thought they'd have given such a key role to a person with more experience. She could have recruited someone herself on a recent visit to Berkeley—so many Tibetans demonstrating on the campus these days.

Youngden wanted to go immediately to the Jokhang Temple and the Potala Palace, but she told him the prudent rule: Rest first and adjust to the altitude. She asked the desk clerk for a room with a view of the Palace. As they were about to take the elevator, Youngden heard in the hotel bar the hollow thumping of beads against a Tibetan *Chod* drum. "My friend!" he cried, rushing toward the bar. She followed, annoyed. When she caught up to him he nodded to the drummer, a Tibetan like himself and explained, "He at UC Berkeley with me. I have drum just like his in my bag."

"*You* were at Berkeley?"

"Sure. Teach Tibetan language—in '87. Year after you graduate."

Bodhi felt somewhat shamed. Perhaps there was more here, she thought, than met the eye. Besides, it wasn't really appropriate for her to question "A's" personnel decisions.

"Maybe we can use your *Chod* drum later." But for now she drew him away from the drummer and the mix of exotics in the bar, and pushed him into the elevator, telling him not to speak to anyone—spies were everywhere and their mission secret.

Youngden went straight to the window to look for the view of the Potala, but the window opened only onto a dingy courtyard. "No view," he said to Bodhi.

"You heard me ask for it," she said picking up the phone.

The desk clerk pretended she had not spoken to him. "Not any view," he told her. This was annoying. She worried that she might be calling attention to herself, but said courteously, "You mean, no view room is available?"

"Modom. No view of Potala Palace in hotel." She managed to contain her scorn until she hung up. "They've built this American eyesore here and not one window looks out on the Palace! Unbelievable!"

Youngden maintained his equanimity. "Maybe Chinese object." He stretched out on the bed in a reclining Buddha posture, and called up in his imagination the tiered rectangles of the thousand rooms of the historic palace where "A" had lived before exile. Here in this hotel where everything was new, he felt a flood of longing for the past—in this his first visit to the great sacred city where his people had flourished in peace. His mind filled with images of rich processionals, of the young Dalai Lama being borne up the palace walk on a royal *palinquin,* under umbrellas of peacock feathers and yellow silk, of helmeted horsemen accompanying him up to the splendid palace rooms, of other horsemen wearing the fringed, beaked hats of high *tulkus.*

Meanwhile, Bodhi had kicked off her shoes and was improvising an altar on the dresser with votive candles and a little mandala she took from her bag, representing Buddha-mind, a display of ultimate reality.

He said wistfully, "I hear of Potala Palace all my life, but never see before. Altitude not worry me. We go now?"

She shook her head as she lit the candles. "Just relax," she said.

Youngden sank back into images of the holy processions at the Jokhang Temple. But other images of all that he had learned of the cruelty of Chinese police around the Temple crowded in on him. He saw a monk struck on the head, another shot, a nun knocked to the ground—all because someone holding a *mala* in his fist had defied a policeman and cried out: "Free Tibet!" Youngden's mind was trained not to dwell upon horror. Yet other images flooded in, of reports he had heard from "B," the Amnesty attorney, and from others, of women whose breasts were amputated, men who were castrated. He saw torturers forcing people to eat salt, then denying them water. He saw a police interrogator giving a monk his own urine to drink. An image rose of an officer dangling a child from a window until his mother confessed to—any crime. Then he saw the man drop the child after all, heard the body thud in the Barkor. Youngden struggled against these images, tried to cut them from flowing through his mind. He called upon the store of cultural memory instilled in him, of huge round drums and long horns sounding, as vibrantly clad lamas danced under a flutter of prayer flags in the courtyard, every dance a meditation, observed in reverence by pilgrims whose hats identified their tribal origins, round and pointed hats, hats of fur and felt and silk and feathers. What it must have been like to be part of all that, of the great sacred empowerments!

He got up and went to the window to glimpse what he could in the street. On the courtyard below no lamas danced; all he could see were a few Chinese people performing calisthenics. And beyond he glimpsed a police patrol.

To recover the old ways, Youngden thought, what would he give? If only their mission succeeded in showing the world what it needed to know to support the Tibetan cause! He was filled with a sense of purpose as never before.

Suddenly, he glanced back and caught sight of Bodhi, and this wrenched him away from all thoughts of the past. She was removing her clothing unceremoniously. Her skin was very pale and glowing. She folded her jeans and T-shirt onto a chair.

"We haven't been given the empowerment together," she said, "but as you often put it, 'Is okay.'" She held out her hands to him with a mischievous smile. "*Karma Mudra?*"

He swallowed, watching as she took a satin quilt with Tibetan-style patchwork from the foot of the bed and knelt to fold it onto the floor. She stretched out in a half-odalesque, and patting the quilt seductively, she said, "Come here."

He stood up. Here was something to wrench him from thoughts of the past, good and bad. He crossed the room shakily. "The bed's too soft," she said, pulling her body into a half-lotus position. "I like sitting up, don't you?"

He sank onto the quilt and gazed at her figure. Her breasts were small but budded upward, erect, and her long black hair flowed about her shoulders. "Oh Bodhi," he said. "I can't believe you do this to me!"

"Not *to* you, idiot, *with* you."

She sprang up, went to the window, and tried to open it. He

glimpsed her back just as he had always visualized the consort of Vajrasattva when doing his guru mantra—a slender waist from which a full hipsaddle flared out. "Too bad," she said. "Sealed shut. I hate air conditioning."

He smiled. "That's an aversion, Bodhi."

She laughed and returned to sit cross-legged before him again.

"Now," she said. "Why don't you take off that lama robe?"

"If you say," he said. "But this not the way, you know."

"Not the way?" Shy as well as nervous, she thought, reaching to help him with the sash.

"For *Karma Mudra.*"

"Oh tell me," she teased, tugging at the sash.

"First, guru help you find consort."

She laughed, dropped her hands to her knees. "Didn't 'A' put us together? He set us on a short, fast path."

Youngden smiled at her joke. The short path in Buddhist study was the most difficult of the paths to enlightenment. Maybe she was joking altogether. He reached out, took her hands, looked into her eyes, and asked, "What you want?"

"Youngden, I'm only kidding about *Karma Mudra.* I just think we should get to know one another better, don't you?" Again she had to wonder if he were all there, or just inexperienced in everything. Did he even know how to handle a camera? Maybe she would have to do it all. In London, she had grown used to the shortfalls of Brits at the network, and as for Tibetans in the dharma, well, multiple partners seemed built into their genes. More than one *tulku,* liberated into the free enterprise system, had found his way to her bedroom, had helped to bring about the state of her readiness now. This resistance in Youngden was a surprise.

He pressed her hands and held his gaze on hers. "Consort practice go by stages. Guru help you all the way. First, in this yoga tell each other things. Talk about teachings carefully. Sometimes all night long talking. So both understand how practice benefit others, all beings. Not just self. My guru say very important. He say another thing. 'Choose someone only gladdens your heart.' This very important." He shook his head gently. "I think maybe your heart not glad."

"My heart—" She looked down and fingered an edge of the patchwork quilt. She knew desire had entered her body without gladness of heart, but—It had been a long time since that came to the notice of any man. She shot a glance at this Youngden. She didn't understand Tibetans. Either they were all over you or full of teaching!

He said, "One thing more. Consort stay together long time. Lifetime maybe."

She said abruptly, "Oh well, forget it."

Youngden crossed the room for her T-shirt. He helped her stand up and put it on. It was a long T-shirt, came down to cover her hips. Her breasts, he noticed, showed through the cloth, still erect. He said, "We try one thing, okay? Sit and hold hands."

"Arcane," she said.

"What mean *arcane?*"

"Romantic, old-fashioned."

"Could be. But want to try?" She gave an ever so slight shrug. "Sit and think what we really want. My guru say second step."

"What we want . . ." She sighed, first irritated, then aware of a tug in her throat that stopped her speech. She sat down. She didn't know what she wanted anymore. Urban living had done something to her heart. Had ambition eaten it away?

"Yes, we sit together until we get answer," he said. "Look at each other." He slid his palms under hers, held onto her fingers. She noticed that his hands were warmer than her own, not at all nervous now. He gazed calmly into her eyes for a long while, and she into his. Her breasts relaxed, her breathing deepened, and so did his. Sunlight glinted through the window, flashing gold reflections on her improvised altar. A fragile light seemed to surround them.

At length a thought arose so strongly in Bodhi that she spoke before she knew it. Something she wanted seemed to come forth as if from another life. She felt a keen rush of thirst; her mouth was dry, her lips felt cracked. Her voice sounded faint, exhausted. Like a small child, she felt—yes, a longing for her mother's breast. She said, "I want—a drink of milk."

Youngden spoke as well. "Me too," he said, and he stood up and reached up to the night table for the telephone. "I call room service."

She stood up and hugged him. "Oh Youngden, I felt so odd, as if you had turned into my mother."

"Like Tara," he said, with a heart-faced grin. "Like all sentient beings, we mother to each other."

Something had come loose in Bodhi's worldly posture as a successful video producer, even her pride at being chosen for this important mission. She had to put aside her misgivings about Youngden. She liked this little guy. She said, "My mother was Italian-American, you know, and very beautiful, not very nourishing. I was always jealous of her. Competing with her." She went on, elaborating on that history as if it still mattered, even as she remembered her mother had lost her looks and now lived the lonely life of an aging divorcée.

When room service came, Youngden took the tray and brought it to her, smiling happily. "It's yak milk," he said. And they drank it down.

In a few moments they were on the street, gazing up at the tiers of windows to the Potala Palace. Youngden turned to her joyfully. "Look, Bodhi, do you see what I see?" A rainbow was arched above the palace, washing the square corners of its thousand rooms with pastel light. "It's like a miracle," he said.

She smiled and said, "Okay, let's go climb all those palace steps."

5

Although Mr. Fu is Tibetan, he is also a Bruce Lee look-alike. He wears a kind-of uniform—a black jacket, trousers, and cap, white socks, and black shoes that look a shade too small. He is such an enthusiastic driver that at the first turn beyond the paved road he runs the Isuzu Trooper into a ditch. This infuriates him. He gets out and although we start to follow to help him, he jumps into the ditch and single-handedly pushes the vehicle out onto the road. A triumph of four-wheel engineering and adrenaline.

The front fender is smashed. He bangs it back out, but the damage is still visible. He stomps around the road, apparently cursing. This will cost him, maybe as much as he'll earn on the trip if body work here is as steep as in the States. Alarmed by this evidence of his passionate nature, we try to calm him down. "Is okay. Will be okay," Lama Mingme says to him. Only when we offer to help pay for the repairs does his rage subside, and his good humor return.

Mr. Fu is in his late twenties, I imagine. He was brought up in Chengdu, he tells Dorje, is not married, did not learn Tibetan from his parents, and doesn't believe in religion, although he has an aged religious mother living in Chengdu. Dorje, as usual, does not hesitate to demand such family data.

Is Mr. Fu Communist? I ask Dorje. He shrugs. He doesn't believe in politics either. This appears to be the way of many urbanized Tibetans, and in fact many Chinese. Ignorant of the horrors of the cultural revolution, or perhaps trained to forget it, Mr. Fu does not dwell upon the past, upon the fact that in Tibet there are now only 2000 monks left out of 200,000, that Chinese authorities stripped the monasteries of valuables, destroyed many of them, then tortured and jailed monks and nuns. Tibetans like Mr. Fu are successes by Communist standards, except for a lack of dedication to the Party (or to anything else) that they keep to themselves.

We try to restore our confidence in him through conversation. A wave of chatter rises between Dorje's mum and auntie.

At the outset, by the time I had finished at the hotel cashier, everyone was settled in the Trooper, Dorje between her auntie and mum in the middle seat, Mingme in the rear jump seat alongside the luggage, his feet propped on giant duffel bags. They had saved the front seat for me. Deference to age? I didn't like that—the American way is to stay forever ageless.

I said, "We can switch around later in the day." But later nobody wants the front. "Too private," Dorje says. Mingme says he likes it in the rear, where he has a clear view for taking photos. It is a kind of seclusion, the front seat, as Mr. Fu and I cannot speak together without Dorje. She likes sitting with Mum and Auntie so that they may chatter in Chinese. Still, I have my notebook, my constant companion.

Dorje's relatives talk nonstop, Mum mostly. Mum's voice sounds strongest in its higher register, but she uses its full range; a rich, actressy tone with a rasp of hoarseness, as if from overuse.

Somewhat younger than Mum, perhaps in her late forties, Auntie is comfortably round, while Mum is very small and slender. Both women wear slacks and T-shirts and have Western-style permanent waves.

Dorje, sitting between them in the middle seat, leans forward, as rice fields flash past us, and confides their unhappiness to me in English. Auntie is married to a man in Canton who apparently oppresses her, and has a couple of grown children. Mum also has several sons and daughters, Dorje the youngest. Mum plans to move to Canton to be near her sister, for she has just separated from her husband, whom I met in their Hong Kong apartment. He sent his wife away because he is very ill and does not want to have her with him in his fatal sickness.

Despite their sorrows, Mum is always on the lookout for a laugh and, spotting it, gives a raucous outburst. Auntie's voice sounds far less frequently, on a faint note of complaint or disagreement. She has a mooning, crooning voice, a moon face, too. It is actually pleasant not to have to think about what the women are saying or to respond to it, to give no thought to the meaning of their musical inflections, just to let them wash over me as I watch the scenery.

A number of farmers up to their knees in water bend over the rice fields, another farmer guides a plow drawn by a water buffalo. Although we see some farm machinery, the buffalo is still much in use. What surprises me is that the Chengdu smog has followed us as we ride the length of the paved road, and some of the workers on the roadside have covered their mouths and noses with scarves.

Mum has taken on the task of looking after our personal needs. She goes into the kitchens of the restaurants as if she had complete authority to inspect the pots on the stove. She demands the owner provide a cup of boiling water, dips the communal chopsticks into it, and wipes them with paper towels. She has brought a large supply of towels, and toilet paper too, which she doles out as she sees we need it. We all have colds, the universal Hong Kong hack buoyed up to full stature by the polluted air of Chengdu, and only she has brought enough Kleenex.

Tonight she checks us into the first town's hotel, where the Chinese personnel, another Mum and sister, eye me suspiciously. There is a discussion. Mum negotiates prices. White-devil woman must pay more than everyone else for room, it turns out. American. Why is she not on a tour? Why not with her own group? Dorje has a discussion with them about this. They are also uncomfortable about taking in Mingme, a Tibetan, though they seem not troubled by Mr. Fu, who must have official driver papers of some kind. She slaps Mingme's Nepalese passport on the smudged glass counter, shames them. "Is visitor here. Don't you know how to treat travelers from other countries?"

Later, Mum comes into our room as I am testing the beds, which are too soft. Mum shakes her head in sympathy. Tomorrow, Tibetan beds. Much better, Dorje assures me.

As we are all her surrogate children, Mum feels in her way what we feel. Now she sets down a basin of hot water for washing up that she has wrung from the management. She tries but cannot succeed in getting tea for us. She shakes her head, does not understand it. Perhaps she can buy some in a shop the next day. I find it quite comforting that Mum takes on these maternal tasks. She is the Tara of our trip; from Tara's Chinese approximation, Kuan Yin, Mum derives her protective qualities.

On the second day at dawn Mr. Fu says we will try to put in sixteen hours on the road. No time for my daily practice of Tai Chi Chuan. In the early light we all take our places as before.

The same dust rises on the roads as in the cities. I noticed few city gardens in Chengdu. Haven't we read that political prisoners become gardeners, the lucky ones? Where are they—still in jail? Landscaping—too decadent, even at the high-rise tourist hotels in Chengdu. In the packed, grassless grounds of Chengdu's museums, there were only a few ancient trees. At the zoo a grimy panda slept in a filthy cage surrounded by weeds, maybe dreaming of bamboo shoots. Caretakers at the home of the immortal Tu Fu, open to the proletariat, guarded a few manuscripts of his poems and also a dusty replica of the terracotta army of the Xian conquering emperor, whose tomb was designed as much for eternity as was the Taj Mahal. An object lesson of a time gone wrong, or a model for today? And in a hallway of horrors, for some mysterious reason, glass cases of preserved embryos bottled for all to inspect—unborn poems? I wondered. No, Communist utilitarianism again; each embryo was deformed by some pre-birth error. And in a dark room beyond the hallway, a few men slouched, watching a film about birth control. The home of a dead poet has a lot of dead space—fill it up with useful lessons from the Party.

In the front seat, I choke on the Isuzu's emissions. Emissions control is probably regarded as a suspect game of capitalist oppression, but there has been considerable rise in China's cancer rate since its rush to industrialization.

I roll down the window, hoping for a breath of mountain air. Only dust and more chemicals enter. Like the farmers outside of Chengdu, I tie a handkerchief around my nose and mouth. Dust rises for miles from oncoming trucks on the unpaved roads.

We pause along the roadside, where farmers with buckets hanging from carrying poles are coming from the fields. Rice fields stretch up into the foothills; farmers are applying crop rotation, both harvesting and seeding their paddies at the same time. The Communists have also created such collective farms in Tibet, giving land to former serfs. I think of Tolstoy, whose effort to distribute his own land to his serfs met first with bewilderment, then scorn. Working among them dressed in white peasant clothes, trying to explain his Christian socialism, his desire to redistribute the wealth and share everything, he could not make himself understood; the peasants thought that lonely, doomed giant had gone mad.

At a bend in the road, a young girl is selling pink cherries piled on a straw mat. We stop and buy some, and not long afterward, Dorje nudges Mr. Fu. "Rest stop," she says, and he pulls over. The cherries. Instant karma, Dorje jokes. Earth Mum doles out toilet paper to her.

Lama Mingme jumps from the jeep with his camera. "I take photos," he says.

Dorje and I borrow a farmer's toilet, a terra-cotta outhouse surrounded by tall bamboo. He will use our fertilizer in rice fields, Dorje says, leading the way into the shelter. Inside, we squat together with our behinds above a deep dugout pit. You must be careful not to stoop too close to the edge or you will fall backward into the excremental abyss.

We have to wait a few more minutes while Mr. Fu adjusts the carburetor. Mum and Auntie sit down by the side of the road, munching treats Mum has squirreled away. I decide to practice Tai Chi now. Mum eyes my movements with astonishment. "Mum never learn this," Dorje says. I offer to teach her what little I know. She shakes her head, but can't keep the suspicious amusement from her face as I continue. What right has this American woman to come and show off knowledge of something that belongs here? Is that her thought? Then suspicion fades and there's a glint of pride in her face. That same look rises up from my childhood, in my own mother's gaze. My child does well to study great things that are beyond my own ordinary understanding. Doesn't everything arise from the great Mother, whether the humble mother understands or not? Mum tells Dorje that we must travel later to the mountains of Emei Shan, where Tai Chi was first conceived, and where there are still great practitioners, and she nods her head possessively toward the snowy peak of Emei Shan. This is her land, her mountain, and her right as mother to offer to share it with the stranger at her gates.

We have traveled beyond Emei Shan in a northwesterly direction but can still see it cresting behind us. The peaks of Emei Shan, one of the four great guardian mountains of ancient China that held the nation's enemies apart and where holy men kept its spirit pure, are almost always clouded over. The clouds, of legendary beauty, are shot through with haloing rings from the sun that are so stirring, pilgrims sometimes jump ecstatically into that light to their death, believing they have attained the Tao of the Immortals.

Suddenly, the farmer's huge mastiff decides to go on the attack, bares ferocious incisors, and chases me. A practical opportunity to test my skill at the defenses of Tai Chi, and my limits become woefully apparent. The animal's ferocious teeth grip my skirt. I manage to turn before they sink into my leg, but my cool has vanished. I stomp angrily back to the jeep. Mum laughs hilariously.

The duffel bags in the back of the jeep under Lama Mingme's feet contain Indian brocades. Fifty rolls of brocades. Hundreds and hundreds of yards. We brought them with us into China as a gift for "C's" sister. A Hong Kong connection of Dorje's saved us walloping overweight charges at the airport. These coals to Newcastle weigh one hundred kilograms.

"C" purchased the brocades last year in India, and stored them at the home of one of his students in Hong Kong, where we picked them up. Lama Mingme brought along the two other duffel bags that day, and divided the brocades into three separate bundles, one for himself, one for Dorje, and one for me. Bolts of decorative Indian patterns threaded with gold and silver. Heavy as lead.

Packing away her share, Dorje had fingered the loosely woven fabric and sniffed. "These are not so good as Chinese."

Mingme: "No, but it's what Tibetans like."

"What are they for?" I asked.

"For the Khandro," said Mingme. "For rites in the temple."

"Oh, rituals," said I.

"Yes, *pujas*." Prayer meetings. "Help with visualization."

"Rituals," I muttered, then, "Don't you think rituals signify an attachment?" He did not reply. "Attachment to the past," I said.

He was silent. "Attachment, a major cause of suffering," I insisted, good humoredly.

He said nothing, knowing I did not want to carry the large bundle he had handed me. We staggered under our load.

"Lama Mingme, I don't believe in ritual," I said. "I think there's a conflict between ritual and the concept that we should give up our attachments." Still no reply.

"Brocades!" I said scornfully. "They have no function. They symbolize the archaic spirit of the East."

Lama Mingme, aware of my failure of charity, practiced the *paramita* of patience, at which he is very good.

Auntie croons happily as we turn a curve and again the range of Emei Shan stands out behind us. We glimpse the snowcaps, surrounded by the seductive, glowing clouds.

As we pass a freshly manured field, suddenly Auntie sniffs and her voice rises above its customary gentle croon. She shouts several syllables, with a joyful smile. Extending her arm across the back of the seat to her sister, Auntie pulls Mum closer to hug her, drawing Dorje between them into a spontaneous embrace.

Dorje: "She says, 'Oh the sweet smell of China.' She loves China."

Auntie Moon's memory would go back to pre-industrial China, before the rapid change that gave her permanent waves and polyester slacks. Despite all this country has done to itself, she loves it. I imagine her memories: Ragged beggars in foul streets, rickshaws drawn by barefoot men in coned hats, women hobbling on bound "lily" feet through the splashing color, reek, and fragrance of an open market. But I realize these are images from my own *National Geographic* file—what had the ordure of freshly turned earth actually stirred in her mind? She hums a song of attachment. The Battle Hymn of China?

After a few moments Dorje adds, "Me, not so much. I feel human with Tibet." Where she has never yet been. With luck, we shall come to the land that Dorje is conjuring in only a few days.

In the evening before Mum goes to the room she shares with Auntie, I see that she is not feeling well, and I offer her some Diamox, ask Dorje to tell her it may help prevent altitude sickness as we ascend further. She refuses with a friendly, knowing headshake: Western medicine no good.

Lama Mingme pokes his head into our room to say good night. Dorje is saying mantra; I am writing in my notebook. "I pray Tara for you good sleep," he says.

"Can Tara read and write?" I ask somewhat idly.

Lama Mingme squints at me and after a moment says, "You are too politic."

I laugh and ask him, "Did you know there was practically no separation of church and state in Tibet?" He shakes his head. "Never mind," I say. "Tara is omniscient and doesn't need book learning."

In the next bed Dorje prays with the help of a *mala* that was a gift to me from "C's" wife. It is made of pale round seed that she said came from the Bodhi tree in Bodhgaya where the Buddha attained enlightenment. Dorje, coveter of *malas,* saw that I never use it and took it in hand. As I write, the *mala* moves through her fingers, and one of the round seed pauses above her thumb. It magnifies in my mind and becomes the bald head of that Chinese officer, the character haunting my notebook. Another seed pops up, then another, each one an aspect of the man's shiny dome.

This character is so depressed I can't get him out of my mind. I may as well give in and write about him, see where it goes. Let the Bodhi seed germinate. Perhaps the Khandro woman is my muse, to suspend my disbelief for a moment. Conjure—an Indo-European root, *yewo jurare,* "to pronounce a ritual formula." Strange that this inspiration comes as I watch Dorje pronouncing her own ritual formula!

THE GOLDEN ROAD

Captain Bao Yen was burned out and deeply anxious. The orders for his relief of duty in Qinghai were more than a month late. How much longer could he bear it here? His entire company of military police were growing more than restive. His orderly, Wang, had told him that all 137 men planned to petition Beijing for leave, perhaps already had, for which he could expect a reprimand.

He ran his hands across his denuded scalp, which held ridges suggesting a much greater age than his fifty years. Some weeks ago, Bao made a report of troubles at his plant. He felt apprehensive about the report. The problem would be hell to deal with, made him appear critical of a team of scientists and technicians who had installed sealants in his plant the year before. Today an inspection team was scheduled to arrive. He listened for their plane, watched the airstrip apprehensively.

He gritted his slightly separated front teeth. A year was as long as any officer was supposed to stay at 07 Base—they had promised him that when his assignment came up. This was his third year. Command of Operation 07, top secret, the mountain refuse depot.

He stared out at the massive mountain rising in the distance beyond his office window, and reached down for the binoculars he wore on a strap around his neck. In the midday sun a lone Tibetan in maroon robes was walking up the trail that curved out toward that vast, almost circular range. The mountain had a number of domes of snow that, as the sun rays crossed it, changed to the color of a pink lotus. This was one of the many mountains held holy to the Tibetan race, and was believed by some of those foolish people to be the center of the universe. Bao laughed at that, yet as he watched its curiously changing colors, the way the light played about its petal-like peaks, he sensed there was something different about this mountain. A Tibetan prisoner had confessed that it was not even on their map, it was so sacrosanct and secret. It wasn't on China's map either, Bao thought—at least on no official map released to the public, for it was here they had built their great nuclear waste dump.

Not many Tibetan pilgrims made the journey up this path nowadays, but once in a while someone, like this single monk today, struggled up the heights.

Bao's stocky frame sank into his swivel chair; he held his bare head in his hands. His cough started in his throat with a wheeze, then convulsed through his trunk and down to his groin. That was as much as he ever felt in his groin now, he thought, spasms of a cough. He had sent in a health report on himself and his men, but still no reply from Beijing. Three years. One year was too long to stay at this post—even a day, an hour, could kill you. He knew now what the brass had withheld from him at the beginning in the name of national security. He knew that the whole desert was hot. Even the tumbleweed was lethal.

Most officers knew. At headquarters, they were buying their way out of compulsory desert service now. But that was beneath Bao. He was a victim of ground-in soldierly dedication to duty—yes sir, no sir, whatever you say, sir, and it was more than training—it was his character. Just the thought of bribery and the ghost of his old father rose up sternly before him.

Long ago his superiors had "corrected" the ghost out of him in *thamzing* sessions. There are no ghosts of ancestors, repeat a thousand times, submit to a thousand beatings until you know it. This is called internalization, and the self-struggle sessions are only for your own sake, so that you internalize what the cadres know to be fact. But Bao's father, in the way of many ghosts, was caught in an indestructible fixation: honor. His father, a farmer, had fought with Mao. A valiant soldier in the Long March, he had sometimes trooped sixty-five *shili* a day, suffering from scabies, diarrhea, starvation, hanging on with fierce loyalty even after being wounded half a dozen times. His father would not yield to exorcism. He dwelled constantly on the ancient tradition of Chinese warriors steeped in the Confucius code of honor and duty to family, and had even secretly worshipped Kuan Tí, the God of War whose story he had instilled in Bao Yen as a boy.

Bao couldn't stop the ghost—here it was again, reiterating the story. His father's gaunt face with its long, stringy beard stared through him. There had always been a little mound just off the center of his forehead, like a cyst, where he said a bullet had lodged when he was wounded on the Luding Bridge. It had never been removed. Now in his transparent state the bullet was markedly visible. It put Bao in mind of starbursts of light the Taoists claimed to see in their meditations. The old voice quavered in its patient reiteration of the story: "How the great Kuan Tí came to have two graves: When still a mere mortal, before he was canonized, his enemies decapitated Kuan Tí, and bore his head away from a fierce field of battle. His enemies so venerated the great warrior that they called in goldsmiths, who wrought a new body of gold for him and buried it together with his head with full military honors. Kuan Tí's grieving troops recovered his real body from the field. And what did they do for his state funeral?" Bao mouthed the end of the time-worn story along with the ghost: "They made a golden head to bury with the body."

Satisfied that his son's memory was intact, the ghost faded away, the glints of the bullet in his forehead waning last. The story always moved Bao, even now. A chill of boyhood faith went through him as his father vanished. It was hearing the story as a boy that had sealed Bao's destiny as a soldier. The ideal of those tributes was bred into his bones—honor from both ally and enemy. The transcendence of it!

He heard a plane overhead, and lifting his binoculars, Bao saw that it was the small plane of the inspectors. He went out to the air strip to meet the team, a geologist and mineralogist, both wearing heavy-lensed glasses and carrying briefcases. With a sinking heart, he recognized them as having been part of the team that had installed the sealants.

They brushed off the dust their business suits had gathered in the short walk from the plane to Bao's office. They set down their briefcases and wiped their glasses. He said, "Lucky you got here before the windstorm, due tomorrow, I think." He told them that the wind would whirl up sand that would seep everywhere, even through the concrete walls of his quarters. "Sometimes it sifts into the video security and clogs the electronic surveillance board." The mineralogist whipped out a pad and made a note of that. Bao laughed tensely. "Stones as big as basketballs roll around the landscape, knock down anybody in their path. They have caused a few deaths." With a wheezing laugh, he told the scientists these things. He didn't mention that radioactive silt also lodged in everyone's lungs. The visitors were already shuddering.

Just then they heard the roar of a huge air freighter overhead. Bao passed his binoculars to his visitors so that they could see the plane's logo, a red-faced skull and crossbones labeled TRU-RAW. "That tells me it's from the US," he said. "Typical American joke. TRU-RAW is an acronym of TRansUranic-Radio-Active Waste."

"Do you get many shipments from them?" the geologist asked.

"Shipments come from everywhere," Bao said somewhat evasively, aware he had already talked too loosely. The loneliness of his post was driving him, he knew. Actually, shipments from the US had vastly increased ever since their Yucca Mountain fiasco, but he said nothing, as he showed them to the washroom behind his office, showed them the decontam suits and helmets to wear.

His men called their outpost "garbage detail." Most material was shipped overland by railway, or conveyed by truck. This batch airborne from the US would be followed next week by junk from Germany and the Netherlands. Lots of trash from private companies, everything transportable used in industry—from huge canisters of spent reactor fuel to small bales of contaminated tools, wiping rags, gloves, worn-out machinery, even the carcasses of experimental animals, monkeys, dogs. The other day a few thousand quick-frozen white mice arrived. The world's refuse, compressed by compactor and baled, freighted up, and shipped out. His men would take the casks and canisters below to the mine. Some would be encased in concrete-lined salt beds, some simply buried.

His visitors were suited and helmeted to go below. Bao saw they noticed a model of the works on his desk that his orderly had made; it looked like a child's hand-held game of a maze—an intricate interlacing of mineshaft hollows. He said, "You probably remember what it looks like below. Tilt it to get a steel ball into Start." He laughed again, but his visitors only peered at the model and back at him through their thick lenses. Bao punched up the elevator that led from his office to a monorail car.

The car, sealed with thick protective glass, gave Bao private access to the underground storage operations, and facilitated his daily inspection of the work. It ran down through a long tunneled drift into the depths of an exhausted uranium mine.

Bao said, "The trouble's in Tomb #3. The canisters. Leaky canisters. Could be a nightmare to fix." The visitors were gazing through the car windows and made no reply.

Suddenly a pounding roar reverberated down the drift. "What is that?" one of the men asked.

"Drilling," Bao explained. Drilling to deepen the mines went on daily. "Like quarry sculptors grinding out headstones," he said with a grim smile. The old mines were, after all, being transformed into a massive graveyard. The air became eerily misted from the oil and watery fog spewing out of one of the drills down the line. "It's like the desert dust. Seeps through even the reinforced concrete of my quarters."

The workers were Tibetan prisoners mostly, and a few Mongolians and Chinese dissident prisoners, too, all overseen by his troops. They were steel-gloved and helmeted, but underneath the helmets, all of them were also bald, and many had begun to lose their skin.

Bao stopped the cab at the huge titanium and zinc alloy canisters where he had detected seepage. Water in the tombs meant corrosion, then eventually seepage into ground water. It was a very dangerous situation.

The men took from their briefcases some small testing vials and got out of the cab. They asked Bao to leave them there to do their testing. Bao returned in the car to his office.

As he waited, Bao thought of the contents of the vault behind his desk. There he kept an extraordinary invention. This was a weapon of his own design, which he was ready to offer to the Minister of Defense in Beijing. In his spare time there in the desert he had developed it in secret. He knew that it warranted a Medal of Auspicious Distinction, if he ever had a chance to make a presentation at the Ministry. As soon as he could get leave, he would take it into Beijing.

It was not long before the signal for the car below lit up. The inspectors were quick to return. In his office, they gazed at Bao to the point of discomfort. One wiped his lenses studiously. Their tests, they told him, indicated the tanks were neither corroding nor seeping. Proved his speculations improper, in fact. One said, "The cells are adequately blocked with the sealants we installed last year."

Bao looked out the window at the sweeping mountain view. After a moment, he said, "Do you know how close we are to the source of our great rivers? That mountain—"

One of the scientists shrugged impatiently. "That mountain probably has no springs. It isn't even on the map. There is no danger."

"It's just a few hills," said the other.

"Hills!" said Bao, wondering if the man needed those heavy lenses changed. "We could contaminate the water of all China."

"Don't be superstitious," said the other, making a note. "There's no proof of a river source anywhere near here."

"I believe this entire installation is a mistake," Bao muttered. It sounded like treason, even to his own ears. "I mean, I believe we could create another depository deeper in the autonomous regions, further West where we did the testing. All that vast basin and beyond could be safer. I have suggested to Beijing—"

"No danger. No way," said the other, also writing something down, then gazing at his wristwatch. "Beijing will stand by our analysis, I'm sure."

"The sealants are safe," said his associate, folding his graphs and charts into his briefcase carefully as if they were sacred text.

Bao offered the men tea—perhaps if they sat down together they would see reason. But they refused—probably out of fear of contamination, he thought to himself.

And so Bao saw the two determined men off on their plane, and returned his office. He sank into his chair. Perhaps the only result of his reporting the leaks would be another reprimand. Or worse. He shook his head.

Denial of the danger seeping through this base would destroy his life and the lives of his men. The prisoners, too, he thought, as he glimpsed again that lone ant-like Tibetan figure making his pilgrimage up the mountain path. Eventually, the drinking water would be lethal throughout Tibet, then wherever rivers flowed, slowly wherever rivers flowed …

He swiveled around to gaze at the vault. The way his reports were handled, he might never get to Beijing with his invention. He was beginning to doubt the wisdom of even trying.

The fax machine jerked into action, bringing hope back to tug at him. It had to be word of his relief. At last, his orders! He crossed the room to the machine. Perhaps now he could tell his men their reprieve was in hand.

"Kuan Tí," he whispered, "please deliver me."

6

A mighty whitewater that can be heard across the entire town of Luding sweeps below a suspension bridge. We walk across the bridge above the churning Dadu River. Dorje and I grasp the side chain railings and one another's hands like scared schoolgirls, as the loose planks of the flooring shift under our feet. This bridge, held up by chains suspended from rocks at either side, looks sketchily built, but it has been here since 1701.

The sweep of history rushes with this dramatic river. The town rests in a deep valley cut by the water on the ancient "Imperial Route," along which tributes to Peking emperors were brought by dignitaries in sedan chairs suspended on poles. Here in 1935 during the agonizing 12,000 mile Long March, the Red Army took the bridge from Chiang Kai Chek's forces, who then set fire to its planks, and the Reds dashed across hand over hand by the chain railings. In the Fifties when established in power, Mao Tse Tung sent his People's Liberation Army here to invade Tibet and to create the roads that have enabled them to hold the region.

In the open gaps between the boards, the water churns thirty feet below us. Dorje and I cannot hear one another speak over its roar. At the other side, she translates Mao's slogan inscribed on stone: *All China United.*

Branches of broad-leafed trees meet above the busy main street. The trees, not very old, may have been saplings planted some thirty years ago. I imagine these streets, with PLA soldiers crowding the many snack bars and cookstands, sitting at the small outdoor tables to eat steamed dumplings and noodles and to suck on the stewed feet of chicken, before the start of their march into Tibet. Did this town, with the passage of its rushing water, make the soldiers also aware of time passing and of change? Did they think of the heroism of the Red Army or guess at the terror they themselves would bring to Tibet in the effort to unite "all China?"

Mum has insisted we pay for everything only with Chinese RMB, not FEC, tourist money. Dorje says that Mum will pay for all the food and I am to repay her when we return with dollars, which she can then change on the black market. Sounds okay for Mum but rather an inconvenience should there be anything I need to buy. There isn't, however. At every stop only absolute necessities, usually made of plastic. We have lunch at a semi-outdoor grill, where a row of ducks is being roasted. On our table, unabashed, a roll of toilet paper. Which turns out to be there for use as napkins. Again, no tea. What is going on? Who ever would have thought we'd need to bring tea to China? Worse than bringing brocades.

Afterward, while the others go shopping for road edibles, I prefer to sit alone in a teahouse overlooking the river gorge. Mum objects—I should stay with group. But I hold my ground, and insist they go on without me.

An old woman with hunched shoulders and an amiable smile brings a teapot and serves me. Delicious green tea. Mum should be here.

Two young men at the next table nod to me. At their feet, backpacks. One of them wants to practice his English. Architecture students in Beijing and on school break, they are headed into Erlon Shan to hike.

The student who can speak English tells me in a low voice he has seen police violence at the student demonstrations in Beijing and testifies to seeing friends beaten. He says he fears that worse things are coming, but believes that Communism has to end in China. Everyone says so, he says. "Did you ever hear Mao's slogan, 'Let a Hundred Flowers Bloom, Let a Hundred Schools of Thought Contend'? Now it's really happening." His expression is a study in conflict between disbelief and hope.

I notice a policeman in the street, watching us. He moves into the café, fixes his gaze on the three of us, and braces his stick between his palms. It comes to me that mine is probably the only white face in town. I can sense fear in the policeman, that he fears having to take some action against these school children. I ask them if the police can understand English. No, of course not. "But they don't like us to talk to Westerners." The policeman stares until I become concerned for the students, remembering what they have witnessed in Beijing.

I turn to my notebook, find some notes about the Cultural Revolution given me by one of my Tibetan women friends, and lines from a poem, "Those Men, So Powerful," by Stanislaw Baranczak:

> always
> you were so afraid of them,
> you were so small
> compared to them, who always stood above
> you on steps, rostrums, platforms ...

In 1960 the Chinese took Nyima's father to prison, when she was eight. She and her younger brother Tashi had been raised in the country by a beloved stepmother, Damcho, in a complicated polyandrous marriage common in Tibet. But when they took her father, the Chinese moved the family downstairs into the sheep's stable. The sheep were bumped outside. In the cold early morning, Nyima and Tashi saw them huddling together, the knobs of their knees shaking. Upstairs in their house, a Chinese family moved in—a noisy, angry Chinese mother with three children who taunted them and called them names and said they looked ugly. Then the Chinese made them leave Damcho to go to school. Forty years later Nyima tells me: "I still dream about the school."

On the way Nyima saw ragged people lying in the streets of Lhasa, and hundreds of big, wild dogs. An old woman, shivering with a chill, grasped one of the dogs and held it against her body—trying to keep warm with a wild dog. Just outside of Lhasa they would go to school, away from Damcho.

"This school is special. For the 'high-born,'" the China man in charge said. "Used to be a monastery. Place for lazy monks." Nyima saw that his muscles looked stringy; his head was like a large-toothed skull, like a beggar's. Now she understood why her people had always called the Chinese "beggars."

After several months Damcho was allowed to visit them. She walked two days to the school to bring the children a basket filled with fruit and barley bread.

There were so many things Nyima wanted to tell her. She could scarcely speak. Her brother went easily to her, sat on her ample lap, fingered the silk of her striped apron. But Nyima held back, gazing up at Damcho's center-parted hair. She wore no ornaments in it today. "Why no coral in your hair?" she asked.

Damcho laughed. "So many things Nyima must have to tell her, and she asks about her hair. How are they treating you, Nyima-là?"

Badly! she wanted to blurt out. Where could she start? How she and her brother were sent to the fields to cut the tea and tie it into bundles. How Tashi began to cry because the bundle on his back was so heavy, how she tried to help him when nobody was looking but got caught and beaten for it.

So much had happened to them at the school. Just the sight of Damcho made her choke with desire to tell and tell, how their only food was watery broth, how they were punished every day for reasons they did not understand. But something made her want to keep Damcho from hearing how hard it was. She fell silent.

Peasant children also came to the school. They fared better than the rest and were allowed to go home at day's end to their families. They were called upon for a lesson about barley and weeds. The Chinese administrator glowered at everyone, and said to the peasants, "These rich children can't tell barley from weeds. Do you know why?" Nyima and Tashi lowered their faces. They knew he would answer his own questions. "Put your hands out," he demanded. That meant he would hit them, but they did as they were told. "You didn't know barley because you were pampered, taught only to enjoy the fruit of the labor of others, to live off their backs. Look how dainty your hands are!" And his whip came down on their hands, flicked their cheeks, slashed their shoulders. But that wasn't enough. He turned to the peasant children. "You know the difference between a weed and barley, don't you?"

The peasant children did not understand him at first. They knew their parents, too, were confused by this new order, these punishing

Chinese lords with their questions. "How is it that you know things these privileged children do not know? You had no schools before we gave them to you. You were allowed to learn nothing! Ignorance—the Buddha called this one of the three great causes of suffering, yet your monks kept you ignorant. Understand? You were slaves in a Medieval world!" He held whips out to them, told them they could repay their ancestors now for the evil done to them for centuries, by punishing these terrible children.

The peasant children drew back, afraid of being hit. But the guard was patient. He was used to stupidity—he said so. Education took patience. Eventually, one by one, all of the poor children took the lashes into their hands as they were told, were drawn in a spell to the whips as if they were strings of licorice candy, and they all moved toward Nyima as if she were to blame that it was not after all a treat placed in their hands. Every child was seized by a terrible common scream, then, as if they were all caught in an instant sandstorm and were struggling for shelter, they began pushing, shoving, trying to squeeze closer and closer to Nyima and Tashi. The whips screamed in the air and red worms grew on Nyima's legs, on Tashi's arms.

"Now you will learn the difference," the Chinese shouted in her ear, "between poison and food. You will not be so dumb again." But Nyima felt dumb, and still didn't know the difference. This is how those in the animal realm must feel, how the sheep numbed by the snow must feel. She thought she would never know the difference, as new pain sprouted in her heart like weeds, with other hurts so dense she couldn't tell one from another. Everything that happened seemed to create another hurt she couldn't name.

By this time she knew that if she said nothing, there would be less punishment. This is how she learned to put up with abuse. Dumb! Yes, she fell silent, like an animal who cannot tell a weed from barley. What was food, what was poison? With Damcho she was dumb as well—to speak to of the pain would only make it worse.

On Damcho's lap Tashi began to cry. His tears fell down upon the cloth that covered the fruit, the barley bread. "Have some food," Damcho told them, folding back the cloth, handing Tashi an orange. He held it on his lap, made no attempt to peel it. He gazed at the orange. "Stones this big," he said.

His words released a flood of images for Nyima, making it even harder to speak. The two Chinese women at the school, Lin and Fae, sent the children to gather rocks "the size of oranges," they said, and they had to pile them in the courtyard. "Good exercise! You Tibetans do not get enough exercise. Holy walks around idols are not exercise!" Then they made the children smash the Buddha statue with the rocks.

Damcho took the orange, broke into its peel with her thumbnail, carving a single tangy-smelling coil of peel. "I know about the statue," she said. "Never mind." That made Nyima's eyes sting.

"It was only to avoid beatings," she said.

"Do what they tell you to do. They can't take your mind away," Damcho said.

But that was what they meant to do! Nyima knew. When the whips broke on her legs she felt a break inside herself as well. The lamas had taught her that thinking came from the heart. No wonder she felt dumb—it wasn't just because the Chinese said so, it was because she could no longer think, because her heart was broken. "You thought you would become like your mother," Fae taunted her. "Wear turquoise and coral and jasper from your crown to your navel!" They wanted her mind more than anything, they wanted to twist all her truths into superstition.

"I sleep with the thousand buddhas," Tashi muttered soberly.

"Do you now?" smiled Damcho, pressing her forehead to his, caressing him, trying to coax a smile. But did she really understand? Did she see the sacred cloth scrolls, folded on their pallets, for them to use as sheets? Before the Chinese came their father had sent a great artist to the monastery to paint the tanka of the thousand buddhas, but Fae made Tashi use it for a sheet, knowing that he still wet the bed at night. All the children had to sleep on tankas painted with revered images, of Tara, of Chenrezi, of the peaceful and wrathful deities, of all the Bodhisattvas. "Idols and superstitious nonsense," said Lin. "Many Chinese children have no sheets at all!" said Fae, who also made them use the fine paper of the holy texts for toilet paper. She heaped scorn on Tashi: "Were you planning to become a lama, little boy? To tax the poor of all they earn, to sit with your delicate hands holding these idolatrous texts and drinking *chang* until the Buddha took you to the Pureland?" Stinging taunts were always followed by stinging slaps on the hands, to make sure they were toughened up.

Tashi slowly chewed the orange wedge, juice sliding down his chin. He seldom smiled these days, although Nyima tried to make him laugh. When they had to kill flies, she tried. The Chinese had brought many horses with them, and the horses were followed by many flies. They swarmed throughout the stables and courtyards. The school official with the large-toothed head thrust small cardboard boxes into each child's hands, empty shoe polish boxes that had the sharp smell of bootblack. He smiled as if at a private joke. "Be good little children. Kill the Buddha!" He told them to kill the flies, then place their corpses inside the boxes, that they must fill each box. The children had never killed a fly before, or anything else intentionally, for they knew that compassion was indivisible, could not be given one creature and withheld from another. Every child knew such things. However much a pest any creature might be, it valued its own life as much as a human did; it feared death and all suffering.

Behind his back, Nyima said to the children, "The Chinese brought a whole army of their ancestors for us to kill!" Everyone laughed, except Tashi.

At the end of the day the school official inspected the boxes, made sure each one was packed with corpses, then he led the children to the courtyard to a hole in the ground, recently left there when the rubble of the broken Buddha statue was taken away. The guard made the children upturn the boxes in that place, piling the dead flies on top of one another in a mass grave. This they did day after day, trying to diminish the number of flies around the steamy horses.

A fly's wings are delicate, lacy, and translucent. In a certain slant of light they can reflect the colors of the rainbow. A fly can lift its forelegs to close its tips together, as if in a *namaste* greeting. Nyima noticed these things, looking closely and speaking respectfully to each insect before taking its life. Perhaps the school official didn't realize he was giving the flies a sacred burial ground, Nyima thought to herself.

One day she heard him say, "There's no end to them. You kill them, and there they are again. How will we ever get rid of them all?"

When Damcho was ready to leave, the teacher Lin came out and thanked her for bringing the fruit and barley bread. She took it inside, and that was the last the children saw of it.

Once Nyima ran away, ran several desert miles to her father's prison. The guards there let her see him, and she told her father she had come to tell him about a quarrel she had with another child, how she had pulled her hair. For such a thing you came all this way? he smiled. He told his guards about it and, amused, they agreed to let her stay overnight. But then her father saw the welts on her legs, the scars. He asked her about them, but she could only cry.

When she came again a few weeks later, the guards remembered her, humored her. This time her mother had sent her, she told them. She said to the guards that a dying relative was begging to see her father. Actually, the family was greatly disturbed over the suicide of a cousin who had been tortured and who had flung himself in despair into the river. The guards finally agreed to let Nyima's father go home for one night. Nyima's uncle, a prison trusty, was allowed to go as his guard. They were even given horses. Nyima rode before her father, touching the horse's coarse mane. As soon as darkness fell, the father and the uncle gathered the family together, mindful of the fate of their cousin. That night the entire family escaped.

Except for Nyima's brother. The school would not allow him to go home to see his father, as he was being punished for some misdeed. And so Tashi was left behind at the school.

Damcho, several other children, and Nyima's grandmother all traveled along a mountain trail above a river. Nyima remembers that her grandmother, walking on the ledge and guiding the horse, let go of the rein for a moment and the horse fell into the abyss. They lost the animal and most of their supplies, and were without food for days. At last they crossed a flimsy suspension bridge on the Indian border. Knowing they were being chased by Chinese soldiers, Nyima's father cut the rope of the bridge after they had safely crossed. She remembers the flash of his knife, the rope going slack, the bridge sliding into the water below, the subdued cheers of the family. She remembers the reflection of the moon shattering when the bridge struck the water.

Damcho got a job as a dishwasher, her father did coolie labor on the roads. Nyima herself eventually became a trader of Tibetan art in Kathmandu.

I asked her about Tashi. She said she hasn't seen him since she became a refugee, had only heard of him from others. "He goes in Chinese mind," she said.

I become uncomfortable for the student hikers. The policeman does not go away, but continues to glare at them. I fear their fearlessness, both an encouraging and forboding sign. I wish them luck, and gather up my things, shake hands with them, say good-bye. As I watch them walk away with their knapsacks, the sound of students singing outside my balcony echoes.... *"The Internationale ..."* I realize I want to telephone my son.

When I rejoin the others, Mum expresses disgust with the town. No tea here either. What a mystery! What has happened to all the tea in China? Perhaps my tea house would sell her some, I suggest.

I tell Dorje this may be the last chance I have at international telephoning. I had reached home once from the Chengdu hotel, and my son had told me that my mother was weaker.

Dorje goes with me to the local police station, where she insists that they let me use my calling card. After an intense and lengthy discussion, a policeman throws up his hands. Gritting his teeth, nearly outdone by Dorje's insistence, he dials for an international operator. "Dorje," I say, "you should join the democracy movement here in China. The Communists could never stand up to you." She laughs, but says, "Politics too worldly."

She speaks to the operator, gives the number, and we wait. Again a great deal of heated discussion as Dorje talks to the operator. It is amazing how much Dorje has to say. What can it all be about? After a while she hangs up, says we have to wait half an hour. "What was the argument about with the operator?" I ask.

"I told her is emergency. I said doctor have to talk to you about putting Mum in hospital. I told about emphysema, what you said other day, that lungs so sensitive she can develop pneumonia any moment."

"All that?"

"I explain your son need help."

"But he doesn't, he's every bit as capable as you are." That may not be true, of course. He has none of her presumption. But I must defend him against Dorje's blind assessment.

"He can manage okay?" She smiles. "Anyhow, don't tell operator."

The police make us wait outside in the street, where we watch the market crowds with their baskets. One man goes by with a carrying pole that contains nothing more than a woman's purse at the end of it. Two men struggle at each end of another pole bearing the weight of an automobile motor.

But at the end our wait, the operator calls back and says the lines are down. I cannot get through.

Dorje says, "Is okay, I know. Like Mingme says, 'Will be okay.'"

The ruts in the semi-graveled road deepen, and we grow weary from jolting. Every day we try to travel between fourteen and sixteen arduous hours, not a vacation as I had warned Dorje. Late in the day, we come upon a horseshoe curve where repairs are being made, and realize the workers are Tibetan. This encourages us, as they're the first Tibetans we've seen on the road, broad of face, sturdy of limb. Their cheeks are chapped with rouge-like puffs. They differ so strikingly from Chinese that just a glimpse supports their claim to an historic identity of their own. Lama Mingme calls out to them, and they reply, grinning at him. He becomes elated by the bond of language.

"Your own blood!" Dorje cries to him.

The workmen are gathering up rocks from landslides, repairing cliffhanger openings at the side of the road. Many Chinese and Tibetan youths died in the building of this road; such a death was thought to be as valorous as death in battle.

Mum starts to sing, and Dorje and Auntie join in. Even Mr. Fu in the front seat knows this song and sings as well, a rousing march. *O Erlan Shan*. Every Chinese schoolchild has to learn this song, Mum says.

Dorje translates for me and I write it in my notebook:

O Erlan Shan
Higher than ten thousand feet
Ancient trees and flowers
on every slope
Big the rock and mud away
heroes of building road
have no fear of wind and rain
and patient for hungry …

7

Even though we notice a Tibetan checking in at the Guest House, once again the manager offers suspicion of Mr. Fu and Mingme, which Dorje has to argue about. Uneasy glances at the white foreign devil. It is a tense moment. The landlord could lift the phone and ruin everything, we think.

"Guest House" is a euphemism for rectangular concrete cell blocks. Originally built for traveling Party dignitaries, and spaced along the route at intervals of a day's travel, they also enable the truck drivers to bed down after a hard day's drive.

We are finally admitted, but to rooms four flights up from the outhouse, a fact we do not learn until after having climbed the stairs. When I groan over this, Mum beckons me into the dark, odoriferous hallway. A vent pipe stands at the end of the hall; she peers through the hole cut in the floor for the pipe—you can see all the way down to the ground floor. She pantomimes a suggestion that I use the pipe hole for peeing. The smell declares others had done so, she seems to assure me. The corners of her mouth lift encouragingly, maternally, as she gropes in her pockets for some tissue. I shake my head. Is okay. Not to worry, I say. I'm not so feeble I can't climb the stairs. "For 'Guest House' read 'Flop House,'" I mutter to myself, descending. "We are born between feces and urine ..." St. Augustine should be posted on every Guest House door.

Afterward in the room, Dorje is reciting her mantras. I lie down without testing the bed, and sit up immediately. Rock hard. Running my hand under the edge of the mattress, I find wooden slabs laid underneath the excruciatingly solid mats. I thought I liked a hard bed, but I didn't know hard. Dorje sees my comedy and her fingers go to her lips in her classic satire, even as she continues her mantra.

After her ritual, she says, "At least you have your darling pillow." It amuses her that I've brought along a small down pillow, but it is getting me through many a hard night.

I turn out the bare overhead bulb. The chatter of Mum and Auntie comes through the thin wall separating our rooms. It is as if there is no wall, and they talk without ceasing far into the early hours. Agnes Smedley once wrote that she thought foot-binding was a clever device intended to make Chinese women silent and submissive. I can almost understand a man driven to extreme measures by the likes of Mum and Moon!

We are all anxious as we load the jeep. A twitter of rose finches in the solitary tree inside the concrete wall reaches us in the breaking light. This morning we found that the guest house, grim as its sleeping quarters were, had a restaurant, with a cauldron of steaming white *conge* in the center of white-clothed tables, as well as other delights, pork buns—and tea! Mum barged into the kitchen and tried to buy some tea from the management. Nothing doing. She came away rebuffed and puzzled. This small town lies on what used to be called the Tea road. Where is all the tea in China?

"I am nervous as you today," Dorje says to Lama Mingme. We are hoping to reach the border checkpoint before officials arrive. Mr. Fu starts up the Trooper, and the arduous, bone-jarring day begins.

Mingme has insisted on sitting in the rear, but as soon as we reach the rutted road prolonged groaning begins to come from his corner. Shortly we all begin imitating him—Ahgh! Ahgh!—even anticipating his cries as we approach potholes. As soon as the jeep starts up today, his groans come forth, and Dorje, Mum, and Auntie imitate him good humoredly.

Dorje says: "It's good to have someone like that on a trip to make fun of!"

Mum tells a dream she had. She was riding south on a giant pig, which kept falling down in mud. It sounds comic, but Mum was terrified by it. Dorje tries to reassure her by saying that we are actually going north and that the dream reminds her of a Tibetan saint and namesake, called Dorje Phamo, "Thunderbolt Sow," who may be looking after her. I keep to myself the thought that the dream may mean Dorje shouldn't have brought her mother along.

There are checkpoints on this road, but none is manned in the early morning. "Maybe no guard at any checkpoint," Lama Mingme says. If we are turned back, we can simply go back, we reason. We have not discussed the possibility of imprisonment and other Communist response to outlaws.

The road narrows as we ascend. High above us, a ribbon waterfall trickles steeply down from the rocky face of the mountainside. Low rhododendron bushes are growing along the mountainsides, gold and russet. There is no right-of-way for uphill traffic in these mountains. You barge ahead. Whoever has the strongest will wins. We hear warning horns from oncoming traffic at every turn, which makes us even more watchful for patrol cars.

At one turn, Mr. Fu comes to an abrupt stop. Caterpillars driven by Chinese workmen are moving away a landslide directly in our path. Piles of rock and dirt cover the road, and the machinery is lifting it to dump it down over the side. A few Tibetan workers are helping in this with shovels. Mr. Fu turns off the motor to wait and we get out to stretch. A spray of tiny lavender irises grows along the roadway, endangered by the Caterpillars.

When one of the workmen pauses to let traffic go through, horns of trucks sound for us to make way for them. We pull over to oblige. This passage is no place to stand up for your right-of-way.

No police in sight at least. That makes us hopeful.

At length we come to a checkpoint where there is a roadblock, with several trucks parked behind it. But the booth is unmanned. "Auspicious," says Lama Mingme. We stop and enter an outdoor café beside the road to inquire about this.

Mum begins talking at once to the café owner, but not about the roadblock. Food first. Mum always gets the best possible food everywhere we go. At every stop, she singles out a café owner whose place may look very discouraging outside, but from whom she is able to command amazingly fine cuisine.

Dorje seeks the information we need. Road closed, the café owner says.

"What! We cannot get through?" asks Dorje.

Not until afternoon. The road has eastbound traffic mornings, westbound afternoons. Too narrow for two-way traffic, too many landslides. Most of the trucks waiting for afternoon passage have no cargo, which puzzles me somewhat—aren't they headed to Lhasa for trade? Mr. Fu pulls the Isuzu behind the last one in line. We are close to the checkpoint booth, which is empty, with no official to demand permits. Yet.

"What if we just drove on through?" asks spunky Lama Mingme.

Dorje advises not. We might run headlong into irate truck drivers. Better to cross the barrier along with the afternoon truckers; a number of others have already pulled in behind us. But by then won't there be a guard? We decide to wait and see. It will be a long, all-morning wait.

I walk down the road and stretch out on the grass in the shade of an official building, away from the buzz of Mum and Moon, and draw my straw hat over my face hoping to sleep off a fresh cold. However, instant karma, as Mingme would say. Flies buzz about me, making sleep impossible. I sigh, sit up, and open my notebook, write about a fictional Mr. Fu. My plot requires him to understand English, which I have to make the common language. I have a feeling Mr. Fu may become pivotal.

THE GOLDEN ROAD

Now that the jeep driver, Mr. Fu, was on the road, he was beset by emotional turmoil. His passengers puzzled him—What was their mission? He had seen at once that they were traveling in disguise. The monk and the old nun had some hidden agenda, yet made no attempt to conceal the fact from him. They seemed to think he knew all about it. But he didn't want to know about it. He wanted to stay out of trouble. He tried to eat at a separate table from theirs, but they appeared to have proletariat views, and saw his effort to sit apart from them as submission to lower status. "Join us, do!" they insisted from the start.

Their every expression was kindness itself. That was part of the mystery. Kindness was too simple. Mr. Fu was accustomed to other qualities—suppression of opinion, lies, concealment, distortion of history. He was used to Chinese Mind.

The second morning out, the monk took from his duffel bag a pair of running shoes, Pumas, and at the curb outside the restaurant he stooped to put them on.

The old woman, waiting beside him, peered out under the brim of her straw hat and said, "Don't you miss all your attendants rushing to tie your shoelaces?"

The monk said, "You know I don't allow that." He turned to Mr. Fu and said, "I think these leather shoes weaken my disguise, don't you?" The question shot alarm through Mr. Fu—who was he anyway?

The old woman grinned at the monk and said, "You can step in a ditch next stop," she said. "Get some grime on those sneakers."

"I love your common sense," he said fondly. This also bothered Mr. Fu; they were like a pair of old cooing lovers.

The monk made some solicitous queries about the woman's health problem. He pulled from his purse a little packet of Tibetan palliatives. Mr. Fu's mother took something like these, herb balls the size of marbles. They had always reminded him of deer droppings.

The monk said, "I know you have defied authorities often in the past, have been called onto Roman carpets more than once, especially about your agenda for women priests."

"But why should the Church keep women down? Don't you think I'm right about that?"

"I do. But with me, you have to take your medicine." He indicated the little brown pellets. Mr. Fu found this quite cloying.

Then the monk turned to Mr. Fu and offered him the shoes he had just removed, of fine Indian leather. Mr. Fu's own shoes were somewhat down at the heels, so in some confusion he discarded them in favor of the monk's. That bothered him too. He did everything the monk suggested; he wondered if it was mind control.

During his job interview with the Amnesty International attorney, Fu had experienced a rise of the resentment cultivated by his Chinese schooling toward all white foreign imperialists. The man had asked him probing personal questions that stirred his conscience: "Do you have a family? Only a widowed mother in Chengdu? Does she want to go home to Tibet?" Mr. Fu seldom saw his old mother these days; all she ever talked about was going back to Tibet to die, which depressed him so much that he stayed away. And the Brit asked another odd question: "Can you keep a secret?" But when Mr. Fu asked what the secret was, the man had only laughed and said, "You shall see." He gave him a card with his telephone number in London. "Call me if I can ever help you later on," was all he said.

One evening at dinner the monk spread a map on the table. The secret, thought Mr. Fu, must be in the map. He decided he didn't want to see it and took a chair at an adjacent table. They wouldn't hear of it. The monk pulled out a chair and urged him to come and sit beside him.

The map just lay there, tempting Mr. Fu, while the monk and the old woman continued their flirtation, if that is what it was. The monk confessed to her that in other lives as a younger man, the flesh drew him. He said, "In my youth, I was stimulated by images of female incarnates."

"What kind of images?" she wanted to know. "Not porn!"

"Of course not, dear lady," he said. "In one lifetime you and I were lovers. A few centuries ago. Some historians think I was dissolute in that life." Now what in the world could that mean? Mr. Fu wondered in vexation. "Actually," the monk went on, "it was a life of intense inner creativity, a life of poetry and deep song, *bhakti*, as Indians say."

Mr. Fu's feet hurt. The new Indian shoes had sucked his socks down into themselves and blisters had appeared on his heels. He tried to shut out their talk. The monk, still concerned about her health, said, "You will have to let me teach you how to relax through meditation."

The woman, unskillful with chopsticks, was spilling rice as she talked. "I pray a lot," she said. "And you know we have a relaxing practice, from St. Ignatius of Loyola. He called it 'composition of place.' You locate yourself in a place, seeing such things as the trees in the garden of Gethsemane, or any holy place, and you envision the locale entirely through your five senses."

The monk grew excited. "You are describing a mandala," he cried. Then he enlarged upon the involvement of the senses in his own meditation rites, the meaning of mandalas, mantras, mudras, incense, bells, and on and on. Next he described one of Mr. Fu's mother's favorite saints, the scary Machig Labdron. "She taught the *Chod* meditation," he said, "which means 'to cut,' a method Tibetans use to overcome the fear of death." Mr. Fu grew depressed. He hated their religious talk.

The woman wanted to know if Machig was the one who went into graveyards and drank blood from a human skull, and had a horn made from the thigh bone of a pregnant woman. When the monk nodded, she said that someone had told her about Machig—only she said "Macha." "So primitive whopping and howling at demons," she said. "But I like her name, Macha; she had balls."

"It's a bit more complex than whooping and howling," the monk said somewhat defensively. "You are sharing your blood with hungry ghosts, nourishing them."

"Something like a Tibetan Eucharist, I suppose," she said more thoughtfully.

Mr. Fu was becoming acutely conscious of the throbbing in the round raw places where the tender flesh had lifted from his heels. He didn't like being reminded of his mother, of his neglect of her, of her nearness to death. He wished he hadn't thrown his old shoes away.

The monk pressed the old woman's small, withered hand. "It is your concentration that will do the job ahead for us. You have direct access to Vajra Mind."

Mr. Fu stood up and excused himself from the table, fearful that he might start to weep. Whether about his mother or out of frustration with all this theology he wasn't sure. He knew he could not listen to an explanation of Vajra Mind. He pulled out a cigarette and went into the street to smoke.

Through the window he could see the monk turn to that map, which he and the old woman pored over. And when he returned, they made no move to put the map away. It still lay on the table beside Mr. Fu's chair.

"Look at this, Mr. Fu," said the monk. "Here is where our teammates have been." He pointed to *X*s that marked bomb-test craters. Chinese missile sites were carefully detailed all over the map. It showed that in Nagchu, Kongpo Nyitri, and Powo Tamo there were ICM's and ICBM's. It even noted the ranges of the missiles. The map indicated weapons directed at New Delhi and Calcutta, within range of Sikkim, Burma, Kampuchea, and Vietnam. At Gonggar Airport, southwest of Lhasa, an *X* marked a squadron of J-7 fighter bombers. The monk pointed to another site and remarked, "The most recent installations actually show that China is capable of making a first strike anywhere in the world."

Mr. Fu was shot through wth fear, but was silent. After dinner, he took out another cigarette, and started to go back outside.

The monk detained him, "First, let me have a match, Mr. Fu," he said, taking up the map. "Here's where my photographic memory comes in handy." He struck the match and pressed the curl of flame to the paper. With a kind smile, he said, "You will forget some of these details, Mr. Fu, but you must never forget the truth." It sounded like a riddle, and only compounded Mr. Fu's mystification.

"I have a map out in the jeep," he said anxiously.

"But from here on," said the monk, "you are to follow my directions, not the map."

Lama Mingme calls me from my grassy refuge near the checkpoint to come to lunch. When I look up, I see that the road is jammed with trucks for perhaps a mile behind the roadblock. From the outdoor café we watch the checkpoint station for an official, but none appears.

Mum has gotten the café owner to prepare the best meal of the trip—freshly picked bamboo shoots in a delicate garlic sauce. These are unlike any bamboo shoots I have ever tasted, pale green, divinely tender, like a cross between white asparagus and artichoke hearts, only better. No wonder pandas look like such spoiled darlings. Pandas thrive only on a special bamboo shoot and were becoming extinct because of the scarcity of them. Now a new strain of bamboo has been developed that grows abundantly, and so the pandas may come back into abundance themselves.

No tea, however.

No official comes, and so honor system rules this roadblock today. No bribe necessary. "Good karma," says Lama Mingme. Bureaucratic laxity, I say. Truck motors rev up down the line. As we are the only small vehicle waiting, the first driver kindly signals us to pass before him so that we may zoom ahead unimpeded. Mr. Fu starts up the motor of our jeep of fools.

The sky is like a lake in which a snow peak shimmers. Am I looking up or down? Our jeep has stopped by the roadside, and I get out stiffly. Every bone aches. The crest of Erlon Shan stretches before us. Here the road is more than 2000 meters above sea level, the mountain range more than 3000. For miles we've felt a disorientation, unsure of whether we were ascending or going down into a valley.

"Photos, must take photos." Lama Mingme leaps from the jeep in his skinny jeans, with the zoom lens he purchased in Hong Kong. His hands are shaking more than usual, and so I worry about the altitude. Also shivering in the clear, cold air, I join him beside a snow bank that stretches across a vast white-clad meadow. From there, the snow reaches out to finger the green velvet of the mountains.

"This light!" shouts Lama Mingme. "My lens maybe not good enough to catch." The light plays around us, a daylight strobe; it beckons and vanishes thrillingly.

A vivid expanse has opened before us, and kindles in us the possibility of some other, internal expanse. A distant row of prayer flags above a roadside shrine pulsates in the wind like the signal of an enormous vista of the spirit unfurling. These flags are hung in strips of five rectangles in vivid colors—red, blue, yellow, green, and white—each color standing for a complex of things in Tibetan mysticism.

The flashes of silver and gold seem near, then far, airy thoughts spinning close then flying off. The clear lake-sky appears more boundless than the mind. It must be such light as this that creates the famous visions seen by Tibetan wisemen in Lhama Lamtso, the lake where signs are said to appear to show the way to new incarnations such as the Dalai Lama and other *tulkus.* Lake Lhama Lamtso, the Tibetan star of Bethlehem. The sky yields many signs for Tibetans, who often report seeing their enlightened ones ascend from the earth in a "rainbow body." No wonder—the light makes us feel we could levitate. No wonder the Tibetan science of mind: Such vastness invites reflection upon the nature of being, the dream of existence. An ego cannot stand up too well against such space.

Dorje doesn't like Lama Mingme's show of enthusiasm. It is too time-consuming. "Come back into the jeep," she shouts after him as he darts into the snow.

"Perhaps he needs a break from getting bounced around," I suggest.

Lama Mingme is beside himself with joy at returning to the place of his birth. There seem to be literally two of him, running along the roadside with his camera, bandy-legged, dogged, indefatigable. He shouts as he darts into the snow meadow and up the mountain slope to catch a better angle in his lens. Two Lama Mingmes: One a wiry, grinning Tibetan whose origins no skinny jeans can disguise, home after lifelong exile; the other a clown dancing on the edge of a precipice.

Dorje calls to him again. "Come back right now, Mingme!" she orders, tossing her long, black hair. He grins at her, pleased by this attention from her, any attention from her.

She hasn't minded his delight in the sight of the first Tibetans on our journey. But this picture-taking won't do. She keeps our purpose firmly in mind, finds his distractibility childish.

"Mingme!" she calls out. "We are losing valuable time. It is getting late. Never mind photos!"

Bossy Hong Kong girl! But he grinningly obliges and clambers back in. Soon he is groaning again from the bouncing, but this time nobody jokes.

Glancing at Dorje's mother and aunt, I see them grip one another by the hand as our jeep veers close to an unprotected shoulder with a deep crevasse below. Suddenly I understand the antipathy between Tibetans and Chinese that exists on a personal as well as political level. People forced to move to Tibet under China's population transfer program are said to dislike it intensely. Many suffer from the altitude. Few Chinese live within their own sacred mountains, only holy seekers. Of course that can be said of mountains almost anywhere else on the globe. Many people fear this glorious elevation where Tibetans thrive. Their love of this high, risky land has to mold their character, has to underlie their balance in acceptance that all is impermanent.

8

On the road, I ask Dorje, "Do you have a question for the Khandro?" She doesn't understand me at first. I tell her there's a traditional notion of asking the wise woman for the answer to some important, burning question. The Khandro is such a woman. The idea is new to her; she sinks away from her chattering relatives and falls silent. A distant white-capped range emerges in the morning light to the south of us.

We were up early today but not earlier than the ferocious dogs hanging about the Guest House, strays, about thirty large dogs, like dirty white bears, all howling most of the night, and still alert for any handout. We had heard the Chinese had rounded up all the dogs of Tibet and slaughtered them. Like flies, they may be ineradicable.

Breakfast in the Guest House consisted of hot water and some cookies Mum bought from the management's display case in the lobby. Still no tea. Nobody can understand this. Mum laments not having bought tea bags at the grocery in the Chengdu hotel. But we weren't preparing for a trek, and who could have imagined no tea!

Mr. Fu glares intently at the road, which demands his constant concentration, with its abrupt character changes, its sharp turns, its crevices, its rock piles. To distract myself from the suddenness of his halts and swerves, I reach into my pack for my journal, thinking that perhaps Dorje is unaware of the powers the Khandro is supposed to have. Bracing the book against my knees I stabilize the page enough to read some passages about the Khandro to Dorje.

The Chinese officer newly assigned to this remote village during the Cultural Revolution examined the records about the Khandro. She was a problem. The officer thought he would probably have to execute her. The common lore about her powers of mind was cause enough. All over Tibet, the Red Guard was at work making sure Tibetans understood what Chairman Mao had in mind for the Cultural Revolution. New jails were being built to house the recalcitrant. Cadres were being trained in new punishments for those who might not comply with correction. This woman would have to be brought in line.

The record showed that a former commander ordered the statues of Buddhas and other idols in her monastery destroyed. One of the soldiers stationed there set about it, meaning to break up the main statue in the courtyard with a hammer. The occupants of the place went inside and gazed down upon him, the lama's sister among them. The soldier was left quite alone with the statue.

This monastary was in the high desert, some distance from the forest. The wildlife was confined mostly to foxes, wild yaks, and goats. But suddenly the soldier caught sight of two tigers, streaking forcefully across the sand as if after prey; and there was no mistaking it. He was the prey. He could only retreat hastily. The tigers stayed there for days stalking about the statue.

That was only the beginning. There was another sacred statue that soldiers made an effort to destroy. Monks had stored it in a wooden box, clearly in an effort to hide it. The soldiers found the box, but were unable to budge it, even though they knew the statue was small and light. Yet the box was like a dead weight, and stuck stubbornly to the ground. One soldier who tried to move it had a terrible streak of bad luck. In the weeks that followed, his son was drowned and then he himself went mad.

Next, there was the issue of the soldiers who threw the Khandro, bound hand and foot, into the river where she met with a lucky upstream current. The commanding officer at the time relieved those men of duty, in embarrassment over the issue. All this made the woman very popular with the locals, of course, and something more than a nuisance.

Now the order of the Cultural Revolution must be put into effect. The officer was full of zeal for Chairman Mao's cause. He sent for the Khandro.

He also sent word out to the peasants for miles around to come to bear witness to her "self-criticism." The gathering took place under the bright sunlight. The officer placed her upon a platform, surrounded by soldiers on one side, villagers and peasants on the other. The woman stood in a skirt and jacket of skins, her black hair radically tangled. The officer found her eyes difficult to look at; red coals seemed to burn behind them.

The officer held before her a picture of Chairman Mao. "Do you know who this is?" he asked.

She gave a shrug as if to say, "Who doesn't?" But she said nothing. She was not given to excessive language. Even as a child, it was said, she had spoken more to spirits than to people, and she often went alone down to the river where she talked to bridge trolls and hungry ghosts. One peasant had even told officials that she was the reincarnation of a troll magician. Very early in life, it had been clear that she was quite different from other people. Now she did not waste words. She stared at the officer silently.

"It is your duty to make a tribute to our great Chairman," said the officer. "Do you understand? This is an opportunity for you. To correct your past errors."

Her face took on a more ferocious aspect, and her eyebrows rose and fell above the red glints of her eyes, but still she said nothing.

"This you must do. You may as well make up your mind to it. Everyone is here to witness this. Your people understand, you know, that we all live by our glorious Chairman's grace. You must strengthen that understanding for them."

Suddenly, she forced air rapidly through her lips—Westerners know it as the "raspberry." The peasants broke into laughter, which was stopped by the crack of the officer's whip on the platform floor. She stood quite stony faced. He was furious.

The officer shouted a command to two of his junior officers and they grasped the woman by the arms. The people fell silent. Would they execute her? They watched, humiliated for her, as the two men stripped her naked and bound her hands.

The officer took a marker from his chest pocket and drew on her belly a red circle, turning her navel into a target. At that several of the monks from the monastery rushed up to the officer to appeal to him. They pleaded with him not to shoot her then. If she had to die, they wanted to say certain rites. To prepare her. They pleaded for time.

"Ah, Tibetan funeral rites! Let's prepare her by all means." And he whispered orders to his men, who went into his headquarters, and returned with some paper flowers. Mockingly, he ordered the men to drape the flowers about her shoulders. "There, now she is prepared to die."

The officer shouted another order. A Chinese soldier raised his rifle, aimed at her, and pulled the trigger. His gun misfired. He reloaded and aimed—it misfired again. The commanding officer became infuriated. He wrenched the rifle away and reloaded it himself. This time he aimed it at a post of the platform, and the bullet shattered the wood. Reloading again, he aimed at the Khandro, but he too could not touch her. He felt the pull of the rifle slightly to his left as it misfired again. He heard an apprehensive murmur of satisfaction among the people.

The officer had to reconsider. These powers of mind she seemed to have must be dealt with privately, not before an audience of Tibetans. He ordered his men to untie her hands, to allow her to dress herself. He told them to disperse the crowd.

As soon as she had dressed, the Khandro turned her back on the soldiers, lifted her skirt in their faces, and gave a loud, memorable fart. Then she leaped on a horse they had stolen from her and rode away, with the wild shout of a Kham warrior.

After these events the Chinese officer sent out word that she would not be punished further because she was totally insane. Crazy wisdom.

Dorje loves the story of the fart, repeats it to her Mum and Auntie. Mum laughs with hoarse delight.

I find another magic tale in my notebook from a woman who now lives in Sonoma:

A stocky woman of about my own age, but looking much older, Serong is embarrassed by her broken English. In Lhasa, the Chinese used her as a translator of Mandarin into Tibetan. Today in Sonoma County there is no call for Tibeto-Mandarin-English translation. "English not good enough anyway," she says. She cleans bedpans in a nursing home.

I make her uncomfortable. Probably she isn't used to telling her story. She glances about the restaurant furtively, as if afraid of being seen there, then she laughs at herself. "At home we never took guest to restaurant. That was thought too low. As if you had no home to entertain." Here that is the case; Serong rents a room in someone else's home.

As children, Serong and her cousin lived in a nunnery not far from Lhasa with nuns who taught the children *pujas,* prayers, and to sit long hours in the meditation hall, their maroon woolen robes gathered about them.

The nuns practiced secret rites forbidden to children, who, the nuns warned, would be struck blind if they ever saw them. To learn these higher practices took years. "You have to be empowered," Serong explained. "Children not empowered." No child risked spying with her eyes, but when the nuns went to the outdoor shelter beyond the nunnery, the girls crept close to the wall where they could hear the empowered nuns. Serong and her cousin listened through the wall to curious thumping noises. Then they understood—these were attempts at levitation. Bodies falling to earth. The girls recognized the heaviest sound: That would be their great aunt, who was very fat. "We children laughed and laughed." Blessed disrespect, one of childhood's stolen joys.

The nuns were probably practicing *lung-gom,* Serong said, the levitation that enables rapid trance walking. The practitioner appears to skim miraculously along the surface of the earth at an inhuman rate. The skill takes profound concentration, and, it is said, can be fatal to the practitioner if interrupted. Some who believe Jesus spent his adolescence in India suggest such adepts may have taught him to walk on water.

"The nuns also practiced *tumo,*" Serong says. I feel a little thrill when she confides this. *Tumo reziang.* "They would go outside of their secret place in the coldest weather, wearing only white gauze over their bodies and a red band from shoulder to waist, and they would meditate in the snow." In this practice the body heat rises along the spine, warm enough to melt the snow, a practice that can come in handy when stranded in the wilds.

I say to Dorje, "What freedom, what *liberation—tumo reziang* in the snow! Just the thought of such naked power can make your body heat rise!"

She laughed. "My guru tell me they have to wring sweat from the white gauze three times. To prove skill."

I turn back to the notebook to read the rest of Serong's story.

Serong's discomfort isn't really caused by her unfamiliarity with restaurant dining. She doesn't want to tell me the worst that happened to her. Too hard to speak of it? I ask, for I can see that she still carries the pain of what she went through. No, not that. She doesn't want to call attention to herself. "Not Buddhist way," she says.

I order lunch and talk to her for a while about the Jewish Holocaust, and the decision of survivors to tell and tell so that it may never happen again. "If you tell your memories, they can be a powerful weapon against other abuse," I suggest. I tell her of something I read on the Venice ghetto wall: "Nothing shall purge your deaths from our memories, for our memories are your only graves." I told her that burying the truth can sometimes turn it into a lie, can make the wrong version of what happened sound like the truth. She sinks into silence, mulls it over; finally she talks.

1960. Scene: a large meeting place in Lhasa. The hall is crowded. "You have to go. If they send for you, you go." Serong stands before a table, where young Red Guards have set up an improvised judgment seat. These children of Mao, none much over twenty, are offering help to the People in correcting their error-stained lives. They have bound Serong's hands behind her for this help. "You must examine your failure to serve the People," commands the lean young interrogator, a schoolboy, she thinks. A crook in his right wrist suggests it has been broken, perhaps in just such a session as this. *Thamzing.* It made everything crooked. "Try to remember who you really are. Understand your deception. Take your time." He is patient, he knows that to help others correct themselves in this way takes forbearance, a willingness to repeat yourself, as well as ferocity. Over and over he repeats the charges against her. He is utterly dedicated to the Cultural Revolution, and is so earnest he appears ridiculous. But he is very dangerous, she knows. He will do anything to make her confess, anything.

"We must help her remember her true identity." The young man with the twisted wrist burns his gaze into her. "You have deceived us. We know that you are the queen of Bhutan." She laughs inside, not out loud. She is not now nor ever has been the queen of Bhutan. It is true that her cousin may be the queen, but she has had no news of her since she went there after the fall of Lhasa. She herself has never been to Bhutan. "Tell us about the fortune you have sent to Bhutan," says the cadre. He will repeat the lie, she knows, until she is confused, begins to believe it. She is not her cousin, has never been her cousin, she continues to remind herself.

The cadre turns to the witnesses, all of them Tibetan people, many already self-tamed; his crooked wrist lifts in a gesture toward Serong. "You must help her remember. Come, let's help her."

Quite a few Tibetans present are willing to strike her, having had lessons in the class struggle. They now believe that when her mother fled, gold coins and jewels of coral, jade, and turquoise went with her. They have imagined the old woman, her hands heavy with rings, grasping gold necklaces and headpieces, stuffing them in large sacks—the Chinese have told them. Serong recognizes an elderly couple who will not meet her gaze; they were once devoted servants to her mother. The young questioner and his assistants provide the sticks, call her mother's servants by name to come forward, for they are the ones who must strike first. Others close in, and as Serong feels their blows raining on her head she mercifully blacks out.

Probably the creation of the Red Guard, turning youth loose on dissidents or suspected dissidents, Chinese as well as Tibetans, was the shrewdest and cruelest of Maoist strategies. Here were True Believers, lacking life experience to complicate their thoughts, still endowed with the primal cruelty of children. Having completed their own internalization, they were empowered to indulge in any form of torture. They raped, maimed, aborted, tormented by any means—cattle prods, electric shock, starvation. They tortured Serong by tying her feet together, bending her body at the waist, pinning her arms behind her back and securing them above her shoulders, like the wings of a plane. They called hers the "take-off position." New kind of levitation. The practitioner stays in "the airplane room" for weeks.

Witnesses have reported seeing many men and women locked in the "airplane room." Such terms allow the torturer to objectify their victims. Here is the magic of the cadres, dehumanization.

In the Kali Yuga we learn the full extent of man's psychosis, but it is not a new magic. Agnes Smedley has described this very torture by the secret service of Chiang Kai Chek's Chinese Nationalist party. During the late 1920s the "Blue Shirts" taught it to the Communists first hand, by submitting them to it.

We glimpse partridges and several hares disappearing under low hanging branches.

Now Dorje nudges my shoulder. "Too many questions for the Khandro-là, not just one." Then, "What about you—do you have a question for her?"

I tell her I'm thinking about it. At that moment, swooping over the jeep, on its way down into a broad crevasse dense with pine and juniper scrub, the outspread wingtips slightly lifted, a golden eagle shows us its power of flight.

Dorje turns to Mingme in the rear seat, and asks, "What about you, Mingme? What is your question?"

He hasn't followed our drift. He smiles and asks, "Will you be nice to me again sometime?"

9

THE GOLDEN ROAD

Youngden folded his camera into its case with a heavy sigh, as Bodhi drove the jeep away from the crater site. This was not a natural crater, but man-made, they knew—the craters they had come to put on videotape. She had seen their like strewn throughout the Nevada desert.

They were both exhausted. The inside of their mouths felt caked with grit. A layer of dust had settled over their sunglasses.

The terrain was covered with saline encrustations that made the ground appear white. Bodhi complained her eyes hurt as if from snow blindness, even behind her sunglasses. But it was not yet time for snows to begin; this was the season of sandstorms, although they had seen only a few substantial dust devils so far.

She had done nearly all the driving, on roads sometimes barely visible in the desert sand, winding through the Quaidam Basin into Xinjiang, and north toward Lop Nur, to nuclear testing grounds. The Chinese had given the province they traveled through a name meaning "new domain," yet, only decades before, these highest deserts of the world had stretched far beyond the haunts of ordinary folk. Its vast regions had seen an ancient procession of travelers, from early holy men, spreading both Buddhist and Muslim teachings, to Marco Polo, who recorded that the desert was the abode of evil spirits that created illusions in travelers, causing some to see mirages of armies advancing toward them, luring them to their deaths.

Now evidence of human invasion lay on all sides of them, throughout the vast stretches of sand. They came to a firing range with deep crater scars, a more bleak landscape than they had yet seen. Youngden photographed the bomb-test craters with his wide-angle lens. To distinguish the scars on this desert from those in Nevada, Youngden used his macro lens to take a few identifying photos of the Chinese ideograms on signs attached to the electrified fences. He took pictures, too, of yellow posts spaced along these fences, for they signified the presence of radioactivity. His video camera captured details of a lead brick wall intended as a radiation barrier. Bodhi soon realized she did not have to teach him how to do anything.

Next they were glimpsing the southern edge of the Gobi Desert and turning onto the road toward the installations at Malan, a city the Chinese had created for the development for their A-bomb. There they were only able to shoot from a distance outside the enclosures of cyclone fencing.

"Danger Force Field Not Protect." Bodhi translated a sign literally for him and laughed. "Remember that neon sign over the disco in the hotel in Lhasa?"

Youngden smiled. "Yes, in English said: 'Punk, Latest Thrill Stimulation.'"

Their Amnesty International lawyer "B" had cautioned them not to attempt to go beyond the fencing where there would be increasing levels of security. They would encounter ground sensors to alert security depots of their approach, which would soon detect them on video screens, and if they went a mile or so beyond the barbed wire, they would encounter land mines. "B" had also told them that some Chinese travelers, who missed the signs or couldn't read them, had "disappeared" by simply wandering too far within the forbidden territory. Eventually, Bodhi knew that she and Youngden might have to take that risk, if the code they had for gaining entry through the electronic gate at the ultimate rendezvous should fail. Once there, however, they would be able to rely upon the help of "A's" master plan.

At length they turned north again, to make the approach toward the rendezvous point. They hoped to arrive the next day. The air was still, almost forebodingly still. The vast and desolate sands stretched far ahead.

They came to a geothermal station not far from the road and drove past it quickly, undetected. It was the dinner hour; perhaps all personnel sat over a hot pot with their chopsticks. At nightfall they reached a turn that led to a murky spring, which had either run off from the foothills they were approaching or from the geothermal works, and had created a small pond. Scrub pine grew beside the water, and a few marsh reeds. They had only a small amount of water left in the skin tied to the grill of their jeep, but fearful of contamination they dared not refill it. They still had tea from large thermoses they had brought from Lhasa.

The air was so quiet they decided not to pitch a tent, despite the possibility of a dust storm. And if they had been detected by the station, they could make a swift getaway. They did not build fires at night for cooking but munched on their stores of trail mix and dried meat. It was dusk when they fell gratefully into their sleeping bags. An almost-full moon rested like a gold melon on the horizon.

"So tired," said Bodhi, as her body sank against the sand.

"Like a sack of bones," said Youngden. "I can feel my whole skeleton."

"You Tibetans! Always death." She sighed. "I'm so tired I don't think I'll ever have sex again."

Youngden half sat up, grinning. "Tell me!" he said. "No *Karma Mudra?*"

"Never," she said. "Cured by exhaustion." She closed her eyes, smiling as she thought of the old-fashioned rituals for choosing a mate Youngden had described to her.

She said, "Yet I have to think of 'A' and 'Mother,' so much older than we, and they have traveled more than 2000 kilometers."

"'A' so wise," Youngden said. "I remembering the words he say about hour of courage."

Bodhi turned her head and looked at him. "You're not afraid?"

"Sure, is scary stuff we do."

Suddenly in the stillness they heard a gliding movement overhead. Straight above them they glimpsed the white underside of a huge bird. The bird, with a wingspread of at least eight feet, hovered above the water. Its head was crested with red, and black feathers cloaked its neck like a sheath halfway down its long white throat. It was a black-necked crane.

They watched as the creature drifted down to the marsh. Its wings, turned ochre-colored by the dusky light, compressed for a slow descent. It settled on the pond with the moon lifting above it. The great bird was so close to them they dared not speak. Silhouetted against the darkening sky, its neck curved down as it slid its beak into the water. It raised its head and remained standing there for several moments. Then it drew one foot upward, and they could see the four prongs of its claw coming together and sinking back into the water. It stood on both feet, swiftly preening itself for a moment. Then it lifted its other claw and held itself motionless for several seconds. Next, it turned its head three times, stopping with its beak poised in their direction. Everything was still for a moment, then the bird's wings lifted, spread, gave a firm flap. The claws drew up, and the great creature soared away southward, in a strong ascent to the open darkness.

They were speechless for a while. "Migrating from Ladak," Youngden said at last.

"So rare," Bodhi said in a hushed voice. "I will always remember this."

She reached her hand to his sleeping bag, and they linked fingers. The stars beginning to come out seemed very close, nearer to them than the distance the bird had climbed. Their fatigue had soared off into a vast sky of waking stars.

They talked, as they had every night, about the karma in their lives. Bodhi had confided to him the cruelty of the convent where her beautiful mother left her, and where she resorted to constant prayer to the Virgin Mary; and she had also told him of her Chinese father, killed, it was thought, by small-time mobsters in the numbers racket in New Jersey. Youngden had confided his orphaned childhood, a failed marriage, a child he fathered in India, and numerous American girlfriends who tried to dominate him. Tonight, as Bodhi started to speak of the men in her life—this one, the indelibly married London politician involved in a banking scandal; that one, the playwright, who seduced her by saying he wanted to die in her arms—talk about arcane!; then the actor who was a closet gay and tried to dress her like a Mafia moll—even as the pain of each situation arose still intact, it all sounded unutterably trite. Was everyone's story totally—samsaric? Was everyone caught in some intense pursuit of ignorance? Surely Youngden's experience with his girlfriends was as absurd as her own. And so their talk turned to the Dharma that they both loved, and they talked of the Four Noble Truths and the Great Perfection, until the constellations had traveled halfway across the sky.

As they became sleepy, the crane rose again in their minds, that miracle that had come and gone in only a few brief moments.

"I thought they were extinct," she said.

"Almost," Youngden said. He told her that the black-necked crane's nest was hunted for its eggs, a delicacy. "We lucky to see."

"It was so fast, here and gone in just a few moments. Like a space between breaths. And yet, I will always remember this. It was forever."

"Maybe enlightenment like that," Youngden said. After a while he added, "I think 'A' take us on this trip for our own benefit. Benefit me to come home for first time, even if is sadness here in Tibet. And benefit you—"

"To learn about my life. What I want …"

Youngden said suddenly, "I can explain something, about how certain birds follow holy customs, like cranes and cuckoos in Tibet. They mate for life."

"Cuckoos!"

"They maybe model for *Karma Mudra.*"

"Youngden, I've never known you to make a joke about any sacred rites."

He laughed at that, and when he laughed her heart felt lighter, felt—yes, almost glad. But she said nothing about that to him. Wait, she thought. Wait and see.

Dorje says, "Not so much trees here."

We have come to the historic forest of Kham. How do we know it? Only from the old map I brought along, which shows names no longer in use, rivers that have run dry, the kind of map that in the times of the great explorations used to contain landmarks like: "Here be monsters, here be dragons." The map shows a gigantic forested area.

Broad stumps cover the entire mountainside. As the rutted road winds upward, acre after acre, mile after mile bear witness to clear cutting. A rotten pine stands alone, lopsided, on a cliff side. Ragged bushes strew the mountain slopes; the soil erupts in perpendicular spines of erosion. A long vertical gap upturns the roots of severed trees. From the top of the ridges, streaks of exposed forest floor extend down to the road. Terrain once enclosed by trees now shifts and slides, loosening piles of stone that come crashing down the steeps. Mr. Fu stops from time to time; we all get out to push rocks from the road.

"This is not what I thought the forest of Kham would look like," Dorje says.

Tibetans lived for centuries in harmony with the forest, sharing in its cyclic self-restoration, respecting its wildlife. Fires were made with yak dung, not wood, houses were made of packed earth. We noticed yesterday some reforestation in Western China, a stand of young pine that rose up a hillside. But now having crossed the disputed Kham border, there's a distinct change.

From the time of Tibet's great warrior-liberator Gesar, in the eighth century, until the latter half of this century, the forest near his birthplace was the home of fox, bear, and wolf. Monkeys chattered in lofty branches of juniper, spruce, and cypress; pandas fed upon the tender shoots of rattling bamboo; and in the sky over the high grassland ranges hawks and eagles soared above gazelle and yak herds. The forest, the largest high altitude area in the world, spread across the vast snow-peaked mountains of historic Eastern Tibet, a myth-inspiring presence. For all its empty-mind study, Tibet has a great store of legend, often told in the way that Christ used parables, though sometimes describing acts of guile and treachery in admiring terms. The forest gave rise, around the sheltered firesides of river basins in the black tents of nomads and in villages scattered throughout woodland and plateau, to Tibet's epic poem, *Gesar of Ling.* Of a Homeric scale, these bardic songs, sung for centuries, depict Gesar's secular triumphs in destroying the enemies of Tibet's greatest saint, Padma Sambhava, on his mission from India to spread the teachings of the Buddha. Even today nomadic travelers will chant fragments of Gesar's story as protection against attack by enemies.

Gesar, born of a virgin, could magically transform himself into a lion, or enter the body of a departed tiger, if it suited his purpose. He had self-cloning power, could duplicate himself a hundred times over and create phantom armies that vanished like clouds after vanquishing the enemy.

Marco Polo may have heard such legends. Gesar rode a great flying horse named Kyang Go Karkar, on missions both merciful and vengeful. Padma Sambhava is said to have secreted many teachings, called *termas,* in forest caves and elsewhere in Tibet, where they lie hidden until people are ready to receive them, at which time a sage advanced in knowledge of the mind discovers them. Many have already been found, others still remain undisclosed.

Often Mr. Fu must pull over to the side to allow the passage of oncoming trucks. Now we see why so many of the trucks at the checkpoint were empty. Eastbound trucks carry loads of logs of varying sizes, some of them no more than eight inches in diameter, saplings. They have obviously come into the forest empty to bear loads back to Chengdu and other points east. Many of these are old army trucks, maneuvering around precipitous curves, and are not really long enough for logs, not like trucks used for this purpose in the States. I think of those freeways of Northern California down which logging trucks, bearing enormous redwoods, travel to lumber mills. Here even the new trucks are small, the same size as the army convoy trucks; but of course these winding dirt and gravel roads could not support logging trucks as we know them. The dust is continuous. Again, I tie my handkerchief over my mouth and nose.

We pull into the guest house parking as some of the trucks are arriving for the evening. Many drivers are Tibetans. They look rugged but tired. Hard work hauling away the forest of their ancestors for the support of their historic enemies.

The restaurants everywhere we've been are run by Chinese, although the streets of this village are filled with Tibetans. Some of the men are drunk. I had heard the Chinese are selling them alcohol called *San Jui* and *Ban Jui,* hard liquor that is bottled in Chengdu for Tibetan consumption and that no Chinese will drink. Mum and I go into a store and buy a small bottle of it to taste, hands-on research. It is like stove fuel. Later I pour it out; a bottle of vodka in my pack is backup enough.

At the sidewalk market, which is closing up, I glimpse a tired woman folding away her merchandise; at her belt is a *purba,* a tri-sided blade, its carved handle set with turquoise and coral. I think of the New Mexico and Arizona reservations, with turquoise and silver and firewater.

By bedtime I feel as if the day has had a surreal quality about it, as if the bleak mountainsides and the procession of trucks are a dream from which we must awaken, thrashing and gasping for air.

Today I have decided to make a count of the logging trucks in my notebook, marking them down in lines of five, as my sense of outrage intensifies. Earlier visitors counted flocks of gazelles or antelope or deer; we can count logging trucks.

At length we come to the wide section of the river and a village where a small lumber mill is in operation, although most of the forest logs are leaving Tibet. Here it is possible to see the logging strategy—chutes send the logs from the high side of the river down into the water, where men use grappling hooks to push the timber out into the current. There's a tremendous backup, however, as they've not been able to get the logs trucked out as fast as they were cut, despite the traffic on the road. Trees in the water below have created several miles of log jam. Some logs float with the current, but many more are clumped together in piles or are stuck on rocks and waterlogged. They could have been in the river for months, and will not be worth taking out. The whole maddening enterprise clearly suffers from bad planning, and the result is a waste of natural material and, worse, complete disaster to the ecology.

There've been no police on our route at all, and only one checkpoint, unmanned. We could probably go all the way to Lhasa if we wanted to. I realize that the well-known efficacy in brainwashing and torture by Communists has led me to the false expectation they would be generally efficient. I had confused efficiency with a matter of attention. Here the attention, as blind as rage, was given to killing trees.

This village has a doctor, whom Mum insists we all see for remedies for our Hong Kong hack. Her dream life is getting more intense, as is her vertigo. Last night she was chased overland by a giant flying fish. "Bad Tibetan sign," says Dorje. Perhaps the forest landscape caused the nightmare, I tell her.

The doctor's office is a storefront really, with a sidewalk window counter where you buy vials of Chinese medicines. Mum hustles us inside. The benign, elderly doctor bends his head with its thin strands of gray hair over Mum's wrist, taking her pulses, the Chinese way of examining the total being. I think of a friend and colleague who in the past year says she has seen twenty-seven "health providers," one referring her on to another—from the podiatrist, to the internist, to the urologist, to the cardiologist, oncologist, dermatologist, gynecologist, to the orthopedist, the radiologist, to the dentist and periodonist, to the ophthalmologist and the optometrist, and on up to the shrink. No wonder the US has a serious health care problem. None of our "providers" can consider the complete human being, only parts.

In the Chinese holistic view, privacy is not a factor, as we are all part of the whole. Through the open storefront counter, passersby stop and peer in at our treatment. I look out the window at the road, continuing my count of logging trucks.

The doctor tries to interest Mum in an injection, says she needs to protect herself against altitude sickness, tells her she is in worse shape than the rest of us. She declines, insists he give her some tiny bottled pills, which she serves up to Dorje and her sister afterwards at mealtime. I submit to taking them, too, as the doctor prescribed them for all of us, but I also rely on my vitamin C, which Mum refuses. Actually, I take both Eastern and Western medicine, to hedge all bets.

Next door to the doctor's is another stall, where a Tibetan seamstress is at work. Her face is wreathed with gray-streaked hair into which turquoise beads have been braided with a red scarf. Coral globes hang from her ears. Creases are seared into her ruddy cheeks. Lama Mingme wants to have a long conversation with her, but Mum pulls him away. Come and let the doctor look at you, she insists. He complies, but as soon as possible, he dashes out of the doctor's room to the one next door. After our consultation, we find the dressmaker has made tea for us, salty Tibetan tea, which I find delicious. Mum gulps it down, as it is the first she's had on the road, though she also says she doesn't like it. Do the Tibetans control the tea market? Most unlikely. One of the mysteries of travel.

The cheerful seamstress listens as affectionately as if she had known Lama Mingme all his life, as he explains that he is going home for the first time.

"We escape Chinese police so far," he says. She wishes all of us good luck.

In the village restaurant, Mum strides into the kitchen, and at the stove pulls off the lids to the aluminum pots to inspect the steaming cuisine; then she orders an enormous quantity of food. Whatever her ailment, it has not interfered with her appetite.

The restaurant's only window shows a sunny view of the lumber mill, bright amber slices of the plundered trees visible through a square from this dark, functional space with its chrome table. I face the window and continue marking my lines of five as the trucks roll past.

As the food is brought to the table, I give vent to vehement feelings about the destruction of the forest, which are fueled by the apparent indifference of my companions. I say to them, "The forest has been emptied out."

Mum and Moon busy themselves serving the rice. Mingme, giving Dorje a neck rub, shakes his head. "Much impermanence," he says.

"The armies of Gesar of Ling couldn't hide in these trees, Lama Mingme."

He smiles, but is intent upon Dorje's neck. I go on with some indignation. "Little information comes through in the media at home because the networks can't get in here, just as they can't get into Lhasa. The forest of Kham was once the largest high-forested region in the world. The consequences of losing it are as serious for the world as losing the Amazon Basin. Don't you understand?" Mum and Auntie, eating, do not understand my words of course, though they gaze up at me as they chew, wide-eyed and wide-mouthed at my sudden speech. Dorje, enjoying Mingme's stroking, doesn't bother to explain to them.

"Where Amazon Basin?" asks Lama Mingme, truly puzzled.

A brief geography lesson, then I say "It's the monster greed at work again."

He asks, "Where monster greed?"

"The forest monsters moved to the cities, disguised themselves as men."

He brightens. "Gesar magic."

"Think of Hong Kong. Perpendicular monuments to greed covering every inch of land. The island is a mile-high cemetery. The people rush about in a Dance Macabre!"

Lama Mingme laughs. "This very good," he says. "Good place for doing *Chod.*" *Chod,* the mantra practice of Machig Labdron, the graveyard goddess.

His levity arouses my ire. I call up images of Beijing bureaucrats working to make US trade with them desirable, so that it becomes profitable for the privileged of America to build more monuments to greed on this continent. I suggest that luxury hotels and office towers made with lumber from this desecrated mountain will turn Beijing into another mile-high cemetery. Meanwhile, the holes in the sky enlarge all over the globe, where ordinary people swarm like dying termites, and the rulers seal themselves off from reality on private estates. I lay it all out.

Mingme listens to my diatribe in wonderment, then shakes his head, grinning. "You very good on this. I like."

Mum and Auntie are exchanging glances as the chopsticks go repeatedly to their lips. Sauce dribbles upon Mum's chin. Rice sticks a trail on Auntie's sweatshirt. Usually exhaustive but not sloppy eaters, they are disconcerted at hearing my voice raised this way. Dorje murmurs to them, a brief explanation. They shake their heads.

I say, "We all take part in this, too, at least by taxes and silence."

"I tax-exempt," Mingme says, then adds, "Vote exempt too," recalling his immigrant status.

I throw up my hands. There they are, embodiments of the human disaster, mired in ignorance and sensuality. Oh, to arouse them with half the power of the stomach's first growl! I fall speechless with frustration.

Mum asks, "Does she have a fever?" Earth Mum and Sister Moon—I can count on them to trash my loftiness.

Dorje and Mum confer, shake their head sadly. Thinking over what I have said? No, they are reluctant to tell me the ultimate truth about the restaurant. No tea.

By nighttime I have counted more than 150 logging trucks. That many in a single day, each bearing eight to ten tree trunks, careening and churning toward China.

The forest of Kham is no more. It is gone, together with much of the animal and bird life that once thrived here.

Tibetan mythology shares the universal death and resurrection theme of other cultures: Gesar will come again. Like Kalki of Hinduism and Quetzalcoatl of Mexico he will come, not only to overthrow Tibet's enemies but to save the entire world. This will be accomplished by his righteous but ferocious army. The myth says that Gesar will ride a white horse, and the horse itself will be a former Bodhisattva with the power of flight; this leaves his return open to a contemporary interpretation that he will arrive in the company of airborne warriors. After a very lively battle, which may take place just outside the kingdom of Shambhala, Gesar will lead the fortunate and deserving into the kingdom for a reign of peace and justice. He presumably will have a benevolent rule of enlightened subjects never before known on earth, devoid of the defects of ordinary mind.

Gesar comes to change cowardice, the companion of greed, the enemy that is in our own minds, into courage; his work is transformation, like that of Maitreya, the Buddha who is yet to come, and the long-overdue Messiah.

The forest of Kham hovered over the Gesar tales in mystery and magical potential, a primeval world where any miracle is possible for a hero who by faith and force of justice, or even by strength and duplicity, promises deliverance. The myths of the forest inform the imagination that conjures Tibet. Where do the myths go when the forest is destroyed? Where the power to conjure?

Late at night during a cold run to the bathhouse under flaming stars, Dorje is still brooding about questions for the Khandro. She asks me if I have one, and I tell her that I do, but I'm not sure I know how to phrase it.

I sit on my bed with my notebook during Dorje's mantra practice. She has to leave the light on in order to read her ritual chants, and so I find myself watching the Bodhi seeds of the mala again, as I think of literature, its transformative power. The strength of fiction lies in its ability to transcend the principle of noncontradiction that says a thing cannot both exist and not exist at the same time. To be and not to be ... Metaphor breaks all the rules. Probably that principal is what the contemplative seeks, too, but not using words. The Diamond Heart Sutra says that Enlightenment is uncontainable and inexpressible; it neither is nor is it not.

THE GOLDEN ROAD

They drove on northward, the mystic direction. One of "A's" earliest lessons was that paths to the North point the way to supreme emancipation. They were approaching the village of his birth, but they would go farther, on toward the secret mountain where he had always imagined one day making a pilgrimage. The direction was propitious, but in keeping with the Tibetan notion that an auspicious event is likely to be balanced by an ill-favored one, their destination was also a place of toxic malignancy.

An image of the bronze Buddha partially melted by the A-bomb that he had seen in the Hiroshima Peace Museum floated into his mind. The temperature on the ground beneath the exploding bomb reached 7000 degrees F, and although bronze melts at 1600 degrees F, the Buddha had survived, arousing the superstitious to marvel. His reasoning, however, was that the brevity of the heat pulse could account for the statue's survival. Ever since boyhood he had been fascinated by science, but his calling had led him on a different path.

Yet his present task was in part scientific—an intervention in science at least. His life, filled with inner practice of a spiritual nature, now turned to the innermost secrets of governments. Those secrets must become the outermost, exposed to the light of truth, just as nirvana and samsara must be seen as one.

They were drawing near the part of the forest he knew well. He was pained to see clear-cut acreage where great trees had stood. He had heard of this disaster, but to be in the presence of these forsaken hillsides was overwhelmingly troubling to him. Bedrock glared out from among the brush, where spongy, mineral-smelling humus, built up over centuries once lay below the giant trees, and which now was already washed away. He reminded himself of the impermanence of everything, fixing his mind on regrowth, change for the good. But nevertheless a prophetic vision suddenly passed before his eyes. People he knew in the West often talked of how the ozone layer above the atmosphere thinned when forests were destroyed. Now he saw a part of the future, fully developed: Not of a slow burning of the globe through a hole in the ozone but a sudden eruption, not of fire but of water, here in this already deeply damaged segment of the world.

This river, which normally carries more water than any other in the world, suddenly chokes, its current turns and flows upward, a sign of disaster.

The monsoon, the worst monsoon in human memory, has come, and the rain beats against the stumps and brush on mountainsides that once held lush hardwood growth. Unrestrained by the enormous trees with the containing power of root and humus, entire mountains are turning into mud, crashing down onto the roads, sweeping them away—all the labor forced upon Tibetans for years swept with it—deluging whole villages and river towns. Thousands of people are caught in this onslaught of water streaming from the denuded peaks down through river gorges and churning into all the cities of Western China. Here is a karma almost as cruel as that which China has brought upon the Tibetan people in the last forty years—accomplished in a mighty stroke of the elements. A Chinese logger forced to work here rushes out of his house as it crashes down like pick-up sticks. A farmer grips his arms about a cherry tree in his orchard that, uprooted, dashes a hundred wrens and jays huddled in its branches into the storm and bears the man into the seething abyss below. A village street has become a river of mud, where a lone, drunken Tibetan wades knee-deep; he too is swept away, as village shops and their shopkeepers tumble down into the wash. One of the greatest perils from which the goddess Tara gave liberation was the peril of floods, which stand for lust in the human heart, but no Tara appears in this vision. The monk sees the whole mountainside turn into dense ripples of mud, overwhelming everything in its way. Within those perpendicular slashes of erosion tunnels form like open sewers, down which hundreds of people, Chinese and Tibetans alike, slide and thrash helplessly. Their bodies plunge into the engorged streams, as if they have been pushed onto logging chutes. Shrieks and cries from those falling into the river rend his heart. On the shores people reach out to loved ones with grappling hooks, but they too are quickly tugged into the current with the others, all beyond rescue. The roar of the water sounds in the monk's ears like the quenchless fire from the realms of hell, where in his meditations he has seen fire and ice torment victims of their self-created karma, hells where ice heaps blister upon blister on the flesh, and torrents of fire engulf the being without diminishing its consciousness of pain, where there is never even relief in death. And as the rain slackens, the massed bodies become waterlogged and float in clusters, rotting, swirling in the ebbing flood, piling up one against another like logs in the deep hollows of the river basins.

The vision rushes on, wrenching the equanimity of his mind into a weakened state, which he knows he must correct. He must draw his own thoughts away from this terror through an opposing power of mind. He must clear himself completely of this portentous vision, or the presence and usefulness of his mind could be disabled, perhaps for good.

And his mission still lies ahead.

IO

Six AM: A loudspeaker blares Chinese propaganda across the rock-strewn courtyard of the Guest House. It wakes us up with a great din of verbiage, and a band plays a march that blasts us as we go to the outhouse. Inside, an open row of holes with concrete foot slabs on either side awaits us. Chinese women stare in surprise at me, white foreigner, and observe my masterfully casual squat above the accommodations. One of the women is stepping into day-glow underwear.

Mr. Fu, his hair rumpled, sits dejectedly in the gloom on the stoop outside his door, scratching his straw toothbrush across his teeth. He spits on the ground. Lama Mingme follows suit. Chinese fellow-travelers, men and women, do likewise. The morning conversation of Mum and Moon is undermined by the blast of patriotic chatter and Chinese marches on the loudspeaker. Morning washing is brainwashing.

Parked beside our jeep is one of the old army convoy trucks; we see that the grill has been painted with huge dinosaur teeth—to suggest the coming extinction?

Mum and Auntie Moon are murmuring together before getting into the jeep. "What did Mum dream last night?" I ask Dorje, increasingly intrigued by her mother's symbolic night life.

Dorje shakes her head, doesn't want to say.

Just outside of the village we see rock quarries on the deforested mountain slopes, which are surely contributing to erosion.

Over the roar of the Isuzu, I can hear the ticking of Lama Mingme's crystal *mala* in Dorje's fingers. Glinting in the rising light, it send rays throughout the jeep. Mantra is Dorje's preoccupation on the road, her refuge from Mum and Auntie, I suspect. No wonder she is such a devotee, with their incessant chatter. She clicks the *mala* as Lama Mingme, his feet propped on the duffel bags, clicks his camera in the rear of the jeep.

The lighter air as we ascend makes us feel heavier. Everyone has a headache. We have risen beyond the once-forest of Kham toward the sweep of grasslands, and begin to see many small creatures funneling the ground. Not all wildlife has been destroyed. These creatures are here because the hungry foxes who used to eat them by the dozens for dinner are gone, having been trapped for the Chinese skin trade.

After her mantras, Dorje nudges me. "Actually, Mum had a very bad dream last night, of a tree growing from the top of her head, with a bird building a nest in it." She ends with a chilling murmur: "In the teachings this is a sign of approach of Lord of Death."

In the distance I glimpse a row of prayer flags, slung from a single tall tree to the wall of a shrine. Several strips are strung together so that they hang as if on a laundry line above the ground. At closer range we can see that exposure has faded the primary colors of the flags to pastels.

"Stop, oh stop!" cries Dorje, shaking Mr. Fu's shoulder. "A Kalachakra shrine!" It is a small roadside stupa whose dome is crushed on one side; it looks like a miniature ruin of a Mayan observatory.

The shrine appears too small to have warranted bombing, but as it is built alongside the road, it could have been shelled years ago. "We must see this!" cries Dorje enthusiastically. Lama Mingme says nothing about this display of tourism on her part; he is glad to stop to take photos here too. Mr. Fu pulls the jeep to the side of the road.

Outside the shrine gate we stop at a pile of prayer stones, small carved slabs of slate, some lettered with the full mantra: *Om mani padma hum. Mani*—jewel, *padma*—lotus. *Hum,* very like the hum of Winnie the Pooh. Or the ecstasies of Tantra, depending on your angle of repose. These *mani* stones look as if they've been gathered and tossed there casually.

Dorje doesn't object to Mingme snapping photos here. "Take these stones," she orders him.

A single monk is caretaker, and comes out at Dorje's bidding to tell us the story of the place. He stares at me humorously. *"Mieguo?"* he asks. By now I've had plenty of confirmation that Americans are a source of amusement.

The shrine was not bombed, he explains, but has fallen victim to neglect because there are no funds for repair. He leads us away from the crumbling stupa, into an adjacent shrine room. At the doorway Mingme pauses to photograph the dharma wheel above the entry, the wheel with eight spokes leading inward to suggest that suffering is overcome by inner work on the eightfold path of right—understanding, aspiration, speech, conduct, livelihood, effort, alertness, and concentration. The shrine has a small altar to the Kalachakra deities, with only the essentials: seven offering bowls, a *dorje,* and a bell. There is one tanka at the altar, of the benign Avalokitesvara, or Chenrezi, offering his multi-armed generosity to humankind while his wrathful aspect, Mahakala, the Lord of Death, dressed in skins and a necklace of skulls, stomps upon the writhing bodies of mere humans who know nothing better to do than copulate.

"We were approaching the Lord of Death—maybe this is all Mum's dream meant." I say to Dorje, and she prostrates herself hopefully.

To one side there is also a small statue of the mother goddess Tara, in her traditional posture, hand extended in compassion, right foot forward, as if to come toward you to offer help.

The neatness of this altar is not typical, for Tibetan shrines are usually as crowded as the one in Dorje's Hong Kong apartment. This shrine, however, almost evokes the aesthetic austerity of the Zen temples of Kyoto, where clutter never offends.

Zen offers the ideal setting for seekers concerned with both Western hygiene and aesthetic appearances. Rows of meditators clad alike in black, sitting on black cushions precisely lined upon tatami mats, in a clean-swept hall, with the simplest of altars, muted candlelight, a perfectly arranged vase of three fresh flowers signifying man, earth, and sky set beside a simple carved Buddha—impeccable! To surrender one's ego in such an environment, contemplating a mind-clearing koan—what could be more pleasing? But such is not the usual Tibetan style. Tibetan monks in monasteries in India and Nepal may be in need of a bath; one may find them dozing in their dusty robes in a shrine room that may smell of rancid oil from the unceasing butter lamps. The flowers may be wilted and the altar pictures lopsided. In Bodhgaya, where the Buddha attained enlightenment and where there are shrines from many Buddhist countries, the Western visitor will probably prefer the style of the tidy Japanese retreat.

Style. "That is not my style," said Chekhov when urged by a relative to press the collection of a sum of money owed him. The statement is a legacy of his admirable personal style. Its echo is in Hemingway's belief that style is all that we can leave behind, is the message. Leaving things out, especially the meaning, has become the literary model for many writers. I've sometimes expressed a whimsical fantasy of disappearing into a Haiku line or even a syllable. Om? The reverberation of eternity? Three syllables. Ah-oo-um ... Yet there's a difference between inner and outer style. When Chekhov spoke of his "style," he may have been surrounded by an unholy mess of books, correspondence, and manuscripts, not to mention tea trays, vodka glasses, and handkerchiefs stained by his fated lungs. The head of a Tibetan order, the Karmapa, on his deathbed is reported to have smilingly reassured grieving attendants with, "Nothing happens." An echo of the Buddha's core teaching, "Nothing becomes other than emptiness." That too is style.

In this shrine where the monk maintains clutterless order, he picks up a small covered bowl, opens it to show that it is filled with white round pellets, *ringsel,* which look rather like tiny homeopathic pills. His eyes crinkle as he allows Dorje to hold them in the palm of her hand. They are both very careful not to spill them. He explains that they magically appeared one day during the funeral of an important *tulku,* falling down from an unknown source among the mourners.

Very carefully, Dorje pours them back into the bowl. *Ringsel* are Tibetan manna, but they are to treasure, not to eat.

"I will always remember this!" she says happily on her way back to the jeep. As we are driving off, a mild wind rises, lifts, and inverts the prayer flags hanging from tree to shrine, making them look like a fractured rainbow.

We ride until dusk, when the sky becomes gold-streaked above parallel shadows that seem to extend to an infinite horizon. Our jeep moves like a fly between these stretches of dark and light.

At night while Dorje tells her beads, I'll write about Captain Bao. I like this suffering officer and hope that he is leading me more deeply into Chinese Mind.

THE GOLDEN ROAD

Captain Bao ripped the paper from the fax machine, and stared at its message in dismay and grief. A compensatory leave—that's what they were offering him. That was all—a week in Beijing. And there would be no relief for his men, no leave.

He flung himself into his chair, burying the ridges of his skull in his hands. How could he face the men, tell them this?

Wang, his orderly, stood at the door. When Bao lifted his head, Wang saw the fax on his desk and understood everything. His skinny shoulders sagged; he hadn't stood like a soldier for months. And now with this obvious news—Wang compressed his full lips. They would have to stay for another year, if they lived that long.

"Shall I pass the word, sir?" Wang asked.

Bao gazed at the fax, then slowly shook his head. No. He would have to tell them himself. "Call the company to assemble in the outer yard at two tomorrow afternoon," he said. "And give the prisoners the rest of the day off." The prisoners of course would never be relieved. At least his guards had another chance a year from now. If they lived. Wang left to comply with his orders.

Bao gripped the fax, and in a fury hurled it into the wastebasket. What could he do? His entire career rose in his mind like the seepage from the mines that drifted into his office, a slow poison. From his humble beginnings to this command post—all delusion.

Few others knew the range of the nuclear operations as well as Bao, for his assignments had taken him to a number of widespread operations. Versatile! his commander in Xinjiang had said. The thought of that made Bao's mouth twist with irony. In the early years, the halcyon days of the eager volunteers, the days of Bao's youth, the great, secret Ninth Academy was built. The Bomb—China too would have the bomb! China would create a league of scientists greater than at Los Alamos. The site for the headquarters was chosen, in the gold and silver sands, that northern desert plateau, so high that at first everyone felt dizzy and asthmatic after only a few steps. Yet what a fine spirit of dedication filled them! Everyone worked with such patriotic fervor. Built a city that had not existed before, Malan. "Magnificent" was the byword of the great technological institute, China's own. It was greater than Los Alamos! All the space they had, the vast deserts on the roof of the world. Eventually headquarters would realize Bao was right, that they would have to build other disposal plants further west. Eventually they would have to make use of all of Xinjiang and Xizang, and Ladak too. They would have to take Ladak eventually. China's gigantic strategic resource—what fools Tibetans were to think they might ever reclaim their territory! As crazy as thinking Mongolians could start up their empire again!

As money poured into the desert project, the Great Leap Forward came to an end in famine. The volunteers were promised bonuses of tinned pork and sweet potatoes that never materialized. They went on lean rations during the "three hard years." Even with all farming in collectives, China endured the worst famine in human history.

The commander of the post ordered several platoons to start a truck farm, giving them a ration of the scarce water. Bao was assigned to the potato and mushroom detail. What a humiliation! They put him on the farming detail because his heritage was farming, for many generations. But he could never tell his family of this demotion. Instead, he wrote them that his work was secret like everything else at the Academy, which was true enough. Bao built shelters for his mushroom banks, where multicolored tree-eared fungus thrived, bursting out of their stacked nests. The post commander visited the structure, and rewarded him with, "Magnificent!"

Once Bao went on a brief leave down to his parents' home near Hunan. As his train pulled into the station, he saw emaciated farmers carrying strange wares on poles, and setting them down at a market alongside the station. Bao recognized it—perhaps only a few in the village would have known what they were shipping out on the train. He knew that uranium had been discovered near there, and that the Army was giving farmers short courses in mining it, with no regard to its dangers, telling them nothing of the early mining martyrs already sacrificed in Chenxian. Farmers were scrambling for it. In the famine, it was all they could find to sell. Bao saw them pile it up on straw mats as if it were grain or cherries and oranges.

Bao's old parents would have been glad to taste his potatoes and mushrooms. Farmers like them were not allowed to keep enough grain to feed themselves. Everything went to Beijing bureaucrats and to the secret nuclear operations. Some grain rotted in storage silos. He found his parents with empty bellies. Many of their neighbors had died, and Bao could only help them with the little grain he could buy in Hunan before his leave was over.

Later he would learn the truth, that thousands, then millions, had perished, but these figures were kept from the desert forces. Like many others, his father and mother ate roots, tree bark, then white clay before they died. Rats foraged the countryside ravenously. His mother was so weak she could only look on as his father's body was devoured by rats, knowing her turn was next. Bao had to suppress thoughts of the nation's resources; if so much had not been poured into the gold and silver sands— It was a line of thought he could not pursue and keep his sanity.

He received a promotion—to work as a machinist, a big opportunity, and his first real intimacy with nuclear danger. He and his friend Wu were sent further west, to the component plant in the Qilian mountains near the old Silk Road. That was when the terrible, powerful appeal began to reach him—to be so close, to work so much on the edge of destruction! Everyone became infected with the tension, the—yes, beguilement, of it. There was something seductive about nuclear energy that all the workers shared, the burning urgency, the thrilling secrecy, though no one spoke of it that way. It was deeply, deeply—erotic.

Bao became one of the inner team then, the machinists who practiced month after month, competing for the task of fabricating the first ball of uranium for the bomb, which would fit snugly inside its shaft, secreted in its enclosure as if pressed through a woman's vagina to lock into her cervix. He hadn't been the one who finally won the competition. His friend Wu gained the honor of being the first master lathe operator. He had worked with such fierce concentration he lost thirty pounds.

He'd never forget the day of Wu's triumph: All gloved and masked, Wu took his position and placed the uranium in his vise. The brass who had come for this special occasion waited expectantly for him to create the very first uranium ball in China. Wu suddenly realized his position, what a responsibility he had won. This was lethal uranium. There could be a far-reaching deadly accident. Wu froze. Then when prompted to begin, he reached violently trembling hands toward the vise. So many witnesses, all the important cadres who had worked on the project, had come for this event. Wu broke into a sweat, and dropped his hands. He sat like an impotent, shamed boy with his first woman. Everyone had to leave until he could pull himself together. Bao went to fetch him a cup of warm milk. The witnesses returned, and on his second attempt, Wu succeeded, measuring, adjusting, and finally machining until he had the nuclear core ready for the tight, perfectly fitting nest of its shell case. Secret and close with promise and mystery and terror. More beautiful and terrifying than a woman's inner depths, more thrilling. The cheer that rose from the witnesses was one of orgasmic ecstasy.

After that triumph somebody from headquarters sent a box of T-shirts to the plant printed with the radiation symbol, three wedges surrounding a Yin-Yang circle, and below it ideograms reading: "Tao Glow."

Still, Bao began to feel sickened by the enthusiasm at the plant, the fatal allure in which all were caught. His superior must have seen his state of mind, and soon sent him to his present job, to oversee the construction of the refuse depot at the site of the uranium mine. It was then that his old father's ghost had begun to appear to him.

Very early in the game officials had thought of using Tibetan political prisoners to mine the uranium. They removed more than a hundred Tibetans from Gutsa and Kong-po prisons to build a reform-through-labor camp at the mines, *laogai* for monks who had shown resistance to verbal self-correction. That was his big promotion. Coordinating shipments from the Tibetan prison camp to his Security and Protection Bureau, as waste disposal was officially called. Another lie. There were many children, boys, working the mine. Tibetans were blamed for the presence of children, of course, because they had always sent their sons to monasteries to become monks at an early age, and the monastaries of course were a primary source of prisoners.

Once he passed a few of the boys laughing among themselves. He stopped beside one of them, who fell silent, went back to his digging. Bao prodded him. What was so funny? The boy looked up at him and finally answered, with a shy grin. "We are digging a hole deep enough to get to America." Bao gave the boys a wink and walked on.

Then a day later the emergency bell sounded and the hoistman brought the man-cage up the shaft; the faces of seven Tibetans under their helmets were covered in coarse green dust, and one of the men held the limp, bloody body of that boy. A chunk of sandstone had jarred loose from the face of the cave and crushed him. All these years and many other deaths, and he had never got that one out of his mind. One day the boy's face grinning up at him—and the next, nothing. Those men under their dusty helmets—all of them doomed men as well.

That day, as he thought of the dead boy, his father's wrathful ghost had come toward him, in another reproachful visit. The bullet in his father's head from the old war wound gleamed like a miner's lamp. He said, "My son, this work of yours is an offense to Kuan Tí. You must go back to the farm. Only old women are left to reap the crops. Go home." But he could not go home without becoming a deserter.

Meanwhile, the building of the missiles went on up in Malan. It had all become a crazed cycle: build, destroy, and bury. Nobody knew just how many times his once-great nation could blow up the globe.

Sometimes at night Bao would go out onto the desert and look up at the sky, which shone so closely with such neighborly brilliance because of the altitude of the immense plateau, a sky to all appearances unaffected by the poison of his own star. And he would think of the down-slanting tunnel of the drift below ground as some malevolent counterpart to the astronomical phenomena he had learned of from a scientist at Malan, the red drift and the blue drift, galaxies in outer space moving toward a black hole. He would ponder the possibility of some synchronistic connection of language that linked this planet with his underground drift, the color of green, to those red and blue galaxies and all starry existence in a hidden movement toward the ultimate black hole, and the end of everything.

II

This morning our departure is somewhat delayed because Mingme wants to visit the large monastery here. Before Earth Mum and Sister Moon have finished eating, he goes down the road talking to Tibetans. They are happy to see strangers and since our arrival have crowded around us, curious, eager to talk when they realize one among us can speak their tongue. It is a relief to see their brightly colored clothing after the drab conformity of Chinese dark blue. Even though the woolens of their garments are shabby, their vibrant, gaily-colored embroidery has outlived the skirts and jackets they adorn.

Last evening when we arrived, we had stopped at the monastery and asked them to take us in, but they had no room for travelers and sent us to the Guest House. They showed us around first, however. The outside of the building is surrounded by large number of prayer wheels, one hundred and eight, Dorje says, the number of beads on a *mala.* These tubes of colorful print cloth stretched over wires and mounted on wooden wheels are meant to be turned by visitors, each turn crediting the visitor with a prayer. At the front passage, Dorje and Mingme took off their shoes to go inside, placed them before the curtain at the entrance. A Chinese man offered to sell me incense, which I declined. He entered ahead of Dorje and Mingme, rudely kicking their shoes aside. Others, Tibetan and Chinese alike, followed, but Mum, Auntie, and I preferred to go down the street to check into the Guest House. Later that night, we drifted to sleep to the deep intonations of mantra from the monastery.

Now after Mingme leaves the breakfast table, I realize that I have left my down pillow at the Guest House. I tell Dorje that I'll run to pick it up, only a few blocks away, while the three of them finish their breakfast. I take off as she is translating some explanation to Mum and Moon.

I come to a schoolhouse, across the road from the Guest House, where recess is going on. A group of smiling Chinese girls, aged eight or nine, stop me, ask me to sit on the steps with them. They wear school uniforms, white blouses and navy skirts. "Eng-lish," they say to me. "No, American," I tell them. *"Mieguo."* That makes them laugh. They want to practice the phrases they know. "What-is-your-name? How-old-are-you? Where-do-you-come-from? Where-do-you-go?" They want to tell me a few Chinese words too. *"Xie xie,* Thank you ... *Wo yao cha,* I want to buy some tea." I try, but of course make them laugh at my failed inflections. We are having a nice time. Body language and cheerful spirit transcend our shortcomings. The girls giggle, and so do I.

Looking at the downside, I realize there are no Tibetan children at this school, where the girls are so tidily attired. Tibetan children may go to the official schools if they know Chinese, but failing that they go to separate, poorer schools. The language barrier is a catch-22 that demotes Tibetans to second-class status in their own country. These Chinese children are here because their parents have taken government inducements of land and money to move into Tibet. But this is home to these children, more so than to their parents. As much as any immigrants anywhere, they are at home here and nowhere else. Even some of their parents apparently worship at the Tibetan monastery.

I think of the outcry against immigrants the world over: Back to Haiti and Mexico, back to Laos and Pakistan, back to Africa, back to China. Back, back ... A few decades ago American liberals had a notion that once racial discrimination ended people would blend together and everyone would become a pleasant shade of suntan. This would come about because of the unity, mutual respect, and love among races. But that naive notion didn't consider that cultural values are not skin-deep. "Where do you come from? Where do you go?" Words from a song from my childhood, *Cotton-Eyed Joe.* Joe was black, newly from Africa when that song was first sung. We cannot go back, neither to Europe nor to Africa nor even to China.

I am thinking these things when suddenly, there comes Dorje, trailed by Mum and Moon. They find me sitting with the children, showing them where we are on my map. Despite Mum's poor health, she and Auntie have followed Dorje, in a state of alarm at my daring to go off by myself. Independent action is not allowed. Mum and Moon are very upset. I am a stranger here where I do not know the language, where women are sometimes grabbed and cut open for their kidneys, their eyes.

Of course, I find their alarm absurd. I try to tell them I am all right, I am among children. It is a bright, sunny morning in a friendly rural town, no lurking scavengers of human innards around.

The recess bell sounds. Dorje goes across the street to the Guest House and retrieves my pillow, which she gives me with a reproachful look. "We are all same group, must stay together," she says. Mum and Moon start back to the jeep, mumbling disapproval.

I wave good-bye to the girls. Where do any of us go? I wonder. We cannot go back, we have to go forward; we have to find a solution to these conflicts of race and culture and share the wealth of everything we are. Enjoy the riches, as children do before they learn to fear that they may be abused, captured, forced into some form of slavery or extinction, stolen for their livers, their hearts.

When we get into the jeep, a tall Tibetan presses his long, ruddy face to the window, flattens his nose against the darkly tinted glass trying to make out what's inside. He has high cheekbones like the Navajo's. I realize that he is drunk, like others we have seen, drunk on that cheap alcohol made for the exclusive recreation of Tibetans.

The sight of the Tibetan at the car window makes me think again of magic—our jeep might have been transported to Navajo and Hopi territory. Cheerful, self-contained native inhabitants are transformed into abject victims. They drink to forget their mothers who were tortured and humiliated publicly, their brothers who may have starved in a death march to prison, like our own Trail of Tears. They drink out of helplessness in the face of these facts: Their kind are so reduced in numbers that they will soon become a tourist freak show, their land is being systematically repopulated and undermined, clogged with toxic waste, ripped open with neutron bomb tests. Tibet is being transformed into a nightmare reservation. There is a difference. Native Americans are no longer routinely curious or friendly when visitors arrive, for they thoroughly understand how they have been pressed to extinction, poisoned by alcohol and uranium.

We bump along, across a sandy plateau. The morning light spreads into a deep green and purple shadow on a bank where an Alpine tundra ground cover creeps with tiny blue and yellow flowers. Here an occasional wild yak in his shaggy coat appears, where once there were herds of uncountable number. There are still hundreds of small burrowing creatures, seemingly intent upon destroying the terrain in their search for food. What is missing from the food chain? It is recorded that the Chinese slaughtered thousands of yaks, at the same time that they replaced the barley crop with rice, which doesn't like this altitude, and that this effort at crop substitution caused a famine that brought suffering also to the occupying Chinese. Now they are raising barley to sell to the Tibetans from whom they have taken the farmland. This ecology needs more than study.

The powerful nations do nothing to support Tibet and yield to China's version of history. I wonder if that is because the old superior attitude toward indigenous people still holds in favor of nations bent on "progress." Having no production lines, or profit agenda, the natives do not matter. They chew blubber, scalp enemies or eat them, leave their dead to vultures, and so why not improve the US reservations with mines, and scatter plutonium across the Dreamtime spaces of Australia? Why not use up Tibet?

Tibetans believe that the ordinary, every-day mind, busy with its creative and destructive action, puts impermanent things together into composites—people, places, and things—or destroys them. Take a relative composite like forest, for example. If any part of forest is taken away, its impermanence becomes noticeable. It has no inherent, continuous existence. You might even say it is substanceless. There is no single thing you can call forest. It can be destroyed. Loggers can take it down, haul it off, make skyscrapers out of it. And so it has no constant condition. Even if it were to renew itself, regrow, and return, it is constantly subject to change.

To me the story of Tibet is a metaphor for all that is wrong in what we do to our world. But when Lama Mingme considers the destruction of the forest, and prefers not to assign blame, he is taking a longer view than I. Thoughts of impermanence enable Tibetans to feel forbearance, which may sometimes have the appearance of passivity and submission. The forest is impermanent, not part of what Tibetans call Absolute Mind, which doesn't come and go, is not dependent upon conditions, and is, like heaven, mysterious to our ordinary mind.

Absolute Mind is undegenerate from beginningless time, eternally changeless, unconquerable. Tibetans also say that these distinctions are conveniences of language; the absolute and relative are inseparable conditions of the great web of being.

As I turn to the lighter fantasy of my notebook, I realize that Bodhi and Youngden are drawing closer to Absolute Mind tonight.

THE GOLDEN ROAD

Bodhi's heart pounded; her hands on the wheel trembled like Youngden's. Her tension mounted as they approached the rendezvous point. Youngden's altimeter showed over 10,000 meters. "Can 'Mother' survive this height?" she wondered to Youngden. He shook his head, wincing. The altitude made him feel twice his own weight.

There were only tire tracks on the desert now, not a road, and they followed them in a slow ascent. They glimpsed the dazzling breadth of the landscape before them, where the mountain "A" had told them about rose like a great inverted bowl where pink clouds concealed its summits. Foothills of this great range, sweeping along to the east of them, led to a pilgrimage path that had its apex somewhere beneath those clouds, which was on no map, and which was shrouded in majesty and beauty. Rainbows hid within the clouds, grouping themselves in delicate shapes, hanging like clusters of delicate green and purple grapes or tendrils of rare vines.

Youngden shook his head in wonder. "I will try, but doubt video can catch rainbows like this."

Bodhi could scarcely contain her excitement. "They will be here tomorrow morning. I pray to Tara that they have made a successful journey."

He said, "Is okay. Will be okay, I know."

At length, the holy mountain showed itself more distinctly to them, where its peaks stood in a circle like lotus petals, crested by the setting sun, which lent it an aureole light.

She said, "It looks unreal. Is it really on this earth?" She stopped the jeep and they got out. Youngden lifted his field glasses, looking toward the mountain. "Maybe not real," he said. He swept the lens along the foothills. He handed her the glasses, shaking his head. What she saw through the lens was Commander Bao's installation, the fences surrounding the installations built above the mines, and the bold, incongruous diagonals of the huge airstrip cutting across the high plateau. A cargo truck was driving away from a plane. She lowered the glasses slowly.

"How do they dare build something like that in such a sacred place?" She had known to expect it, but had not imagined how invasive the installation would look against the lofty face of the mountain.

Youngden said, "Old Tibetans say holy mountain contain lodes of emeralds, gold, diamonds. But to mine them, not possible. Sacrilege."

"And what they have put here is the deadliest of mines. Not a gemstone in it."

They stood silently for a few minutes. Then turning to her, Youngden saw that she was crying. He reached out and touched her cheek. "Tears make little silver trail in the dust," he said.

She threw her arms around him, pressing her head against his chest, sobbing.

"So sorry," he said. "We talk last night about our little situations in samsara. This big karma, very bad."

She clenched her fists, pounded his shoulders with them. "It makes me so *angry!*"

Brushing the dust away from her cheeks, he bent down and kissed them, then kissed her lips. He sighed. "I think not so angry, wrathful. Good job for wrathful deities."

After a while they spread their sleeping bags, as the evening air chilled. The stars were more brilliant than ever, and shone down on the desert with iridescent sprays of light. They zipped their sleeping bags together, and without speaking undressed and lay beside each other. The moon lifted and bloomed still full above them. Bodhi raised her hand and thought she could almost see her bones through the flesh in the brilliant light. Youngden reached up and his hand too seemed transparent as he clasped hers. Sprays of light cut across the sky, stars seeming to streak weightlessly above the desecrated terrain.

"Think of it as a mandala," Youngden said. "The concrete airstrip, the mines, the mountain. All part of a mandala."

"Yes," she said, as tears still came down. But then they went into one another's arms, and Youngden dried her tears. Slowly they began to chant the mantra of the union Bodhi had suggested so lightly—was it only a week ago? Slowly, slowly, even as the cold night air enclosed them, their bodies warmed, and a hot current streaked up through their spines to penetrate their hearts, open them.

Youngden laughed, and said in a careful, even voice: "I have to remember . . . this practice is for others."

Pulling him closer, she said, "When I was small and wrote letters, I used to add to the return address, 'USA, Northern Hemisphere, the World, the Milky Way, the Universe.' Imagine that."

They continued the chant. The resonance of their sound filled the air, and their bodies felt a more delicate charge rising between and within them, a sensation spreading at the base of their spines flowing gently upward through their hearts to the crown of their heads and suffusing their visual mandala out into the luminous night, then extending the image up around the great mountain, and beyond to the entire country, spreading it south and eastward, and throughout all the provinces of China, and westward throughout all of India, and upward and downward to the North and South Poles, penetrating the teeming crowds of the streets of all Asia and the traffic jams of Europe and the United States, permeating the entire globe of earth, and going beyond it through the moon's globe and all the spinning and shooting stars, like a love letter sent for the bliss and benefit of the vast universe above and around them, the universe becoming a mandala of perfection contained in their mutual being, not to be released intemperately.

12

Out of the early morning darkness the outlines of a number of caves emerge, cutouts in a barren hillside. Beneath the caves, where the morning shadows are receding, lichens cushion the ground. Their low growth drapes the earth with many shades of green and a small yellow flower in a tightly woven carpet, where two domestic yaks are watching us. No wind, but as the yaks move to graze, their manes flow about their legs like skirts. They belong to a nearby Tibetan house. We see fewer thatch roofs as we ascend; the occasional house now has squared off, with painted eaves and flat Tibetan roofs designed so that people may sleep there on hot summer nights, or make love. Today we are above 4200 metres.

In the soft light of dawn, a Tibetan woman walks up a pathway toward the caves with a pail that Mingme says contains food for a retreatant. Someone sits in darkness within, perhaps going blind in order to see.

Solitary retreat—some people have a talent for it. Tibetan retreatants subject their bodies to extreme restraints. They eat, sleep, and live upright in meditation boxes, in which they cannot lie fully extended, and perform numbing sitting and mantra practice. Out of the box, they occupy their time with full body prostrations. Westerners who try these practices sometimes suffer temporary insanity. Yet I also know Westerners whose faith is strong enough to take such rigors in stride, one a woman who recently started a retreat of three years.

In the time of Gautama Buddha, almswomen were allowed eight personal objects—begging bowl, razor, needle, girdle, water strainer, and three robes. I imagine a film about these nuns—it would start with a close-up of a woman's hands putting the objects in their place in her cell. Was she obliged to wear the girdle under her robe every day? I wonder about the function of the razor, perhaps for shaving one another's heads and the heads of monks. The monks, who were allowed books and many other privileges, did not carry a sewing needle but took their mending to the nuns. In one story Siha, driven to despair through seven years of fruitless meditation, took a rope, plunged into the woods, bound the rope around a bough, and tied it to her neck. I wonder if Siha felt like a hungry ghost, or imagined she would be doomed to the realm of the hungry ghosts because of her suicide. Just as she was tightening the rope to end her suffering, illumination broke upon her and she achieved the Great Liberation.

The Tibetan saint Milarepa, in his hermetic life beside the "turquoise lake" near Mt. Kailash, self-condemned to a diet of nettles, scorned as a scruffy beggar on visits to Lhasa, said, "My practice is harder than the salt pressed in yak skin, like a rock. It is easier to carry a load of skins up the mountain than to do my practice." My sense of it exactly. I clearly lack the patience of a saint. Tibetan meditation feels to me like torture. One hour of chant rouses demons of impiety—I turn to drink.

Yet these caves are not so far removed from the way I've spent most of my life, in a small room with a desk, back to the window. Isn't that solitary focus what painters and writers work for? Push themselves to extremes, go mad with images and words, seeking some integrating freedom in the work. The composer Georges Enesco said, "The essential exercise of the composer—meditation—has never been suspended in me. I live a permanent dream that stops neither night or day." So it may have been with Milarepa. And with Euripides, too, who lived out his last years in exile in a Grecian cave.

Dorje's imagination is also stirred by the caves. The solitary Tibetan has disappeared into a dark hollow in the face of the pale cliff. "How about jump out of the jeep, find empty cave, and sit?"

I laugh. "Contemplate impermanence, and hope some friendly nomad will come along with a pail of barley and salty tea."

Dorje: "Maybe find a *terma.*"

"C's" father is said to have thrust a dagger into a rock to release one of Padma Sambhava's *termas,* the hidden teachings, where others had failed. An Excalibur story. Many of these teachings still remain undisclosed, it is said. Seeds to open the mind throughout the ages. They are often discovered, in a meditation process that cannot be described to the lay person, as new mantras, and sometimes they appear in material form like the find in the rock. Although these teachings bear a strong resemblance to one another, each is said to contain a germ of knowledge hitherto unknown. Artful Padma Sambhava. He knew how to string out his gifts for future generations, for all time. Like the best storytellers, even those who write about the sequences of ordinary mind, like Scherazade, Homer, Chaucer, Shakespeare.

Dorje teases Mingme. "Suppose we drop you off here to live in a cave, Mingme? Pick you up on our way back," she says.

He grins, shouts over the engine. "Dorje, I can't believe you do that to me!"

"By then you will be *mahasiddhi!*"

Later in the day, Dorje nudges Mr. Fu. "Rest stop."

He pulls over to the side not far from the black octagonal of a nomad tent. A truck sounds its horn and passes as we park. Now that we are beyond the forest there are fewer trucks. This one is loaded with rolls of woolen rugs, bound for the Lhasa trade.

A drying rack of skins stands outside the tent. The skins are already darkened by the tent's shadow; afternoon shades are lengthening across the sands. This is a small tent, for a family of six or so; Lama Mingme says his uncle "C" told him that there used to be huge tents in this part of the country that could hold 400 people; fires would be built inside as the people huddled through cold and smoky winter ceremonies.

When we get out of the jeep, two children, a boy and girl, run toward us, and halt to wait at a safe distance. Lama Mingme sticks his tongue out and his thumb up at them, which he knows is a historic Tibetan greeting, but they giggle and lean on each other, holding hands, keeping their own tongues inside their mouths. Their ruddy cheeks are like rouge cakes, hard patches of sunburnt skin that we see on many children here who live in the open. Will they all have skin cancer one day?

While Mingme snaps their photo, I go to the jeep, pull a picture book from my bag, and beckon to them. I have brought several books for "C's" sister, color photographs of Tibet's monasteries and landscapes, before and after destruction. The children come shyly. I open the book and show them a photograph of a yak. They stare, entranced. The boy's head turns in amazement to the hillside. Their own yak stands behind their tent, where smoke from a yak dung fire gusts from a top vent. Someone is preparing the evening meal.

We sit on the rocky ground while Mingme takes more photos. As I turn the pages of the book, the girl's eyes widen and glow above her red-caked cheeks, and she stops a page with a small grimy hand, almost slapping it. "Lhasa," I say. It is the familiar image of the Potala Palace, home of the Dalai Lama. A photograph made about this same time of day, in a golden light. She gazes and gazes, her black eyes devouring every inch.

The longing to see Lhasa—it's in her face. Every Tibetan develops early in life this hunger for Lhasa, more than any place in the world. Lhasa, the golden sanctum, not merely the center of things but the home of the living god Chenrezi, the Dalai Lama, no longer in residence but in their hearts in the place of deliverance.

It is their Celestial City. These children may know of Lhasa only from an itinerant lama, yet this child must already have a desire to go on pilgrimage to Lhasa, for her tiny fingers now timidly trace a path on the page where she would do *kora,* the circumambulation of the Barkor, the half-mile sacred path round the Jokhang temple. She would be among many other pilgrims, some of them turning hand-held prayer wheels in which prayers written by a literate holy man might be stored, like Catholic indulgences. Her body would be extended fully on the ground, and she would stand to proceed in the next step only to the point where her fingertips stretched at the last prostration. The most devout carry this to the extreme of advancing the body only by widths instead of lengths, progressing crabwise and slow. One hundred and eight of these *koras* will earn entry into the Pureland at death. Have her parents made a pilgrimage to Lhasa? Perhaps not, for the Chinese stopped all pilgrimages during the Cultural Revolution.

Lama Mingme speaks to her, and she answers without turning away from the picture. No, she has never been to Lhasa. No, she has never seen a picture of Lhasa before. Yet she recognized it. What Catholic child has never seen an image of St. Peter's in Rome?

In remote areas like this, many people never reach the major holy places but will make pilgrimages to nearby mountain sites where regional siddhas once achieved miraculous states. Nevertheless, the people long for Lhasa, even more than for the greatest sacred mountain, Kailash.

I feel very touched by what I see in this child's face. What draws people to such callings as anthropology and missionary work may be just this—the sight of such visible wonder. That is the impulse of art also, essentially religious. Ingmar Bergman said, "Art lost its basic creative drive the moment it was separated from worship." I start to give the girl the book, but Mingme stops me. There'll be others we want to show it to, he insists.

I rummage in my bag and come up with a postcard picturing the Dalai Lama, which the girl presses instantly to her heart, her eyes dancing with surprised excitement. This is another image she easily recognizes. The boy reaches out to grasp it, and so I start to open my bag to give him one as well. This time Dorje stops me. "Mingme, tell her it's for the whole family." He complies and the children rush off toward the smoky tent.

All one family.

When someone wants to know what was in this crazy trip for me, I have my answer. Her face.

Tonight I open my notebook thinking of the unseen world, which novelists and would-be *mahasiddhis* alike try to conjure up, and I come in touch with Commander Bao's ghostly father again, making prophetic utterances like an old conjurer himself.

THE GOLDEN ROAD

Bao wanted to take a rest before facing his men with the failure of his appeal for a furlough. But before he could leave his office, the ghost of his old father came up out of the fax machine. Indefatigable!

The lump on his forehead seemed almost red now, glowing like a coal. The old ghost spoke to him, "Why didn't you go home when I told you to? Better you should raise mushrooms on our old farm. Better to make tree-eared soup for people to eat than this dust. Your hair has fallen out, and you haven't even gone to Emei Shan for a corrective herb."

Bao sighed. This was a signal that the old ghost would give his lecture about the Taoist sages. And he proceeded with it, speaking of the ancient poets, respectful of nature's power manifested in floods and fire storms and in other sudden forces that erupted and alarmed people. "They understood the connection between natural power and divine power. They strove to find a balance of wisdom to guide people through nature's display of terror so that faith in divine law would endure. And to help us maintain our balance, they conceived and wrote the books of the *Tao* and the *I Ching*."

The ghost's litany was familiar to Bao; he submitted to it, moved by the old rhetoric. But now it took another turn, and the lump on his father's forehead seemed to send out a red starry spray: "Now, my son, an awe of technology has usurped our awe of nature's power. Man thinks his own creations are greater than any river in flood, any waterfall, any fire ever before seen, and has created a new dogma: That transmuting elements is the pathway to the divine. What is the meaning of this?" The old ghost raised a yellow, transparent finger and pointed it at the T-shirt Wang had pinned to the wall. Tao Glow! "My son, an alchemical worship is in place, having nothing more to do with the great Tao than fortune-telling coins."

Bao understood this. The homely, irreversible comedy of seeing his hair fall out had brought it home to him. But he wanted to subdue the ghost, to reassure him. He said, "Father, this baldness is nothing to worry about. You too were bald." It was true; his father's dome was as bald as his own. "Perhaps it is genetic," said Bao.

The ghost would not be put off. He said, "A forlorn hope, my son. You have joined a global *cult.* A death cult. Its members take delight in this danger, in the nearness to knowledge of death. A delusion has spread, seeped into your work like poison dust, that gaining power over this destructive energy puts men in a dialogue with their outcast gods. What would Kuan Tí say to this? There is no valor in nuclear warfare, no honor."

Bao could not argue with him. He thought of the transformations believed possible through nuclear power—yet it was in the hands of men who would not admit to the venom seeping into their everyday lives. Into water that half the world would drink.

The old ghost's beard trembled with fury. "This worship is demonic. Like so many other men, both here in China and elsewhere throughout the world, you have joined a fraternity that plays with this new alchemy and believes that the release of nuclear energy had changed all wisdom, all the energy of the universe. This seduction is terminal, yet they try to place the best face, the *divine* face, on their hidden despair."

Tears came into Bao's eyes, and his body shook. This was like a signal to the ghost, who began to fade. His old father did not like to see strong men weep. Bao tried to control himself, almost wishing his father would stay. He would tell him that he agreed with him, that he was caught in a drift with all others in this work, from which they could not extricate themselves and into which they were pulling all the known world, a drift as inexorable in its charting as the red and the blue drifts in the sky.

But he couldn't speak. He felt he was losing his mind, his control was slipping away. He *couldn't* stay here, he couldn't take any more.

And then it came to him what he had to do. He would take his compensatory leave. With him would go his own secret invention, to the Munitions Ministry in Beijing. They would at last know of his personal accomplishment. Probably he would not live to see its use. But perhaps it could help men come to their senses if they could experience the effect of his invention upon his country, for which he still felt a passionate love.

He went to the door of the vault and opened it. Inside, on a plasticine daisy wheel display stand was his stunning weapon, inspired by the early detonators, small enough to be strapped under a man's coat. You did not send it down, god-like, from the clouds—you had to fire it directly at your target yourself. The weapon contained a tiny plutonium pellet, individualized to demolish no more than a city block. Here was a weapon whose effect you could not avoid experiencing as you used it, could not escape by flight through the air.

He would submit it for official testing. He had tested it himself, out on the firing range, going alone into contaminated crater sites. He knew his years of work as a machinist had paid off. It was perfect, and with the rest of the world pretending to disarm, his country could use it.

His weapon was part of the new alchemy, but it would demonstrate that men, not gods, were at fault for its use, were the agents responsible for the sacrifices it claimed. Fire it at a person, face to face, and you must see the consequence of your act.

He turned the daisy wheel; its loaded barrel glinted. The brass would want to manufacture it. Like its ancestor, there would be no turning back from it.

He got on the intercom and called orderly Wang to come in. He reached down to the waste basket and retrieved his orders, smoothed the faxed communiqué out on his desk.

"Wang," he said, gesturing to the weapon. "I want a metal and concrete protective carrying-container built for this."

"What is it, sir?" asked Wang.

Bao shook his head, sensing that there was something off in his self-justification, something wrong with his reason. But he had to go forward, even to disaster. He muttered, "Call it the 'Plu-Gun.'"

13

Mr. Fu is balking. He stops the jeep and says we didn't tell him how far we intended to go. It is too far. We have come to a village with a small monastery and a restaurant, and he pulls up before a wooden bridge, flat and cantilevered in the Tibetan style. Mr. Fu's negative attitude turns all of us grim.

The constant jolting in the jeep, the isolation, the stress of our sixteen hours a day on the road, the common insomnia from the altitude—all this is taking its toll on us. As I look around at the others, I can see everyone is nearly exhausted. And now this brings us to the edge of panic.

Probably Dorje was not entirely clear to Mr. Fu in the beginning; she drives a hard bargain. I suggest we discuss a compromise.

She says to him, "We all one family." He is suspicious of this line. He is no longer in the Tibetan family, has given himself a Chinese name. But he doesn't want to be in the Chinese family either, not this one. He wants to follow his own name and return to Chengdu.

Auntie voices a low, mooning groan. Mum and Auntie literally talked themselves to sleep in my ear last night, for we were able to obtain only two rooms. I was ready to get up and move in with Mr. Fu and Mingme. How these two dear women love to exercise their mouths! How strong their jaws must be, like the jaws of lionesses! Auntie finally fell asleep in mid-sentence. Mum questioned her, then humphed in annoyance when she realized Auntie was snoring. No wonder they appear tired every day—yet they talk tirelessly anyhow. When we started out today, Lama Mingme confirmed it would have been of no avail to invade his room last night, because they too could hear the ceaseless talk through the walls. And poor Mr. Fu could understand it!

As Dorje speaks heatedly with Mr. Fu, Lama Mingme jumps out of the jeep, saying he wants to photograph the monastery. A Khampa woman appears before him. She wears ragged clothing, but her headdress is ornamented with a round medallion set with a large center turquoise. Her face is ringed with coral beads threaded in her hair. He takes her photograph, then starts to rush around the corner to the monastery.

Dorje calls out to him as he races away. "Come back!" She wants his support in her stand against Mr. Fu and becomes quite angry with Mingme. I've never seen her lose her cool before. She shouts after him, "Come here right now, Mingme!"

Mingme obliges. He has never heard this tone either.

"You should help me argue with him!" she declares. She needs more support than mine; she sees a traditional need of the male voice, even Lama Mingme's. "You desert me taking these foolish photos just when Mr. Fu has decided to quit his job. Come and talk with him." She is exhausted, poor Dorje, near tears.

"But I don't speak Chinese," Mingme protests.

"No matter! Use your voice. Show him with your voice that we must go on. He is *your own blood!* Make him understand. *Talk* to him!"

Mingme comes to the jeep window and speaks to Mr. Fu in a gentle, reasonable tone, as indeed I have. It is easy for Mr. Fu to shrug and turn away.

Dorje's temper rises even more. She gets out and brushes Mingme aside. "Never mind, you useless! I have to take care of everything. You like a child. I am sick and tired of it! You only flit around on vacation!" As her voice scalds him, Mingme sinks away, speechless, near tears himself. He climbs into his rear seat and subsides, tucking his feet under one of the duffel bags. Probably there is more to this drama between them than I will ever know.

Mum cannot bear this explosion. We must eat, she decides. She gets out and tells Dorje to stop arguing, to wait a while. At the restaurant, we eat before further discussion. There is no challenging her decision. Mum leads the troops off to food, Mingme following despondently. Mr. Fu gets out of his seat and stands beside the jeep, lighting a cigarette angrily.

Deserted by my appetite, I gather up my notebook, thinking I will write while the others are in the restaurant. As I go to sit on a stone beside the bridge, I say to Mr. Fu, "Don't leave us here."

He shrugs, gives me a sly grin, and blows smoke between his teeth like a dragon. Does he understand English after all? An uneasiness settles in me as I retreat to my notebook, keeping him within sight. I wonder if buses ever pass along this deserted road. What would we do if Mr. Fu were to leap into the jeep and tear off home with a wild yell. But somehow I think he has too much conscience to desert us.

Is there some way, I wonder, to return Mr. Fu to his faith? Doubt may be my own way of being, but it is alien to the Tibetan nature. Although I may think it is all just so much imagery, like the manger and the magi and the star of Bethlehem, something in Mr. Fu still believes, I know. I'm sure he hasn't forgotten the lessons of childhood.

THE GOLDEN ROAD

As Mr. Fu drove on, "A" pointed out to "Mother" certain places dear to his heart, talking on and on about power spots, sites where miracles had happened. He told her where Gesar changed himself into a tiger and ate his enemies one by one in an orgy of greed, and also where Gesar transformed himself into a bee who slipped inside a drink of water so that his enemy would swallow him and get stung to death.

Suddenly, "A" tapped him on the shoulder. "Here," he said. "This is the place."

The old woman peered out the window excitedly. "The place?"

The jeep was approaching a cave beside the sandy riverbank. "Stop here," said the monk. Mr. Fu got out of the jeep and saw that beside the hillside cave an odd rock formation jutted out. Mr. Fu stretched and lit a cigarette.

He heard the monk say, "This is where Padma Sambhava's deepest secret lies. The time has come for me to uncover it." The monk led the old woman toward the rock, touching her elbow. "And it is time for you to move your own prayer power into Vajra Mind."

Mr. Fu watched as they stood facing the rock. The monk chanted in a deep baritone. Suddenly the monk was grasping the handle of a tri-bladed knife. Mr. Fu did not know where it came from. A shaft of afternoon sunlight opened like a fan about the monk's body. The handle of his blade was studded with coral and turquoise, a gorgeous-looking thing, and very lethal. The monk shifted his weight, thrust the blade at a small crevice in the rock. In it went, up to its hilt. Much to Mr. Fu's astonishment, the rock offered no resistance. He flicked his cigarette away, and drew closer.

The monk's chant deepened. "Mother" murmured a name, Saint something or other, then seemed to go into a deep trance.

A chill went through Mr. Fu's spine. The wrinkled face of his own mother appeared before him as she sat in her dark room in Chengdu, praying, always praying. He could never tell her about this scene. She had such faith in miracles, he wouldn't want to fuel her imagination. But now he stood in frozen fascination gazing at the monk and the "Mother," as caterpillars crept up his neck.

The monk removed the blade, grasped something from inside the rock—a leather pouch?—and led "Mother" to the mouth of the cave. In the clear river water, sand glittered with fool's gold. The monk said to her: "This is the place for your initiation." Folding her black skirt under her, she sank down to her knees, still entranced. Then he called to Mr. Fu. "Come closer. You must witness this."

Mr. Fu frowned, torn with mixed feelings, wanting to draw back, to have another cigarette. The monk's gaze was upon him—riveting. He found he could not refuse, and he followed them reluctantly.

"Pray, 'Mother,'" said the monk. "Sink into your deepest contemplation." He extended the tri-sided knife to her, handle first.

"Just like that?" she asked, gripping the turquoise-and-coral handle of the weapon.

"Just like that," he said. She knelt beside the water, her knees cushioned by a bed of lichens with tiny flecks of yellow buds.

The monk went to the river with a small pail, filled it with sand, then knelt down and began to move his hands in a way that piqued Mr.

Fu's curiosity. From the pouch he had taken from the rock the monk drew several little packets and opened them. They contained brightly colored sand—powdered rock actually—of jasper, serpentine, amber, and onyx. Advancing toward his two passengers, Mr. Fu saw that the monk was making a sand mandala. First, he fashioned a cone from a sheet of paper and next began sifting the colored powder and the golden sand from the riverbank through it. The woman was praying and the monk was chanting, a dual-toned chant that seemed to reverberate from the depths of the earth. The effect on Mr. Fu was to increase his sense of misery.

He sat down and leaned against a mossy tree on the embankment, his legs tucked under him. He knew this could go on for hours. Maybe he could nap through part of it. His blistered heels were hurting him, and again when he closed his eyes he saw his old mother's face. She would have made a soothing poultice for his feet ...

He opened his eyes—hours later, almost instantly?—to an intensely brilliant scene.

The light blinded him momentarily—it took a while for his vision to focus. A young, golden-haired woman stood where the old woman had been kneeling. Her hair cropped short at her ears, she was dressed in a gleaming armor with a crimson velvet scabbard at her waist. In her hand she no longer held the *purba* but a long sword that was covered with rust. She rubbed the length of the weapon, and the rust fell away to reveal a row of small crosses along the bright blade. She looked up at the monk; then, gazing at the blade with a bedazzled smile, she spoke in a voice of wonder. "The words 'Jesus and Maria' are inscribed along this blade."

The monk's chant continued as he rose to look at the blade, nodding and smiling.

The woman's voice was changing, becoming more youthful as she spoke: "This is the sword I once carried into battle so that I would kill no one."

"Just so," said the monk.

"No, I meant to say, the sword St. Joan carried—" Her voice faltered.

"It is also a magic stick of invisibility from the lore of Gesar," said the monk. She lifted the blade to her forehead and, resolutely pressing it there, fell to her knees in intense prayer.

The monk turned to Mr. Fu with a gentle smile. "What can you tell me about Gesar?" he asked.

Mr. Fu rose to his feet. His gaze was fixed upon the sword and the glowing figure of the woman. He tried without success to shrug. "Just—a great warrior, the greatest Tibetan warrior." He was surprised to hear himself say these words, for he meant to say that Gesar was just—a myth, meaningless to him. The monk pressed him to say more, and he felt a curious wave of thoughtfulness sweep into his heart.

"Gesar," said Mr. Fu, "could overcome any obstacle, even from the depths of the forest. With that very sword, he could draw a circle in the sand to make himself and his entire army invisible. He knew the minds of his enemies, and could turn them into rocks or even puddles of mud. Gesar's might was invincible; he terrified everyone except the Just. That is why he is loved and remembered. Gesar will come again, you know, to put an end to greed, sloth, and hate. He will ride his great white horse when the world is ready for a reign of peace in Shambhala."

"You are blessed with a good memory," said the monk. "You are also to be given the burden of a mission you will learn of later. It too will become a blessing to you. Now, Mr. Fu, I am going to take your karma."

Mr. Fu was staggered by this statement. If you did not have your karma, there was no point in being in samsara, he knew, which existed for the purpose of working off karma. If the monk could really take his karma—The monk bent over him and said, "I believe you will soon be ready to become a bodhisattva, Mr. Fu." Then he pressed his own forehead lightly against Mr. Fu's.

At this touch, Mr. Fu's body went through a spasm as if sustaining electric shock. Staring at the monk, he stood up, his limbs trembling, his eyes entranced; he blinked as if awakening from a long sleep. He clasped his hands together in a *namaste,* lifted them first to the crown of his head, then his forehead, then to his throat, then to his heart, and he fell forward in a full prostration, arms extended, body upon the ground, his nose pressed into dust and lichen, at the feet of the monk. A Tibetan mantra came to his lips that he had not remembered since his childhood, the words of the refuge vow: "From now until awakening in the heart of enlightenment, I take refuge in the Buddha ..." An insect squirmed against his face, slithered its tentacles into his nose, but he pressed his face more deeply into the sandy lichen, into which he murmured the words of the Bodhisattva vow: "... I vow to work ceaselessly for the benefit of others."

The monk spoke to the woman: "It was not because you were the 'Maid' that I chose you but because you were also the 'Mother.' From the Maid has come your body and raiment, but from the Mother your mind that to my people abides in the heart."

Prostrate at his feet, Mr. Fu lifted his head and gasped through lips caked with sand: "I realize now. I realize who you are!"

The monk smiled at him, reached down to pull him up from the ground. "Do not be too sure," he said, pressing his palm on the crest of Mr. Fu's head. "We must remember that nobody has the final word on who anybody is."

The Mother, or Maid, cut the air with her sword, and gave the monk a subtle smile. "Pretty good," she said. "But will it photograph on video?"

Mum and company have finished lunch. And Mr. Fu has finished his smokes. He has agreed to go on, and so we pile in as he starts up the motor. His accord comes not out of any familial sense, however, or return to faith. He will drive on out of respect for neither the Buddhist nor the Communist way, but rather for the way of Western capitalism. He has settled for my suggestion that we double his pay.

14

The next day Mr. Fu has to stop for directions at stone gates where the road diverges. Tibetans crowd about the jeep, peer through the dark window glass. Should we follow the road through the gates or to the left? Mr. Fu glares at a map that does not show which branch of the road to take.

Lama Mingme jumps out and negotiates with a lean old woman whose jasper headpiece he wants. She shows him her gold *gau,* the portable shrine she wears about her neck set with a dark red stone. A ruby? It holds sacred relics and probably miraculous *ringsel.* Mingme wants the *gau* but she will not part with it. He also wants her face, which is heart-shaped like his own, and snaggle-toothed, framed with a traditional bandanna clasped at the crown with her headpiece. Defeated in his attempt to nab her jewelry, he nabs her face with his camera, and half a dozen others at the village gates.

The rest of us get out of the jeep to stretch. We question a number of people, but no one seems to remember the way to the monastery we are looking for. One person sends for another, who may know, but when he comes he can't remember, sends for someone else. This is hard to believe—perhaps Lama Mingme's pronunciation is off. We are stalled.

"Memory is one of the things that keeps us turning around on the wheel of samsara," a monk once said to me, meaning, I think, that memory reveals our attachments to this world. What is writing something down but attachment to memory? Writers must surely keep turning on the wheel.

I think of Dorje's happiness at the Kalachakra shrine, and her words,

"I will always remember this." Aren't all shrines in the world a tribute to the power of universal memory?

And what feeling Tibetans themselves express about their lost land! Few want to let go of their memories. What depth of attachment I saw in the women in my notebook! One of the most moving moments I've ever seen on film was the return of the Dalai Lama's sister to Lhasa when the Chinese thought their reforms had been successful enough to invite a Tibetan delegation back from exile in India to bear witness to their improvements. Thousands of cheering Tibetans broke through a fence, to the astonishment of the Chinese officials. For a glimpse of the exiles, the people swept the officials aside, ran in an irrepressible wave toward the sister's car and pressed their faces to the window, weeping joyous tears against the pane. Their joy overcame all restrictions; their faces filled with the depth of their suffering and the agony of their estrangement, in an unrestrained flow of memory and testament.

Some thing are easily seen as part of our earthly prison. Auntie Moon's burst of love for country when she cried: "China, China!" ... nationalism, attachment to home—these are samsara. And the brocades—taking gifts to the past is also samsara. Family is samsara, all one family, also samsara. What is family but memory? A chain of memory linking its members throughout generations. It is impossible to visit a nursing home like my mother's without thinking it is better to die than to live without memory. But even in senility, memory must be stored unconsciously in the bones prompting the life force to remain active even in mindlessness.

Perhaps the monk meant only that without memory there is a chance to experience nothingness. Without memory there is only eternity. Something we do not know.

At last someone comes up to the gate who remembers the way, an old man who smells of sweat and fire smoke and wears soiled lama robes that look as if they may not have been cleaned in years. We learn that he has only recently returned from a long retreat in a cliff-side cave not far from our destination. He remembers the way clearly, and so we get back into the jeep. Mr. Fu impatiently starts up the motor, even though Mingme wants to have a philosophical talk with the old man.

Suddenly I realize I have lost my notebook. I jump out of the jeep, searching the ground below. It isn't there. I walk around the vehicle, looking for it, look under the jeep. My lined notebook with its black binding. The notebook is nowhere. People back away, as if suspecting I may accuse one of them of taking something.

I search under my seat in the jeep, distraught, run my hands along the floor; in one moment it was beside me on the seat, now it is nowhere. My companions, talking in a rise of relief at our departure, do not notice.

The others are all settled in their seats now, and Mr. Fu revs the motor, so I get into my place beside him. I open the glove compartment—not there.

My notebook! With all my innermost secrets, some hidden even from myself, now lost, my fiction notes, my dreams, ruminations, questions. It is like losing my mind! I tell no one. It is too important. Who could understand my alarm? The Chinese women will think I am mad if I betray these frantic, lost feelings. Attachment! All that I've observed and thought was in that notebook, not in my memory, which is blank.

Last year—at my computer deciphering my notebook, I could not make out much of my self-styled shorthand. I began to improvise, getting things down from memory instead of notes; images arose, words poured out. The mind at work—ha! I felt inspired. This was the way writing should move and seldom does, and so I was flooded with joy—yes, writing is my meditation! It is there the visualizations come, the divine light. Suddenly, a click and a blank screen. Power failure. Empty screen. Mind a blank. No mind. All that inspiration, gone. I burst out laughing, remembering "C's" laugh. "When you see your own mind, you will laugh," he once said. This was not enlightenment, but it was funny as hell. Nothing there. I laughed. A friend commiserated: "Why are you laughing? This is hard stuff, losing your work like that." I laughed and laughed. Very funny.

Is there a parallel between my own small technology and the worship Commander Bao's ghostly father discerned in his nuclear warfare community? Some divinity hanging us all suspended over an abyss by an invisible electronic net. Some divine joke!

On the road I cannot see the humor. I sink into a complete panic. I stand up and look on the floor beside Dorje's feet, around the stash of water bottles, Mum's clutter of snacks, nut shells nesting in dust angels. Mum asks what's wrong with me, then shrugs and resumes her chatter. The notebook is just paper to her. She doesn't know that it is my *mind!* She cannot imagine what pain its loss causes me!

The notebook—jumping around from thought to thought, unable to stay on one thing, full of fragmentary scenes, songs, half phrases, nonsense, indecipherable shorthand, a hopeless muddle. Yet the notebook is my guru! I need it so! To lose it is to lose memory, my Tibetan women, their history, their suffering, resistance, and flight, their terrible loss. Where is an event when it is lost?

Why have I lost it? Do I really want to disappear, want the world to disappear? "Memory is one of the things that keep us turning around on the wheel of samsara." And the notebook *is* my memory! It is gone.

My body jerks along like a corpse in the jeep. What shall become of it without the notebook?

"C" once told of a Tibetan who went into a monastery looking for his mind. He thought he had left it there when he visited the day before. Said he couldn't remember what shape it was. Couldn't remember if it was a triangle or a moon or a star shape. Said he'd forgotten what color it was. Maybe it was blue or green or yellow. Didn't find it, though he looked everywhere. People thought he was crazy, but he was lucky he went to a monastery, "C" said, because someone there taught him what the mind really is. Will someone at the monastery teach me anything? The Khandro? Impossible, when body has separated from mind!

My mind is black in color, shaped like a small rectangle, it is full of emptiness, and it is lost.

The notebook was, I realized, why I had come on this pilgrimage, to make some sense out of it, with its jottings, its stories, its collection of quotes, dreams, fictive fantasies, my rudimentary understanding of Buddhist precepts, my judgments about practically everything. I needed to try to reconcile all the elements of the notebook, its records of violence, of inhumane cruelties, of my hope of drawing order, meaning, understanding from those pages, to see things whole. If I couldn't do it there, in so quiet a place as a notebook, how could I expect anything of the whole noisy, violent, needing world? And with the notebook lost . . .

15

We have lost our way. As surely as I have lost my notebook. All morning we were climbing the high desert to more than 4600 meters, until we finally reached a river. Although the river is perhaps a quarter of a mile wide, it appears to have only a low, rocky bank. A smaller tributary flows into it. Perhaps it is shallow, we reason, or perhaps the cliff forty meters overhead is the floodtime bank, as there is another cliff in the distance on the other side. However, the narrow one-lane road we have taken was built alongside the water. The midday light, sunny with warm, rather caressing air, encourages us not to feel lost. Merely confused and confounded and, as always, road-weary.

Mum and Auntie have been quiet for the last hour. Mum, her head slumped on her sister's shoulder, is looking aged by ten years. They both are feeling the altitude badly. Although Mum's large mouth hangs partly open, no sound comes from it. Could my jesting prayer for the Khandro to silence them have been answered by telepathy?

After traveling many uninhabited miles alongside the water, we come to a house high on the cliff, a large establishment with several adjacent buildings. The main house has the flat Tibetan roof, and prayer flags fly from it to one of the smaller buildings. We think the house isn't large enough to be the place we are seeking, but we don't really know.

We may have taken a wrong turn when we left the tributary of the highway before dawn this morning. An expanse of mesa stretches ahead, and we can see no other sign of human habitation, although the road must lead somewhere. We stop the jeep and Dorje sends Lama Mingme up the saffron-colored cliff to inquire. He looks unhappy about it, but she is definitely in charge now. It is hard for him to put one foot in front of the next as he climbs the cliff side.

He is gone a long time. We wait in the sunlight outside the jeep, our hands stuffed inside our jacket pockets against the sharp air. We would like to try the water, which glitters invitingly but presents no easy access. Rough stones from the cliff are piled up at the shallow edge of the river, but beyond them the water is opaque. Mr. Fu declares its current deceptively swift, too deep for wading. How he knows this I can't say, but he assures us we would drown. Where a narrow tributary joins the river on the other side, the water level looks extremely low and a center sandbar shows where the waters mingle.

I stand on the edge of the rocks and stoop down, reaching my hand into the stream. It shrieks ice through my hand. Dorje says, "Too muddy to drink."

Dorje and I revel in the air, so clear of exhaust fumes since we turned off the main road this morning. The light sustains sparks of silver and gold, sent up perhaps by the sun rays that dance on the murky current. There is a vastness in this terrain—the one-lane road disappears into a far-off *V* that seems to meet and turn back to us, on a plateau of multicolored sands with very little vegetation.

Mingme descends as slowly as he has climbed up, his skinny legs bowing out. He looks spent, done in, his color gray. He has never at any time complained, but the altitude seems to have gotten to him, too.

"Monastery over there, down that stream," he says, pointing across the river.

"But no bridge," says Dorje.

"Bridge eight, ten kilometers ahead," he tells us. "Town there too."

How simple if there were a raft, or even coracles, the round, shell-like kayaks Tibetans make of yak skin for fording rivers that can be carried on your back. Or if we knew how to do *lung-gom* and could walk over the water.

But Mr. Fu says we would drown.

We come to the village. There is an iron fence with a Chinese police installation behind it, and even a small, improvised outdoor market, where dismal plastic Chinese goods are displayed: aluminum cookware, nylon underpants, and the ubiquitous sneakers. But no Guest House, no hole-in-the-wall restaurant. When Mingme states our purpose, the villagers understand that we want to cross the bridge to the monastery to visit "C's" sister. And when he speaks of his relationship to "C," a town father enthusiastically invites us into his home.

Mr. Fu says he prefers to stay there in the police courtyard. He does not want to go any further with us, will not. Blisters cover his heels, from those too-short shoes. He will wait for our return from the monastery, he declares. But that could be a long time, we reason, and there is no guest house. No matter, he will sleep in the jeep. He will not go to any monastery.

The town father bows his portly frame and leads us around a corner to an entryway off the street, where I notice a pit filled with horns of yak and musk deer like those we saw on the sidewalks in Chengdu being sold for medicine and aphrodisiacs. The man tells us that we cannot take the jeep, that the bridge we see in the distance is a footbridge, that he will send a boy to the monastery to tell them we are here and they will send horses. We feel relieved at that, not realizing that the boy will go on foot. The man tells us that later, after we have been sitting for more than a hour inside his dark house on his packed-earth bench, and the afternoon shadows are lengthening.

I realize that this may be the very village famed in legends about the Khandro, where the Chinese persecuted her and tried to shoot her.

Mum leans her head against the wall, groaning intermittently, her face swollen and ash-colored. Again, she refuses my Diamox. Probably it is too late now anyway, as it should be taken before ascent.

Suddenly, a pot is brought to the table—tea! We smile at one another in delight. Townspeople peer inside the window, which is without glass, Tibetan fashion, amused at our sudden rise of excitement over the tea. When I smile at them, their lips turn up but they look away shyly, puzzled.

The tea is hard to get down. Not because of the salt, which I like, but because of the water. Dorje says, "Tastes like the murky river." Probably is.

As the afternoon goes on, we become very hungry. Mum's little sack of extra supplies is exhausted. When we ask our host if we may buy some food in the village, his wife produces soup for us. Same muddy taste, but Dorje and I go for it. Mum doesn't budge from her slumped posture in the corner. Auntie's head leans now against her shoulder. They rest that way for a long while.

The waiting makes me miss my notebook. I grieve to myself over its disappearance. I'm seeing it as a kind of death-wish, though perhaps only another writer would understand that. I rummage about in my bag for a scrap of paper on which to write. I find a small pad. The habit dies hard, even without my notebook-mind.

THE GOLDEN ROAD

In London, the Coordinator "B" had completed all his preparations, and now stood anxiously in a control booth, smoothing his silver hair.

In all the years of his life that "B" had worked on behalf of political prisoners, daring governments to free those whom they had wrongly wounded, who had suffered at the hands of torturers, he had never felt so hopeful. He thought of the many prisoners he had helped liberate and of the many more he had not succeeded in helping, and he prayed that all the people waiting for his signal this day would bring enough conviction, enough strength of imagination to bear upon the suffering that prisoners endure. He knew that only through the work of the imagination could such things come about. The imagination of the jailers, the torturers themselves must be stirred, aroused. Only that would loosen the chains of suffering. If he and others of like mind could enable the torturers to realize that their own bodies were inseparable from those they tortured, then they must awaken. The pain of torture would arouse them. Human rights, he knew, could be legislated only in the imagination of conscience.

He thought of his team in Tibet. He felt confidence in the skills of his video producer Bodhi, and he knew her assistant Youngden was a brilliant cameraman, with a strong understanding of the View. He whispered a prayer for the project's two elder leaders, whom he saw as forces for good in the millennium. And that Tibetan driver he had hired popped into his mind, Mr. Fu. The young man, the only one on the journey not briefed on the transformations that were in process, would surely not come away from the experience unchanged. An ordinary person, caught up in events beyond his knowledge, can sometimes make a surprising leap.

The moment had arrived. "B" lifted his hands, showing ten seconds to the studio technician before the satellite cue, which would signal people all over the globe to join together in the sound of mantra and intense concentration of thought.

Sitting cross-legged below on the stony floor, which had been covered with rugs for the occasion, was the entire Gyuto Tantric choir, as well as every other refugee Tibetan monk capable of dual-toned mantra chanting, surrounded by a vast number of the faithful. "B" had been deeply gratified by the response to his programming throughout the world, and especially in his own England, where by a special dispensation from Her Majesty he had acquired the arena where the hundreds of monks sat in profound meditation preparing for their ceremony. Now they began their unique bass and baritone resonations that seemed to fill much greater space than any possible enclosure.

"B" gave the signal. The clang of Tibetan cymbals resounded. Chants that had been known to move mountains rose, soaring toward thousands more around the world, to St. Patrick's Cathedral and Central Park in New York, to Chartres Cathederal in France, to St. Peter's courtyard in Rome, to meeting places in New Zealand, Delhi, Bangkok, and Kathmandu, where the assembled joined their prayers with those deep reverberations rising now from Westminster Abbey.

⟷

Orderly Wang, whose task it was to oversee the interment of shipments whenever Commander Bao was not on hand, lifted his field glasses. An unusual activity on the grounds behind the cyclone fence bewildered him. The guards were behaving oddly, milling about in some formation he couldn't quite place. It looked as if they were lined up—in a picket line. They held their rifles as if signs were attached to their bayonets. He looked at the clock—almost two, the hour the Commander had designated to break the news to the men. He had told them to gather there, true, but their behavior was bizarre. Wang touched the intercom to buzz Commander Bao, only to find the line was dead. It could be that dust had clogged it, but he felt a vague alarm. He decided to go to the commander's quarters.

At that moment, a jeep pulled up outside the office. With his attention on the prisoners, Wang had failed to observe its approach. He pivoted around to the radar screen. It had not shown up there. He looked at the video display screens—blank. Something was the matter with the electronic sensor devices. The door opened, and a young woman with long black hair strolled in, brushing off the dust from her garments.

Wang could not have been more surprised. She wore sandals, a narrow silk skirt above her knees—and a glittery jacket. Except for the dust coating every inch of her, she looked as if she might have just stepped out of the disco in the Lhasa hotel, where Orderly Wang had once ventured. She shook dust out of her long, wildly tangled hair, brushed it off her face. "Do you think I could get some water to rinse off with?" she asked Wang. "You've got a lot of dust around here." Her Mandarin was impeccable, but with a puzzling accent. And such skin—almost white. Was she from Shanghai?

He straightened his sagging shoulders and sprang into action, wishing sadly that he still had his hair. "We can do better than that," he said. "We have some stringent clean-up procedures here. I could put you into the decontam unit."

She stared at him as if she thought he were deranged. "Just some water," she said. "And for my assistant, too."

Startled, Wang realized that another person sat in the jeep outside.

Not Chinese, he thought, an official wariness surfacing. When she caught his glance again, she pulled some papers out of her bag. "And please send for Commander Bao. I'm here to interview him."

That sent a chill through Wang. He knew Bao had been grimly depressed by the visit of the inspectors. Immediately, he left to call the commander, then busied himself getting a basin of water. An interview could lead to self-correction and worse. Also, it could be as bad for him as for the commander.

Bao, resting in the early afternoon before the ordeal of facing the men with the denial of their leave, sat up in surprise. Wang said a woman from Beijing? He pulled his pants up over his stocky legs. What could it mean—that they had received the petition for leave from the company? More likely, the two scientists who inspected the leaks had turned in a bad report, and the woman had been sent for a corrective interview.

By the time Bao reached his office, Bodhi had cleansed herself of much of the dust of the road, though her hair still hung about her shoulders as unconfined as that of a wrathful goddess.

"Commander Bao, we'd like a statement from you," she said as he looked over her Beijing papers. She added quickly, "And a full analysis of the operation."

Bao thought that if he had to report to headquarters it would be fine with him, would get him away from the depot faster. But who was she—this gorgeous young woman? No women were allowed here—Beijing didn't risk it, despite official denial of the pervasive contamination. There hadn't been women on any of the projects since the old days at the silver-and-gold sands compound, when women technicians outnumbered the men for a brief, glorious while, where in fact he had met and married a woman who immediately became an impossible nag, now living in Chengdu and talking nonstop to her sister all the time.

He handed back the papers, stamped in Beijing, showing she was authorized. "Tell us," she was saying, "something about your standard procedures. In your own words." Bao stared. Her gaze—she was utterly beautiful. He was so dazzled that he failed to notice Youngden, who had left the jeep and stood at the threshold holding a video camera. It was serious, Bao thought, if they were videotaping the interview.

Nervously Bao took up the binoculars Wang had left on his desk, and offered them to the young woman for a view of the depot. He began telling her about the arrivals, the shipments from France, from Germany. He said, "You see, they go into the ground. It is a brilliant strategy, really, conceived by our wonderful Minister, who has always managed the A-projects with such wisdom, such—" He sought the official language, which he had so recently disowned in his mind. "—such dedication, and courage. You see, there where our men are marching—" Marching? He broke off, realizing for the first time the odd behavior of the men at the plant. "What is going on?" he muttered, unable to understand what he saw through his glasses. It was the hour he had asked the men to assemble, true, but their behavior was unsettling.

Bodhi's lips parted in a smile and she gazed encouragingly into his eyes. "This installation is built over an old mine?" she asked. She took off her jacket and draped it over a chair, exposing the narrowness of her waist, the incredible curve of her hips. Wang stood nearby, gaping, puzzled.

"Mmm. Yes—an exhausted mine actually," Bao said, his gaze drawn to Bodhi's body as if magnetized. "Each section of the mine underground is sealed, with the sealant Beijing developed. You must know of it." He wondered if she knew how baffled he suddenly felt. He had to watch out or a burst of candor could do him in. But her presence seemed to loosen his tongue uncontrollably. He went on speaking as if his mind were under some spell, obliging him somehow to pour out details of the operation. "It's a conversion operation, you see. We haven't simply abandoned the mine in the usual way. After the ground is sealed, we create storage bins and fill them in with the refuse deliveries—from all over the globe. And so the old mines become graveyards, you might say. Ingenious, isn't it?

"This can go on for centuries. We can continue this create-and-destroy operation forever. This is a vast desert—vast! Once a depleted mine is filled, we can move on to another, or deepen the existent spaces."

Bodhi nodded encouragingly. "It must be lonely up here," she said.

Her wide, open gaze suddenly filled Bao with longing.

Wang spoke up suddenly. "We were supposed to be relieved." Bao shot him a sharp look.

"With nothing in sight for miles but that range of snow mountains," she said.

Outside the dust storm was swirling. A stone banged against the door. Bao laughed, "That was just ping-pong size. Sometimes the wind shakes loose much bigger rocks, the size of soccer balls." Sand was gusting through the door.

He moved to close the door, whereupon the woman introduced her assistant. Bao merely nodded to the man with the camera. Why hadn't Beijing let him know they were filming the operation? They were so secretive in the capital. The assistant looked underfed—in fact, he looked like a Tibetan who had once worked the mines.

Dizzy, somewhat dazed, Bao felt strangely caught up in an illusion. Despite her beauty, or perhaps because of it, the woman seemed like a wraith, a ghost blown up in the wind, with her wildly disordered hair. Her questions had a reverberating, unreal quality.

"Commander, tell me your own thoughts about this ingenious operation," she said. "Should it remain unilateral? Do you believe it should go to the UN? Be put under UN surveillance?"

"The UN!" Caution mastered his weakness. He sensed a trap. Had they told her to question him about this? He said: "Oh no, not with their eternal slogans about human rights! We have contracts with many private corporations. UN surveillance is not desirable, would jeopardize the project." Dust coated his tongue, gritted in his teeth. It was seeping through the window seals. "You must tell them in Beijing. There would be no benefit."

"Benefit?" Bodhi asked.

"For the PRC of course." He thought the sand would fill his throat, clog his lungs—surely his damaged lungs would soon be packed with dust. In the presence of this beautiful, sensual woman, the specter of death arose. Bao thought distinctly, I shall surely die.

Resolutely, he grasped his field glasses to look at his men over at the plant. "What is going on there, Wang?" he muttered. Wang drew closer, shrugged his sloping shoulders helplessly; words somehow failed him. Bao slapped his back pocket for his walkie-talkie. He'd left it in his room next to his bed. "Get over there and see what they are doing, Wang!" he ordered. Wang left at once, through the underground drift tunnel.

Bao was so confused he hadn't even noticed that the cameraman had gone outside, had turned his jeep toward the plant, with his camera running. He hadn't even realized the woman held a small microphone in her hand. He stared at it now, confounded.

He strode past her toward his room to get his walkie-talkie.

"You can't get anything on your walkie-talkie," she said in a friendly voice. He ran his hands along the ridges of his bald dome. "My cameraman and I are going to film the plant now," she told him gently. "We will go over to the plant and talk to your men."

And so Bodhi went outside and got into the jeep with Youngden and drove to the barbed wire fence where the prisoners stood in the nuclear graveyard. From the jeep, Youngden had already begun to film the arrival of a plane on the runway. As they drew closer, they saw huge crates that were being taken out of the freight plane bearing the international radioactive logo.

Bao stared through his binoculars. Now the Tibetan miners were milling around among his police guards. Suddenly he stood transfixed, immobilized. He felt bolted to the floor. His own men had lowered their rifles, removed their caps, and they stood with their bald heads exposed, gazing out in the distance, as if toward the snowy mountain.

He turned and hit the hotline to Beijing. The line was dead. He tried the fax machine—dead as well. He slapped the general alarm. Silence. What was this? Was it India? They hadn't been able to find out what the Indians were doing in Ladak for years, even with all the help from the CIA. Or were the Russians screwing them over again? His mind reeled at the thought of all the loose Russian plutonium.

He belted on his pistol. Then he looked again through the binoculars. What he saw sent him staggering. It was strategically inconceivable, undoable. His entire plant was surrounded. There was a battalion out there armed to the teeth, outside the cyclone fence. His staff had stopped their pacing and now faced an alien—was that the word?—army! The Americans? God, not the Americans—impossible. Too cozy with Beijing. He watched in disbelief as his own men drew back in the face of this formidable adversary.

Among them, a brilliant figure sat astride a gleaming mount, a sword raised above the astounded men.

Dorje nudges me away from my writing. Mum and Auntie have revived somewhat. This encourages Dorje, who has decided to mobilize us. The messenger boy is taking too long. We should walk. Yes, that's it, we shall start off—there's no place to stay overnight here. If we walk over the bridge now we can get there by dark probably. Probably we will meet the horses and can ride part of the way. Anyway, better not wait here, with no place to sleep, no place for Mum to lie down. Come—she urges us to our feet—let's move!

16

The people who have fed us assign another young boy to lead us to a suspension bridge over a slow stream. A certain saint, Tang-tang Gyalpo, built the first suspension bridges in Tibet several hundred years ago; he therefore was thought to have power over water, could alter the direction of currents and make rivers run dry. If this is the very river into which the Khandro was plunged with her hands bound, she may have tapped some of his power.

This is historic territory all around us, at least in the lore of "C's" family: The magic cave of the Excalibur story, where his father parted the rock like butter to find hidden teachings; the house of his mother, a gifted *delog,* one who dies and returns to tell about the realms of the dead.

The boy leading us, barefoot and clad in a sackcloth, points the way with an obliging smile. Each of us carries only a small backpack—the luggage will be sent on by horses later. On the village side of the bridge, I notice a distant monastery, terra-cotta in the afternoon light, prayer flags strung in a ranging course from one low rooftop to the next. Like the ones we saw at the shrine, they are faded to pastels by the elements. "That is the home of Gesar of Ling," says the young boy to Mingme.

"What!" I cry when Lama Mingme translates.

Mum and Auntie, grasping the ropes suspended from cliff to cliff above the river, pay no attention. They have no interest in Gesar, and Dorje, following them, is too concerned about Mum to care. The bridge, which allows only single-file passage, is much more precarious than the bridge over the river at Luding, and although the water there was more violent we felt stronger then. This river is in a quiet summer drift, not challenging at all, but Mum and Auntie move with mincing, terrified steps, cannot even turn their heads to see what has aroused my interest—the vista of the monastery. Dorje says, "We have no time to visit there." Mingme: "But must go later. Take photos."

I remember reading that any number of far-flung monasteries claim to be the home of Gesar, from here to Mongolia. This one is impressive, with its packed-earth buildings sprawling across an acre or so. But even I am too tired to want to stop.

Of course, we are all sick. Dorje is woozy, probably from a fever; I too. "I think it is heatness," Dorje says.

Underneath the bridge, Mingme points out to us, there hangs the skull of a yak. Seeing it, Mum shrieks and grabs onto Auntie. Mingme explains that it was put there to appease bridge demons who may have come in the last high water.

After we have crossed the footbridge, we reach an even more narrow ledge. We must lean against the rocky shelf for fear of falling down into the river. Dorje urges us on, and Mum and Auntie try to hasten their pace, but soon fall behind again.

"Dorje," I say, "we should let your mother and aunt wait behind for the horses." But they don't want to be left alone with Tibetans and insist on staying with us. Our young guide points us in the right direction on the other side of the river, and turns back to the footbridge.

After about half an hour's walk along the flat rim of the stream, we glimpse a village of a dozen or so low houses on the cliff above us, surrounded by a wall. This cannot be our actual destination, too near. Mingme and Dorje forge ahead, toward the settlement, where we hear the scattered barking of dogs, which gathers and increases and become a fanatical chorus. These are very typical of the dogs we have seen everywhere, the size of scraggly goats with the faces of wolves. They bare ferocious teeth at us, and we wonder why they do not rush down the cliff side, overpower, and devour us.

Someone comes to the edge of the cliff, looks over the wall, and shouts down to Mingme: No, this is not the place we are looking for. He points us onward. The dogs do not subside until after Mum and Auntie have also passed and are well beyond sight of the village.

Dorje and Mingme lead the way again. They are apparently undeterred by the altitude, which has now markedly affected my own capacity to move. I lag behind, halfway between the Dorje-Mingme pair and the Mum-Auntie pair, a center dot in our five-of-diamonds. Or spades. A far-flung wild card, out of place.

All afternoon we approach no other structure. Perhaps we are lost again. But how could we be lost here on this high desert, where one can see for miles ahead?

The terrain is full of bones. I become aware of death everywhere. Piles of bones and horns in the village behind the house where we had soup. Was there a slaughter of yaks to feed the Chinese army years ago when it came through? Or perhaps Tibetans themselves kill the animals to take innards and horns to the sidewalk markets of China's cities. Perhaps some of the bones are human, I think, trudging along the sandy riverbank.

Auntie calls out to us distantly that she and Mum are going to stop and rest. I turn back to join them where they sit slumped back-to-back in the lengthening afternoon shadows. Oh what can ail thee, Mum and Moon, alone and palely loitering....

Impermanence ... "Uncertainty is continuous," says "C," a vision of his smile rising up in the desert air. "Walking along a path," he says, "you may suddenly die. You do not have much time." That is his caution against laxity. He tells the story of a mother and daughter, caught in a flooded river. The mother tried to save the daughter, the daughter to save the mother, each trying to lift the other out of the flood, each thinking, "If I drown at least she will be saved." Both were taken by the water, but according to those who can see such things both were reborn in the thirty-third heaven, reward for their selflessness.

My own family, my son and my mother, are suddenly before me. This memory rises on a stretch of desert sand, of a beach on Cape Cod. He is about three, and his hand is fishing in the pocket of her sundress looking for treats. No, they are not in memory exactly; they are frozen in a picture cube on my desk. I sent the cube to my mother years ago and now that she is in a nursing home I have it back. I had taken a series of black-and-white photographs that made up a narrative: On one side of the cube the child peers in her sundress pocket; on the next side his head is closer, looking into the depths of the pocket; and in the next his hand has gone down into the pocket and come up only with Kleenex that is gripped in her hand while he continues to rummage for the treat he knows must be there, then next; ah, he has found it, the chocolate kiss, and she has demanded payment, a real kiss. She sits on the rocky sand next to the picnic basket as he leans forward, hand on her thigh, to touch his lips to hers. And, in the last photograph on the cube, he is in her arms, wrapped in a blanket, for he has run into the chilly surf. Behind them, the dot of our small black dog, watching them at the water's edge. The cube turns and shows its images to me, larger than the life in my lost notebook. These are my attachments, my tug of samsara; my notebook, only a poor substitute.

As we press on after a rest, I begin to doubt if we will ever reach the monastery. Mum is stumbling far behind, held up on her feet by Auntie. "We should take her back," I shout ahead to Dorje and Mingme. But at this Dorje stalks on fiercely, charging ahead of Mingme. Once again I envy the sky-walking *lung-gom* adepts.

A great many desert rodents are the only other sentient beings in sight. Yet we know that across the river there is a house upon a cliff side; we remember that—we passed it this morning. Was it only this morning? But we cannot cross the river, have even lost sight of the suspension footbridge. Miles and miles, and our own exhaustion, separate us from all but desert rats.

I look back at Mum and Auntie, who are like a vision themselves. Two dots on the plateau's landscape. Very colorful, dots of their green and blue jackets above the curving streak of wet sand. Holding one another up. Will they attain the thirty-third heaven?

"C" tells the story of Drupa Kunley, a yogi who hunted goats and ate them. People objected, especially the goat owners. He made a pile of the goat bones, then snapped his fingers and the goats came back to life. "In Tibet we have a small animal not well shaped. We say Drupa Kunley put it back together." The lama laughs and laughs before me in the desert. I recall a resurrection dream of my own about that small black dot of a dog of ours coming back after his death years ago, rising out of the ground in our garden where we had buried him. What joy to see him again! What pain to realize it was only a dream!

And now we come to the skeletal remains of a yak, except for the upper skull. Perhaps it belonged to the yak whose skull hangs under the bridge. There is a large jaw, however, complete with teeth. Once Georgia O'Keeffe said, "Because there were no flowers, I began to pick up bones." I would like to pick up this jaw to keep, but I am too tired, bone tired. I leave it there.

A large, white-headed vulture circles overhead. Perhaps a corpse lies somewhere nearby just beyond our sight. Perhaps Tibetan remains await dismemberment, while well-mannered vultures hunch close at hand as the limbs and trunk are prepared for them to eat.

There is a sense of stillness now, as if no time is passing. Something close to desperation grips my belly. Is this where we die, all of us? There seems to be no other human for miles around, nothing but bones. In this stillness, I feel close to non-being. Perhaps we are already corpses.

Suddenly there appears the Tibetan saint Machig Labdron, here in the desert. She has come to make an offering of her body to the spirit world. I have conjured her up, as she conjures up hungry ghosts and demons. Never before have I been able to visualize these difficult Tibetan exercises, but there she is, Machig, the goddess of the graveyard!

She stands before me with flying hair, wraith-like yet commanding, holding in her bony hands a human skull cup filled with blood. Her gaze pierces me, as she invites me to make the same offering. She is offering her own blood to express her fearlessness here in this boneyard. This is her ritual, the sacrifice of her flesh to feed hungry ghosts. Gore is a substance that easily slides down the throats of those emaciated beings. You too, she tells me, you too can perform this sacrifice. Summon your courage, and you can become a goddess yourself, holding your own blood-filled skull cup. You will become Machig Labdron! As I move slowly forward, she advances before me. From a rope of crystal skulls around her neck, she raises a *Chod* drum and twists it this way and that, so that its throb sounds in a determined, measured beat. From the ground, she lifts the femur of a woman's corpse, which becomes a horn, and the desert air fills with its roar. Here there's no such thing as Quiet Death.

I look about anxiously, for lurking hungry ghosts, or other terrifying Tibetan images, any of which would be right at home here on this desert. The roommate of my youth has entered this strange Bardo I have conjured, drawing her cartoon images of "Ghostie," trailing them across the sand ... In the Tibetan Bardo screeching and clangor from deities of awful mien rend the silence to quake and challenge the unprepared being. I understand them now. Scare yourself witless, then you cannot be afraid. But Drupa Kunley isn't here to snap his fingers over our bones. I realize that what I love about Tibetans is that they laugh in the face of death. Such practices as Machig Labdron's are behind that laughter.

The Dalai Lama believes that non-Tibetans do not see the Bardo deities at death but whatever their culture has prepared them to see. He knows that we Westerners are not imbued to the challenges of Bardo, which means "between two," that is, between two incarnations. Our culture does not teach us to prepare for any transition, and not even for death, except to fear it. Machig Labdron understands my fear, for it is a fear she was created to challenge.

Now sudden streaks of light break the horizon, a reassuring sign that we are not beyond time, for they linger in the sky for seconds. Machig vanishes into a light streak as suddenly as she has come.

The Dalai Lama once said that a pilgrimage through wild, open lands provides visions that help shape the proper attitude and awareness for religious practice. *You do not have much time.*

I conjure up my picture cube again. My son appears in it, again at the beach, fully grown now, on the West Coast, surfing. My mother appears on her bed of age and suffering. Is she dying now, or am I? The visions of my family are like a Rubik's Cube, a puzzle I cannot find the solution for. You have to line up primary colors on the Rubik's Cube; it is a scramble of cubism. Rubik's cube has a certain logic—there is a trick to it, though it has thwarted many rational minds. Once at the beach my son and I got so frustrated with it that we threw it in the salty surf. The next day it had washed up on the shore, its colors washed out to pastels. It had become a fractured rainbow; but despite the transparency of its colors, we were still too dense to solve it. I take a leap where primary colors and rainbow pastels overlay one another, like prayer flags washed by the elements and inverted into a rainbow, delicate ephemera arching a play of light above the hard squares of logic. I am the same young woman who put the picture cube together, no longer frozen in an attitude of detachment. The nearness of dank and murky death quenches even the drought of my heart. In the cube's set of pictures my mother, now all skin and bones and dying of emphysema, looks strong and healthy, is no older than I am now. Even though she has been ill for years, she is not prepared. Nothing in our culture has prepared her for death. I do not want her to die without me. A suicidal friend once said, "Too bad really, that you can't kill yourself while your mother or your child is still alive, too cruel." But you can die, you can die.

On the horizon now the sun is setting as if over an exploded Krakatoa. A cloud rises in a burst of beauty shot through with light streaks; I see it turned into a nuclear cloud and under it my mother and my son. I *am* prepared for that. Madonna and child arise, a vision from our culture beneath a mushroom cloud, a global icon Western practices have prepared me to expect. I know this vision created by our most brilliant minds, this cubistic rainbow of family life whose center does not hold, whose colors we cannot put right. We in the West, in our incarnational drift, do not know the key to it.

Dorje turns back from Mingme and comes toward me, weeping. "Oh why did I bring my mother here? If she dies, I will be to blame!" She starts to runs toward Mum and Auntie, then turns back confusedly to me, not wanting them to see her tears. The Buddha said: "If you had to carry your mother on your back for the rest of your life, you could never repay her kindness in giving you birth." I put my arm around Dorje's waist, draw her to me as we painfully put one foot before the other.

It is getting very cold. One of the rapid changes of climate that Tibet is famous for. Night will be falling soon. I feel something like a stone strike my head. At my feet, a number of pellets. No, not *ringsel.* No shower of blessings from above. Not even a sandstone like those on Commander Bao's desert. These are hailstones.

Once when asked for an understanding about grief, "C" said, "Do not weep for the dead. Tears are like hailstones on their heads."

Of all the climactic changes witches were once accused of bringing about, the most common was the hailstorm. And so, as east and west have always met, in a hailstorm of the heart, we arrive at the dwelling of the woman who bewitches her enemies.

17

A wooden cattle gate opens as we draw near. Two monks are leading horses out of the gate, and with them is the young runner who was sent from the village to tell them of our arrival. These are the horses we might have ridden had we waited.

It is a sizable establishment, somewhat smaller than the village we mistook it for, with perhaps a dozen buildings behind its adobe-like wall. In a daze I try to take it in—the broad river that runs alongside the road has narrowed down and curved into this valley, making a quiet *V* that one could easily wade across. The flat-roofed buildings rise up from the sandy ground; no vegetation is growing here, even beside the largest building, a temple set apart from the others: There is only sand and mud.

We return the amazed stares of the people who have come out to meet us, perhaps thirty monks, grouped around, smiling. Many are fixed on my light hair and skin; how curious it makes them! Several of the monks are young, in their early twenties. Two of them are quite tall; they link long fingers as they gaze at us—their open mouths reveal beautiful white teeth. They grin, astonished.

We are too tired to smile. Two monks, seeing that Mum and Auntie are in trouble, run to help. Mum is lifted in someone's arms, carried toward a door.

Mingme, remembering the duffel bags containing the brocades, speaks to the horsemen. They must go back for our luggage, he tells them, and they cheerfully comply, even though the hail still pelts down and it is almost dark.

We are being taken into a newly built structure, unpainted.

Downstairs is the traditional barn, the kind I have imagined in my friend Nyima's house, which she and her family inhabited after the sheep were turned outside, where they lived along with bins of supplies, bales of hay. The stairway is a straight-up pole, with spiraling footholds, roughly cut out of a tree trunk about two feet in diameter. It is difficult to get Mum up this coil, but the monk who is carrying her calls another to help him heft her and they wind to the top of the pole, where there is a sort of manhole opening. I follow, and as my head reaches floor level, I see Mum go onto all fours, crawl to a pile of blankets in a corner, and collapse onto them.

I too go to the floor on hands and knees; the wood is soft, untreated; under my palms, grains of Tibetan dust and splinters. Auntie comes after me, crawls to her sister, and lies down beside her, moaning. Dorje, coming after us, sinks onto some skins heaped on the floor. She says, "No window glass." Only a thin rice paper covers the latticework on the window. We have entered a freezing, wooden castle of medieval times.

The Khandro is away. She is at one of the other monasteries. A runner is dispatched for her. How far away? Mingme can't say really, perhaps a day. But she knows. Everyone knows about us. Word of our coming was in the air, like a drumbeat. She will be here soon, the monks tell us.

Darkness has settled about the castle. How cold it is! These houses are built with the barn as the first floor so that the body heat of animals below will help warm the rooms above them. However, there are no animals below. There are skins of animals—yak, sheep, and deer—to cover ourselves with. Everyone sinks, stupefied, onto them, breathing in the animal scent.

It is so dirty here, Mum murmurs.

We realize that ventilation from the open window is a necessity because smoke from the kitchen fire fills the room. The kitchen, just off the guest room, is apparently a sort of gathering room, for we hear the voices of the monks in conversation.

Food is brought in, buttered tea and *tsampa*—barley cereal—and a kind of alcohol, which I taste. Many more monks arrive, watching us. Remembering the vodka in my sack, I pass it around the room and the contents of the bottle are consumed before it comes back to me again. Spirits rise. The monks stare and stare; they cannot get their fill of us.

Then one of the monks, seeing that we do not care for the unsalted *tsampa,* even though it is laced with their best fermented cheese, goes downstairs. He comes back, heaving something up through the manhole at the top of the stair, then dragging it across the dusty floor. I cannot quite make it out in the darkness, but when he lights a candle over it, I see that it is what I feared it might be—a yak haunch. It appears to be raw, though it is probably slightly cured. He pulls back the outer layer of hairy skin and cuts generous slices for us.

Scrounging for whatever may be left to eat in my pack—crackers, nuts—I come across several rolls of white candy mints. Mentos. I open the packages and pass the mints around. Each monk takes one and smiles thanks but does not eat it. They see that I am eating one and puzzle over that. What is it? they want to know. Medicine to save until they are sick? Something sacred to put into a charm box? Oversize *ringsel?* Dorje and I laugh, with a revival of our old hysteria. She motions to her mouth, "Eat, eat!" They pop the mints in their mouths, and laugh at themselves, fine white teeth gleaming.

They do not leave. The presence of the oldest of the monks, watching, disconcerts me. Doesn't he get tired of being on his feet? Eventually he goes, but the two monks who were linking hands on our arrival stand like sentinels inside our doorway. Others come and go, watching with great interest our every move. Do they need to keep watch? "Tell them to sit down, Lama Mingme," I say. But they have their own agenda, which is apparently to stand up and look on.

I awake intermittently throughout the night to the wind whistling through the paper at the window. Just before dawn the two tall young monks are still standing where I last saw them, at the doorway between our room and the toilet at the end of the hall. Have they slept at all?

Mystifying. I dig around for more covers, another yak skin, and try to sleep until a crack of light appears.

⊷⊶

The two guardian monks take us to visit the Khenpo. The Khenpo is usually the abbot of a monastery, but this Khenpo appears to be more of a resident scholar, as the management of the place rests in the hands of the Khandro. Sometimes a Khenpo will welcome a release from administrative duties, preferring to pursue the study of the mind. When the Chinese came, this Khenpo performed a heroic deed—he hid the monastery books away to save them from burning or other abuse, and so their library is intact. We are taken into his study for an audience. He sits surrounded by stacks of Tibetan texts, in a cross-legged posture on his bed, which is also his meditation box. These are the classical texts kept in cotton and brocade wrappings.

His face is cheerful, highly intelligent. He puts me in mind of another Khenpo, a friend of his, who stayed for a while in my house in California, and who when my son's kitten died sent it to the Pureland with a wry smile and a special kitten prayer. My son, after thanking him, asked, "What is your name? Is it Mr. Khenpo?" No one in Tibet would have dared address him with such a sense of equality. With a vastly amused smile, the Khenpo, who actually had a long respectful title, repeated, "Mr. Khenpo, yes."

It doesn't take much to make me think of my son here, for even though my fear of dying has subsided, I feel very frail and mortal. I even notice, when I see the Khenpo's shoes beside his door, that they are the same brand of sneakers as my son's. Pumas. They are like the sneakers I have put on "A" in my fiction notes, only more run-down.

This Khenpo gives each of us a photograph of a high guru, one who taught the best-known of all the Tibetan lamas who came to America, Choygam Trungpa. This is a tiny print, one inch square, a little treasure for a believer.

The Khenpo also gives me something else that I beg from him, a few sheets of scrap paper. In the afternoon, while Dorje and Mingme go for a walk and Mum and Auntie are resting in the guest house loft, I sit at the window where light comes through the latticework, even though it is beginning to rain, and I write.

THE GOLDEN ROAD

Bao raised his binoculars, trying to identify the leader on the horse. At first the horse had appeared white, now it looked like a roan horse, but it was turning too quickly for him to see its rider moving among his men. He stared at the uniform of the hostile army—unknown to him. Was it a UN surveillance team, here under orders from Beijing? He had been warned one day they might have to consent to inspection, but surely someone would have notified him. Then it hit him between his flared front teeth which suddenly felt loose in his mouth—Tibetan. Impossible! The uniform was not the Tibetan army's—it had a strangely archaic cut to it. But the faces—the sea of faces might have risen from one of his worst nightmares, a thousand Tibetan soldiers all at attention, all identical under their helmets. The faces of his miners under dusty helmets on the elevator shaft swarmed up in his mind, those doomed men. The soldiers facing his fence were all wearing a glittering armor. Armor! He sprang into action, turning toward the stairwell leading to his tunnel drift.

"Mother" was in extreme discomfort. The armor may have been bearable centuries ago to the young flesh of the Maid, but her own skin, thinned down with age for quite some years now, bruised easily. She felt the metal cutting into her breasts, which were probably somewhat more ample than those of the adolescent girl the armor was first designed for. "I wish this garb were lighter," she thought. Immediately as the words formed in her mind they became mother to the fact; the weight of the armor lifted, became as light as cellophane. She was able then to fix her attention entirely upon the men standing beneath her.

She sat her steed beautifully, even though she knew absolutely nothing about riding. "A" had told her that horse-trading ran in his family, and claimed that in giving her that great secret transmission he had also imparted knowledge of the art of dressage. She and her horse moved through the cyclone fence easily, which was enough to cause the men to lower their arms, and stare at her in awe. Then it pranced among them in elegant circles, and her sword flashed over their heads.

The Chinese military police were murmuring among themselves in hushed voices: "It is Kuan Yin. Kuan Yin ..." The Tibetans also called to one another, "Tara, Tara. It is the mother Tara ..." They saw her as a figure from their individual traditions, just as "A" had told her they would.

Gazing down, she realized that these men were very ill, every last man who stood around her, Chinese and Tibetan alike, looking up in stunned fascination. They were completely denuded of hair, but worse, the skin of their flesh, under its greenish coating of dust, was reddened and scaling, their bodies in various stages of emaciation. "Mother" knew the signs of approaching death, had grown familiar with them in the long years of her work with the dying.

At once she knew what she must do. The exchanges of philosophy with "A" came sharply to mind; she understood how her path differed from his. He wished to lead people through the mind. To her, touch was the way, her mission of healing. "If I can touch a dying person," she had often told the nuns who worked with her, "I can show the way to God." She knew that she had work to do here in which she was well experienced. She began to speak to the mute, bedazzled men, and she realized that she was now gifted with the tongue of angels, for her words were instantly transmuted into the languages of her listeners, just as centuries ago Buddha's first sermon in the Deer Park was understood simultaneously among the assembled listeners in all of the fourteen major languages of India.

She told the men that she had come to deliver them from that place, that they must declare a general strike, that they must leave here at once, using the trucks and helicopters of the base, and fly off to their homes. "The good in human life," she said to them, "is freedom from domination, and you must have a taste of the good in life before dying." She told them that she would give each of them a healing touch, that even though they could not survive the sickness from which they suffered, she could relieve their pain and, more important, help them understand their common divinity. And she moved among them with her sword uplifted, and bent to touch each man on the crown of his head with her fingertips, a subtle tap, which opened to each mind the channel, the pathway, to its own divine nature. Each man raised his face to her and smiled as if the burden of years were falling from him.

"And now," she said, "you must dispose of your arms. Take them inside to your mine, place them in its deepest pit. Come, I will go with you," she called out to them.

Orderly Wang, who had come up from the tunnel, stepped forward as the men moved to obey her. He offered her a ride astride her horse down the elevator, which was manually operated and therefore not subject to the odd electrical blackout. And so, sword held aloft, she entered the mine.

Bao staggered to the drift underground. There his monorail train refused to start. He was forced to run along the tracks in the tunnel on foot, groping in the dark scrambling, stumbling. No light anywhere, only the sound of seepage of water from the tunnel walls. He must get over to the men, take them out of their paralysis, scream orders. But when he clambored to the mine, the men had dispersed. He called out; no one responded. Deep silence. Had they retreated from the invaders, and where to? The mine echoed hollowly.

A terror gripped Bao. What was it? He crept cautiously up the stairwell to ground level, his pistol drawn. The alien army seemed to be filtering through the cyclone fence. Now he could see the figure mounted on the horse more clearly; he saw a man in some kind of armor astride—a roan horse. Something glinted on the helmet, blurred Bao's vision. He recognized the figure, and yet he did not. Overhead, he heard the whirring of helicopters rising from the airstrip. Engines of the trucks were revving up. Who had taken possession of them?

In a fit of mad frustration, he fired his pistol recklessly at the leader, then into the massed invaders striding into the yard, until his chamber was empty. Nobody fell. Had he misfired? He couldn't be out of range. He took shelter to reload.

Then, on legs that felt leaden, weighted suddenly by the pull of the earth, Bao staggered out into the open, his pistol at his side, for he had realized the identity of the leader on the red horse. Bao stared up at him.

The tall, resplendent being, swathed in a long gold cloak, with a black beard that fell in straight strands upon the full length of his chest, gazed down at him. Spikes of gold from a corona on his head extended outward like rays of the sun, against the distant background of the roseate mountain snow. The horse gave a restless neigh and stamped at the dust: It was the Red Hare!

Ta Mi Di! The Red Hare, so named for the swiftness and valor with which he bore into battle his master—Kuan Tí! Commander Bao fell to his knees and bent his head to the ground. Kuan Tí the God of War!

He felt he dared not address his captor, yet his voice rasped against the salty ground. "Is this deliverance?"

18

The Khandro arrives when it is not quite dark. There has been a long sunset and now it is twilight. Before we ourselves hear the pounding of her horse's hooves, the entire monastery becomes enlivened. Several of the monks begin to talk animatedly among themselves.

They have never withdrawn from our sleeping-loft, have stood voluntary guard, I suppose you could call it, throughout our afternoon rest. Perhaps it is an age-old tradition, to observe the honored guest who might at any moment require some minor attention, a handkerchief, a chamber pot.

Our every venture to the toilet is observed with the keenest interest. Mum, the first to go, required assistance, which the monks obligingly offered, but she shooed them off and commanded Dorje to come instead behind a curtain-door to hold onto her. Dorje called back from behind the curtain to me. "No walls! Everyone can see what we do here. People outside looking up." Indeed, when my turn came I found a balcony without side walls, open to the view of all outdoors, and just a wooden hole where one aims, and the waste falls down a whole story to a pit in the ground.

The monks stand about as if they are city idlers observing a construction project; we are a scarcely functioning work team, out to lunch. But now as we hear a horse's hooves pounding the sand, the entire household becomes active.

Lama Mingme fumbles in his bag, his hands trembling acutely. "Why I don't have ready before?" he mutters. What is he looking for? Then it is clear. He wrenches a white streak from his pack—a *khata.* The special *khata* for the Khandro, a white embossed length of silk, flowing through his fingers. He races down the stair-pole. Dorje and I creep to the window, look through a break in the rice-paper lattice. We can see her horse coming, dust rising around its hooves. The woman astride the horse, her black hair flying, wears leather boots, a jacket, and skirt of skins. Then at the barn entry below, Mingme appears and stands with his *khata* extended across his palms; he kneels, just as the Khandro's horse stops with a flourish before the door, spraying sand into his face.

She leaps from the horse. Lama Mingme lifts the *khata* toward her. She is looking up, scanning our window, her black eyes gleaming, her face creased with a frantic smile. She strides past Lama Mingme without a glance at his precious *khata,* and we hear her boots on the pole. She stalks into the guest room—not in our hands-and-knees style. Her glance races about, pauses briefly upon my face; she turns puzzled, alarmed even. Then she swings about to the oldest of the men—whom Mingme calls her overseer—questions him, sits beside him. She sits abruptly, cross-legged on a floor cushion, her boots underneath her. She has not taken them off, although the other Tibetans in the room have left their shoes outside.

Lama Mingme follows, looking dashed, yet he tries again, approaching her, kneeling, offering the *khata.*

This time she looks at him, gazes at the *khata,* and a wave of disappointment washes her face. Her brother has not come. She thought sure that he would be here, but he has not come.

She takes the scarf, clutches it at her knees, heedless of ceremony, which dictates that she offer it back to Mingme, yet she does not drape it around his bowed shoulders. After a moment, he backs away. With his hands clasped in a *namaste* salute, he speaks to her.

"C" has sent him in his place, he says. He explains this unwelcome decision on her brother's part, explains that "C" has learned the Chinese want to imprison him or kill him. The monks murmur among themselves at this. The Khandro fixes her gaze on me. She asks a question Mingme does not understand. The older monk offers a clarification. It seems that she speaks with an accent Mingme cannot understand very well. The dialect here is difficult for those unused to it, he says to us. She points to me.

Mingme explains that I am not a relative of "C's" foreign white wife, no, not her sister, just a friend. She shakes her head. Another disappointment. Who are these strangers to come all this way, how dare one of them be white, the others Chinese? Bitterness sits in her eye. I don't blame her. It is so far, and we do not belong here, truly.

Lama Mingme pulls out a letter "C" has written, offers it to her. She takes it and glances at it, nods. Yes, she recognizes the script; it is from her brother. But she hands it back. Is it because her eyes have filled with tears? Because she is so distraught? She speaks to the oldest monk. Tells him that Mingme should read the letter to her. Ah, it is now I realize that she cannot read, has probably never learned to read.

Mingme holds the paper up to the candlelight, and in a clear, undaunted voice reads the brief message, the explanation for our coming in his stead, and "C's" expression of affection for her.

She hears it through, her face working ferociously. Her lips compress, twist; the muscles of her face are in spasms. Her skin turns gray; its mobility is astonishing, painful to behold. When Mingme finishes reading, there is a silence while everyone looks uncomfortable, sad. Then she slaps both her knees and rises, with one strong utterance. "Dra!" She stands and briskly leaves the room. Her disappointment is more than she can bear in the presence of others.

In the morning, Mum's condition is not improved, and Auntie also appears to be worsening, although she may be merely depressed. She too has begun to have bad dreams. Dorje says Auntie dreamed they were both at a wedding where Mum was getting married into a different family, and they were both dressed in red, and were dancing among the shards of broken Buddha statues. Despite the somewhat festive sound of this, Dorje says these dream symbols are also a sign of approaching death. I have awakened with a vision of Mum's mouth, moving but in silence. I say nothing about these portents to Dorje. They want to leave, and probably should; they have had enough of brave adventure.

The Khandro comes up the stair-pole, and looks down at the ailing mound that is Earth Mum. Dorje, Mingme, and I appeal to her. Can she help Mother Earth in her sorry condition?

Auntie Moon wants Lama Mingme to say that Mum must go down, that she is too ill to stay any longer.

The Khandro resists that. She stands with hands on her hips. You have only just come, she says. It will pass. Meaning the altitude sickness.

Auntie insists that Mum feels much worse, and she herself looks swollen and blotchy. Her lips tremble.

Dorje says to me, "Mum says nothing to eat here."

She must wait at least until day after tomorrow, the Khandro insists. That day, Mingme explains, a *tulku* will arrive. He will know what to do.

But how could one *tulku* or a crowd of them know more than she, the mystic Khandro? Auntie Moon shakes her head, repeating that they cannot stay, not wanting to take a risk with *tulku* power.

Not practical to stay, says Auntie. Once again, the spiritual is compromised by the ever-practical Chinese woman.

Dorje confers with Auntie Moon, says to me, "Auntie thinks Khandro doesn't know how to help. Says she doesn't think she has any magic. Living out here in this primitive wildness."

They are clearly in a frenzy to descend to a lower plane where they belong, perhaps rightly so.

The Khandro leaves us, to attend to some business of her own. Auntie kneels beside Mum, who stirs and huddles against Auntie. They stifle their sobs so that the vigilant monks may not be troubled by their distress.

Two young monks take Mingme, Dorje, and me to see their shrine. They speak Mandarin to Dorje, tell her they have been to Xian to study. The building is made of pounded earth, is a smooth russet clay. The beams were painted, and the square end of each beam is adorned with a small oil image of a deity. The shrine is not as well cared for as one might hope. They tell us that the Chinese used it for storage of grain for their army before they gave up on trying to execute the Khandro.

I stoop to the floor and pick up a few grains. Rice? Dorje wonders. They were storing rice? Actually, it is barley, says Lama Mingme. And although I have read in Charles Bell that grain may be stored in Tibet for as long as a hundred years, I wonder. Maybe it was used lately in one of the many rituals in which a handful of grain is scattered. Sweeping up isn't frequent here, but more frequent than every twenty years, Dorje hopes, with her behind-the-fingers titter. Sweeping up isn't frequent in her Hong Kong apartment either, I think but do not say. This has to be ritual grain.

Dorje asks the monks who built the new building, and they say everyone did it. The rafters and stripped trees for the frame came overland. Yaks hauled them attached by yoke two at a time. Wall forms were built for rammed earth, packed, then removed. They are pantomiming this for us, and laughing as one of them acts out a burdened yak.

Outdoors, Dorje and I notice that the stream has risen since last night's rain, can no longer be forded easily. We look at one another. "Why don't they also build a bridge?" we wonder simultaneously.

Mingme hears us. "Not like your country. Or Hong Kong, where never stop building. Concrete walls of gravestones!" He laughs, my outburst about overbuilt Hong Kong etched in his memory. What a rash complicity Dorje and I have momentarily shared—would we really want a bridge to the Khandro, with throngs of Westerners crossing it to ask her for divinings, then trooping off to a nearby Holiday Inn or Golden Arches? Giving up "harmless isolation" has its downside. Even our coming here is too much of an incursion into the nature of their lives.

Mingme has met privately with the Khandro. For once just two people alone in a room here. He has presented her with the funds from her brother's foundation. Yet he looks dejected as he tells me the money is safe in her own hands.

"What's wrong?" I ask. "Our mission is accomplished, right?"

He says, "She not like other people."

I ask him to explain. He says, "You—me—everybody same one day to next. She every time different."

"How she different?" I ask. It's easy to fall into this syntax.

He can't seem to put it into English. "She like different person. Not know what expecting." So it is, too, with the saints.

Mingme cannot explain exactly what he means. He still looks acutely disappointed. He says that she has told him if Mum and Auntie are firm in their decision to leave in the morning, they can go. His shoulders sag. Then he comes out with what is troubling him. "But I cannot go. She say I stay here."

19

She loves Mingme. He is a relative. He cannot go back right away. Let the others go back, but not him. She will take care of him. He must stay with her for a nice long visit. She tells him what she has in mind, that he will ride horseback with her to visit all of "C's" old friends and teachers throughout the countryside. She wants to take him under her wing. Then after he has become well acquainted here, he will arrange for her to go back to America with him for a nice long visit there. Since her brother cannot come, she will go to him.

There is panic on Lama Mingme's face as he tells us of this interview. He does not want to stay behind when we take Mum down in the jeep. He has duties at his Center in the US. He has an appointment there with Immigration. He has a life there in the States, students, a lover even. At least one woman is waiting for him, although Dorje doesn't know about that. Besides, he could stop off for a little side trip in Nepal and India, see a few friends where he was raised. He will have no motored means of departure once the Isuzu has gone. He feels sick, has a bad cough like the rest of us. And now this.

I suggest that I should stay with him. We could ride with the Khandro all about the ranch, visit all the relatives and the places revered for miraculous events, the cave where this one was enlightened, where that one attained rainbow body. I suggest that when the Khandro was ready to part with him someone could accompany us by horseback to the nearest bus route. We talk over the possible dangers. He may be detained for good, for his is a Nepalese passport. I suggest that he needs my presence, my passport. I say, "It's dangerous for you to stay here."

"But she want to go visit US." Buddhist philosophy firms up in him.

Be prepared for death. Imagine its possibility at any moment. He says, "If they kill me, is okay. But I must stay. She tell me stay. She say everyone else go. Better you go, I stay." He bows to the guru. Or at least to her superior force.

In the evening, we sit in the guest house with monks grouped about the Khandro, exactly as I have seen American students group themselves cross-legged around her brother and others like him in the States in a transplantation of a cultural habit. She is smiling, the fierce emotion we had seen in her completely subdued. *She every time different.*

In the candlelight some tea is brought in, a thermos placed upon the floor. Tonight Lama Mingme has cooked, tried to find something to our taste, but the same *tsampa* with sour cheese is offered and again none of us can handle it.

Mum and Auntie lie with our baggage and blankets in the corner, their eyes swollen shut. Dorje whispers to me. Perhaps we have delayed too long already, she says. She feels terrible about bringing Mum now. It was a mistake. They thought it would be a lark, and it was at first, and now this. "My mother could die because of my selfishness!" she cries.

Mingme plays an audio tape for the company, sent by "C," a long, freewheeling talk in Tibetan that makes them laugh. What her brother says puts them all in a celebratory mood. The Khandro especially. Hers is a warm, husky laugh, not unlike "C's" own, but almost alarmingly abandoned. Is this what Mingme meant about the sudden changes in her, that she could become a different person from moment to moment?

I have turned on my own tape recorder to capture the spirit of festivities to give to "C" on our return. I leave it on, hoping she will say something later, particularly for him. But suddenly a young monk sees it, becomes very excited. He wants me to explain the recorder, he wants to play with it. There is something slightly demented in his manner, and I see that she is not amused, that in fact she does not like my taping anything. I ask her if she will say something for me to take back to her brother. She tells Lama Mingme no, not now. Maybe later. Maybe tomorrow or the day after when the *tulku* comes. After the foreigners have gone.

There is a distance between us, created in part by my remote place in the room with the sick Chinese—we sit on skins in the corner—but also by the hierarchical circle of monks at her feet, in which we are not exactly included. I imagine how lonely she must be. Hers is not unlike the isolation of queens or of saints. And perhaps she can only know herself in ways that are transcendent.

She is alone of all her sex. No other women live here, no sister, no children; she has only the company of probably celibate men. I think of the lives of American pioneer women forced into isolation by westward expansion and often driven mad because of it. In the remote life of my mother's childhood in the rural south, the comfort and support of other women was vital to their survival. No wonder the Khandro wants Mingme to take her to her brother in the States. But "C" has said that probably she should stay where she is rather than try, at her age, to make so difficult an adjustment to the outside world.

I remember the photographs in my sack, of the Dalai Lama. Picture postcards. I've bought a quantity with me, and pass them out. The monks pounce on them. Much better than candy mints! Dorje also has some postcards of various deities. One young monk gets a handful, won't share, and becomes quite obstinate about keeping the whole bunch. Surprisingly, the all-powerful Khandro does not intervene to resolve the dispute.

Then I decide to ask my question. I have a now-or-never feeling, not the most conducive to making a friendly connection. But if we are leaving at dawn the next day as planned, this is probably the last I will see of her. The question comes forth on a wave of general merriment, and is perhaps an unwelcome bringdown. I say to her that on our way here I have been very disturbed by the destruction of the forest. I think people must have suffered greatly because many drew their livelihood from it in the past.

As I speak and Lama Mingme translates, her face changes. But it does not resume the wrathful aspect we had seen on our arrival. Something else is there. Mistrust? Perhaps Lama Mingme is right—she not same person one moment to next.

My question: "Will the forest grow back? Will it return?" It is of course a leading question.

She asks him to repeat what I have said, and he does so, and when she shakes her head, puzzled, I ask him to explain—Will Tibet itself come back, be resurrected, regain its independence?

Again she moves her head from side to side—she doesn't understand. She appeals to the older monk, her overseer, then to her younger monks, shakes her head again. There is a long pause. Is she afraid to answer in front of the Chinese women who are sick in the corner and may be spies? Who have refused her offer of help from a *tulku?* Is it possible she really doesn't understand that I am asking for prophecy?

Lama Mingme speaks with her and tells me he has explained.

Dorje offers, "Sometimes they will pretend not to understand, if they don't want to tell you things." *They,* the enlightened ones. I remember "C's" story of a student often turned away from a teaching he had been begging for because he was too eager for it. Not until he had demonstrated patience by making a thousand barley paste altar offerings was he given the withheld knowledge. Perhaps I have not humbled myself sufficiently. She may think that if I want to know her mind I should not be rushing off, should stay and study and learn with the nephew.

Of course, she may not have the gift of prophecy, one possibility contrary to all legend about her. Perhaps knowing how to bend bullets and float upstream does not necessarily mean that you have the gift of seeing beyond tomorrow. However, the memory of her power surrounds her in the people who look to her every word.

She sits, her eyes glittering, a hint of anger rising. I have brought the party down with my bothersome question. As a woman, she was not given education of the mind like her brother, was not even taught to read. Her natural gifts were neither harnessed by discipline nor fostered by training. No wonder she became subject to vagaries of emotion that sent her to the river bridge to talk to trolls! She may even suffer from possession, in Western terms, as Mingme has suggested, from one moment to the next, a multiple personality. I imagine her as a child, talking to spirits, alone, a kind of contrary . . . and I feel a strong affinity for her that I cannot convey. *She not like other people.*

I say to Mingme, "Tell her I am asking if she can see what is in the future for her country as well as for the forest." As they confer one more time, it seems to me that like the forest she has become decimated, that whatever spiritual craft she once possessed has not flourished but has been eroded along with the ground where the great trees once grew and may have vanished with the felling of their leafy protection, that after the oppression she has suffered, she is holding on to whatever control she can, and sees my question as a challenge even to that.

Mingme says, "I think you are too politic. She will not answer."

As I try to read *her* mind, her eyes gleam at me in the candlelight; her distaste is palpable. It comes to me then that my question betrays something about myself that she sees. "Will the forest return?" reveals my everlasting doubt. She sees my doubt that the bodhisattvas can prevail, even a doubt that she can answer my question. Much more than the color of my hair and skin and disappointing failure to be related to her family she sees what, most of all, creates a chasm between us, that I have chosen doubt, a realm she will not, perhaps cannot, enter.

If I would yield up this doubt, some magic could conceivably occur; then I could write up an imaginative account in which the conjure woman transfers power to me and, through a deep sorcery of spells, trials, and purifying rites, endows me with Ancient Wisdom; then I could return again and again to share royalties with her, and write profitable sequels.

But ever the contrary, I believe this: She could have great power or none at all. She could be a reincarnation of Gesar, who also was not the same person one day to next, magically transforming himself into his enemies, into mendicants, into flying horses, into his conquering ghost army. A Chinese soldier attempting to execute him would have been easily vanquished, too. She could also be thinking of her role as a householder, fearful of the lords of the land, or she could be an ignorant country woman like my mother. She could *be* my mother in at least one life, according to the teachings. She could be Mother Tara as well. So too, as the teachings have it, could Mum, Auntie, Dorje, even I.

Suddenly Lama Mingme remembers the gifts he has brought. The duffel bags were brought back from the village, but were somehow forgotten by him. They are in the corner and Mum is crumpled on top of one of them, has been using it as a pillow. He tugs it out from under her with apologies, and unzips it.

The brocades!

Oh marvel of marvels! Here is something worth responding to! Roll after roll is unfurled. How beautiful each piece is! How the brocades will renew and restore the shrine room! The Khenpo's study, the Khandro's room! What beautiful robes for lama dances shall be made with this! Oh loveliness!

The monks crowd about her, draping the brocades across themselves, over the shoulders of their maroon robes, across her shoulders, and the fabric makes a glowing rainbow of color in the candlelight. It is like a painting, her aged face radiant in the center of it, a mandala made up of these weavings with gold and silver threads running through them. They are so happy. This is happiness sent from far away to create happiness in others, themselves. The heart shape of Lama Mingme's face opens in a grin. "Like Christmas!" he cries.

"Exactly like Christmas," I say, feeling suddenly far away from everything. My question—Will the forest return?—hangs like a film between me and the celebrants. A flimsy tissue, like a scrim for a play set in some other forest, irrelevant here in this glinting weave. All is illusion, airy nothing.

20

They are waiting for us at dawn. From the window of the guest room, I see four mules, for Dorje, Mum, Auntie, and me. Mingme is outside talking with the monks in the semi-darkness. The force of the Khandro's personality has prevailed; he will stay behind with her. The two young monks from Xian are going to take us back to the village. They will go by foot, leading our little mule train. We wonder why they cannot ride—there are other animals, the horses—but Lama Mingme doesn't know, doesn't want to ask. This is the way they set it up. With a doleful mien, he comes up the stair-pole and helps us take down the bags, leaving his own behind.

The Khandro sends for us to say good-bye. She receives us in the kitchen, where she sits on a cushion behind a low table. Mingme, clearly under her direction, bows us into the kitchen, lines us up before her.

Clutching her handkerchief, Mum, first in line, removes her jade circle bracelet, and as a parting gift offers it to the Khandro. The woman takes it, unsmiling, turns it over, and puts it on the table. Then she reaches her hand across the table to each woman one by one. Into each palm she places an antique coin with a firm slap. It is not lost on me that she shifts the order of the coins to save the largest one for Dorje. She sees that I have noticed this, and gives me a see-through look. It is the last I will have from her. She is right to reserve the largest coin for Dorje; she knows who among us suffers no doubt.

Bitterly cold, a mist falling. There's a saying: The cold of this country would stop the tea from pouring—and this is only the end of May. It takes a long time to get us all saddled up, and we stamp the ground in our summer shoes to keep warm. I mount and wait ahead of the others, while the monks tie gray-faced Mum, bundled in her blue nylon jacket, onto the saddle. Dorje signals that she wants her mule to ride beside Mum's to make sure she doesn't fall. Remorseful, she reproaches herself again for bringing Mum along on this journey. Auntie in her green jacket mounts, still very groggy, but not as weak as Mum, and pulls up beside me.

"Dorje!" It is Lama Mingme, reaching up to hold her hand in farewell. She leans over to him. Do they kiss good-bye? My mule steps to one side so that my view of them is blocked and I cannot see.

Lama Mingme comes to shake my hand in farewell. He says, "Don't worry. If I die, no problem." Another echo of "Nothing becomes other than emptiness." Nothing happens. No problem. Is okay, will be okay. Is he afraid? Is this courage or submission? I ask Lama Mingme to promise to come and see me when he reaches San Francisco.

Then we start off. The monks hold onto the leads of the mules of Mum and Auntie. They guide us across the part of the stream where my shoes were soaked coming in. They step into the water, which immediately fills their sneakers, and pools around their bare brown ankles. Their feet will be wet and cold the whole way.

I turn and see that Lama Mingme is still waving to us, and I wave back.

Dorje says again, as we reach sight of the road across the river, "The monks could at least build a bridge." Or a raft, to ferry us across, like Gautama.

These monks are ferrying us by mule. "Ferryman" in Tibetan is *tsong chup sempa,* which translates something like "the mind of the hero."

Dawn sunlight filters across the sands, casting long shadows of burnt sienna, fuchsia, scarlet. We begin to see the skeletal fragments again, scattered in the sand. Catching sight of the yak jawbone I had noticed on my way in, I signal to one of our friends to pick it up for me. He bends to do my bidding, and I stash this memento in my pack, much to his amusement.

We ride on for an hour or so. This time, no death panic haunts our visions; rather thoughts of food begin to rise. Dorje dreams up a steaming bowl of *conge* and a hot pot of fish in broth. I see poached eggs, then scallops Mornay, a glass of milk, a glass of Chardonnay. A dinner at Chez Panisse. A dinner on an airline even.

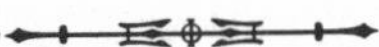

The monks point and motion us to look up. There on the desert ridge above the river are two creatures staring down at us. So distant I cannot make out what they are at first. But as they move about, their tails flaring above their heads, their coats glinting in the light, I realize—foxes. They seem to be trying to decide whether or not to retreat from us, which they do. The presence of these beings helps me draw a deep breath of this clear air, reassures me somehow. Birds begin to call to each other, slow trills; then a distant cuckoo that draws nearer, repeats its call.

The two monks mock the sound. "Cuckoo." We all say it. "Cuckoo," and laugh when the bird calls again. We all try it, "Cuckoo!"

Then the monks try a few English words. "Hello. Hello." Then, "Good-bye." Hello, Good-bye.

Suddenly, tears fill my eyes. How beautiful it is here! They are so young, so seemingly innocent, yet so *present.* So much more present than I, with my note-taking, my visions of food and drink, of flight.

When the flow of the river widens out, we come to the village with the barking dogs. The monks lead us up above the river, close to the village. This time we are passing on the top of the ridge, and must go through the settlement, where we glimpse women beginning to draw water at a well.

"Lot of *mani* stones here," says Dorje. The wall surrounding the village seems made up of them, was perhaps not tampered with by the Chinese. Too remote to tear down. The wall is low. On the way out when we traveled below this cliff, we heard the dogs only from a safe distance. Now as we pass and they again bark ferociously, we see that they could easily leap over the wall. The monks have to shout at them to ward off attack. "C" tells a story about a monk in flight from Chinese soldiers; he came to a *mani* wall, which tradition dictates you must go around only in a clockwise direction and, unable to break with this pattern, he ran toward Chinese imprisonment instead of counterclockwise toward freedom. Is this the same wall? We go around it clockwise.

Just before the bridge, the path narrows sharply above the river gorge, which flows around a sudden turn. We are on a narrow granite ledge, and have to dismount. The monks take the reins of the mules and guide them single file across the path, very slowly. Across the way lie the terra-cotta buildings of the home of Gesar of Ling, rosy in the hue of sunrise, with prayer flags quite still in the early morning air. Because of Mum's condition, no one mentions our earlier plan to visit there.

The monks return for us, take each of us singly by the hand, so that we will not fall from this precipice into the swiftly moving water. Long, firm fingers close about my wrist. We walk across the shaky bridge, holding onto its ropes, the monks protecting Mum and Auntie. We can see the river rushing beneath us through spaces between the planks. Auntie and Mum, terrified, twist their ankles and groan, but fortunately no sprains.

The monks smile at our relief as they help us onto solid ground, where we remount. Again, I am moved by a clear sense of their belonging here, and their diffidence toward us. I give the monks another English word. "Try this," I say, *"Good."*

"Good," they say. "Good-bye?"

"No, just *good.* You are good."

"Good," they say. "Good."

The village welcomes us. People rush out and stand about as we approach. We pass the pit of bones, horns of yak and deer. A young layman approaches the monk holding the tether of my mule, and the monk whispers briefly into the ear of this—friend, relative, business connection, lover? Why a whisper, when he knows his four charges could not understand him? That moment, the monk's lips passing briefly at that ear—it gives me a texture of a whole life, not merely innocence, goodness and devotion—secrecy too.

> In the short walk of this life
> We have had our share of joy
> May we meet again
> In the youth of our next life.

Lines written by the Sixth Dalai Lama, who was known for sexual escapades and love poetry.

Mr. Fu is waiting for us. He appears rested. He no longer limps; the blisters on his heels must be clearing up. There's something else about him—he seems to have an aura of wonder as he speaks with Dorje. He tells her that an elderly nomad has come by the police courtyard where there was a little outdoor market. The man had made a pilgrimage to the home of Gesar, and he began to sing songs about Gesar for the people there, and Mr. Fu could, miraculously, understand him, even though he has forgotten the Tibetan language. It was like a dream, says Mr. Fu.

"Perhaps it was a dream," I say. Yet I am struck by a different quality in Mr. Fu, as if his disbelief has been shaken.

The jeep stands beside the bone pit, where the small horns of musk deer lie, perhaps soon to go to market in Beijing. The Tibetans place our bags into the Isuzu, tuck everything in. All is in readiness. Time to go. We shake hands with them, press into their hands the last package of our Mentos. They laugh, then grow sober as they stand by waiting to wave us away.

Mr. Fu comes around as I am about to get into the jeep and, grinning at me, thrusts something toward me. It is my notebook—Mr. Fu has found it! He points to a crevice behind his own seat, to explain where he discovered it.

I leaf through it thankfully, joyfully. My notebook, with its scattered entries, its fiction notes, with its promise of clarity—or at least its hope! Mr. Fu, I think, in some wonder—Mr. Fu has returned my memory to me.

I reach out to him and, holding my notebook tight against my breast, I grasp him by the neck and press my forehead to his, mind to mind, thanking him in the Tibetan way. Is he taken aback, displeased by this enthusiastic show? As he steps away, I can see in his face something more, some remembrance of touch sinking into him, profoundly wordless, like a childhood thought. Memory rises, feeling deepens, and something discarded from his life, for a moment at least, returns to him.

As he puts the Isuzu in gear and turns toward the road, I browse through my notebook, my jumble of thoughts. I fold into it the stationery I have been scribbling on, scraps of impressions of the Khandro. I did not get the text from her I had imagined, or rather "C's" wife had imagined for me. But synchronicity moves in mysterious ways.

21

I am so happy to have my notebook, I write in it even as we bounce along in the jeep. Mr. Fu, above the boundaries between fiction and fact for me, hums as he drives, occasionally laughing and chatting with Dorje.

I think of Mr. Fu's strange gaze the day he balked and I told him not to leave us. Could he have been so annoyed by my continuous scratching in this notebook that he stole it, hid it away? Haven't we all gotten on each other's nerves on this long trip? And, thinking better of it, perhaps after hearing the Gesar songs, he could have suffered a pang of conscience and decided to return it. Oh, discursive mind forever imagining, conjuring …

I prop my feet on the glove compartment, bracing the notebook against my knees, and go back to Captain Bao and my imagined Mr. Fu.

THE GOLDEN ROAD

When Captain Bao left his compound unguarded, Mr. Fu entered the office, hoping for a smoke out of the wind. As he lit his cigarette, he glanced at the Captain's desk. There he found something that intrigued him: a black notebook. After leafing through it for a moment and examining the sketches and details of weaponry there, he slipped it into his pocket with a sensation of excitement. A little twinge of guilt flickered through him, but vanished in a new-found negative capability. Mr. Fu could now entertain opposing impulses without confusion. He knew he was not a thief, but he realized this notebook contained something that meant the future to him and perhaps to many others as well. This action had to do with the monk's lifting his karma, he thought. He left the office, possessed of a new sense of purpose—more than that, with an unsettling sense of inevitability.

The satellite signal that went out from Westminster Abbey, joining the prayers there with those of many thousands around the world, also carried an image of a communal visualization, a global mandala. This union of concentration, this "composition of place," brought together in the Tibetan desert a massive transfer of thought—belief in the impossible, belief in an irresistible event: The return of Kuan Tí or the return of Gesar, or the arising of Kuan Yin or the Mother Tara, or the coming of the Maitreya or the coming of the Messiah—or a complete transformation of humankind. The event in which "B's" four crusaders took part might be viewed many ways on the relative plane, but concepts caused by boundaries of culture bore little significance in the suspended Ordinary Mind.

The answer to "Mother's" question was clear: Yes indeed, it did photograph on video, even in the world's blackest pits, for all to see.

In the darkness of the mine, "Mother," in her youthful incarnation, stood beside her white horse for a few minutes overlooking one of the pits. When she lifted her arm, the soldiers began to hurl their rifles down into some stuff marked "Green Salt" from South Carolina.

Youngden and Bodhi came to the edge of another pit, where Youngden aimed his video camera at the troops flinging their weapons away. Bodhi held an electronic flash for him, which streaked in the darkness like the star streaks they had seen in the sky. When the flash crossed "Mother's" form, Bodhi said, "Look at how gorgeous 'Mother' is, Youngden."

"What's in that trench?" "Mother" called out, pointing to the pit behind Bodhi. Bodhi turned and looked down upon the stacked bodies of rodents.

"White mice," she said.

"Thousands of them," said Youngden, shocked. He took from his backpack his *Chod* drum. "Mother" drew close to them, gazing down upon nested corpses of the mice. Youngden began to chant the mantra of Machig Labdron, the goddess of the graveyard, and Bodhi joined in.

He twisted the *Chod* drum, and its beads struck single, steady beats on either side of the drum.

Some of the men joined in the chant. Their prayers reverberated through the tunnels of the nuclear graveyard. They prayed that demons might cease to haunt all beings, and particularly they prayed for this microcosm of a holocaust, that the mice might be granted rebirth in human form.

Bodhi cut it short, though, and said, "'Mother,' you must get out of here."

"I do like that Macha woman's prayer," said "Mother." She turned and yelled to the men who had surrendered their arms. "Let's go—my horse is dying!"

The men cheered, "Tara,Tara! Kuan Yin, Kuan Yin!" still disputing her name as they praised it.

"Mother's" white horse was indeed vaporizing, quickly now as they took the elevator back to the surface. They saw that the men, Tibetans and Chinese together, were scrambling into trucks and helicopters, rushing for their taste of freedom. By the time "Mother" had returned to "A," her cellophane-like armor too was replacing itself with her black skirt and blouse and her straw hat, and then the horse vanished in a shimmer from between her legs, leaving her standing on the salty sands. The Red Hare of Kuan Tí or Kyang Go Karkar, the flying horse of Gesar, was also returning to invisibility, and so she and the monk stood facing one another. "That was a joyride," she said.

Impulsively, she reached up to pull his head down to hers. "Let's have a Tibetan kiss. Touching is my way in this life, you know." He stooped lower, and she pressed his forehead to her own, in the Tibetan kiss, two foreheads, two minds, one pressed to the other.

Suddenly, in a dramatic reversal of climate, the dust storm subsided and a light snow began to fall. In the setting sun, the flakes glistened like rose quartz crystals. They settled upon the pathway, obscuring the petaled summits of the sacred mountain. "A" looked up at the scatter of flakes, and came to a decision. It was time for his pilgrimage, the utmost secret of the entire mission. He would send the others ahead of him—they were not yet prepared for the journey he would now undertake, even though they might yearn for it. Even "Mother," even she could not come with him without sacrificing the Paradise she had spent her life preparing for.

"A" opened the door of the jeep. "Get in," he said to "Mother." "You must leave here at once."

Unobserved, Mr. Fu placed Captain Bao's notebook in a crevice behind his seat, while Bodhi and Youngden packed the video equipment into the jeep. They sat in the rear seats. "Mother" got into the front seat, and "A" closed the door after her. He leaned across the window, speaking quickly.

"Something is about to occur," he said, "which is necessary, and a little absurd, like this trip of ours, but do not be alarmed by it. Do not follow me. There is a crowning pilgrimage I must make, to fulfill not only my life but our mission as well. Ask no questions." He gazed down at "Mother" tenderly, reached out, and touched her wrinkled cheek. "Go quickly. And—you may look back, but do not under any circumstances come back or follow me."

His last words were for Mr. Fu. "Be careful, Mr. Fu. *You don't have much time.*"

He turned away, and set his feet upon the long, winding pathway leading to the mountain, his rich voice intoning a mantra. Mr. Fu obeyed him, and started up the jeep. Youngden and Bodhi craned their necks, strained to see—the imprint of his Pumas—were they covered by the freshly falling snow? Did he vanish as well? They gazed and gazed, but his form has vanished. The mountain might as well have opened up to swallow him, and soon the very mountain itself, which had glowed with such an unearthly light before, seemed to disappear in the falling flakes, like a mirage.

Mum is clearly recovering. Within a day of descent she is talking again. She tells Mr. Fu that she wants to see the doctor in the lumber town where we stopped on the way up.

When we arrive, I find that I have lost the coin that the Khandro gave me. It was in the pocket of my black cotton skirt; now it is nowhere. I search all over the jeep, behind Mr. Fu's seat this time as well. Dorje laments a loss too—her guru's picture, the pendant disk with her teacher's image on one side and Avalokitesvara's on the other. What do they mean, these losses?

To Dorje, a source of grief. She cannot get it out of her mind. "How could I lose my guru?" She is as distressed as when her mother fell ill.

I tell her that I understand, and I do. For didn't I feel the same when I lost my notebook, my stubborn way to truth, my own guru? I make a note in my notebook to look for a replacement disk to send her when I get home.

In the doctor's office, we line up as before. This time Mum takes an injection, which she had refused before, fearing the needle. The passersby peer in at our treatment. The seamstress next door who made tea for us earlier in the trip asks what happened to the Tibetan who was with us. We explain that Mingme has stayed behind for a time. She says it is worrisome, and we agree.

22

As we drive on, I chat comfortably with Dorje. The vocalizations of Mum and Auntie are an accompanying drone, but somehow are quieter now, definitely not so intrusive.

I ask about Mum's dream life. Is she still suffering from nightmares? Dorje asks her mother, then translates: "Oh, she had a good dream last night. She was dressed all in white, and rats and pus and other poisons were pouring out of a wound in her heart, and at the end of the dream a beautiful golden fruit fell from a tree and she caught it."

The next day when Mum orders lunch, she demands a whole fish, a pile of chicken with garlic cloves, and inevitable rice. She is ravenous. Soon her voice is completely restored. Every now and then Auntie Moon emits a guttural growl of satisfaction as she eats. They are already planning to continue their travels, to go to Emei Shan and see the temples there, and the clouds haloed with rings into which the devout leap to death. Mum is roaring with laughter again. Her cackles abound, her coarse expressiveness. Perhaps she too will leap.

But no, Earth Mum will not die. She is the earth, encompasses even the slippery sides of the abyss. We have to hope for her endurance, her survival against any odds, talking, still talking.

Dorje demands we stop again at the Kalachakra shrine, and rushes inside. The monk who told its story before is nowhere to be found. She vows that she will collect funds to restore the shrine, and starts by extracting a sizable contribution from me.

I follow her into the shrine room, and stand at the threshold as she prostrates herself. Then she moves to the Tara statue, and reaches out toward the hand extended in compassion to all beings. What does she place there on the wrist? An offering to Tara? As she goes past me toward the jeep, I glimpse it shimmering there in Tara's hand. Lama Mingme's crystal *mala.*

As we approach the rice fields on the outskirts of Chengdu, at the periphery of the city's smog bank, other trucks of all kinds join the lumber trucks on the highway. Their produce of poison settles upon the produce of the fields.

I say, "Back to smoky Chengdu."

Dorje sighs. "I cry when I think of what 'C' has suffered, and of his sister's life there. So far away from everything."

"Yes."

"Still—we learned."

"What did you learn, Dorje?"

A pause. She seems not to have expected my question. Its difficulty makes her frown. "I learned—what to say—I learned about myself. How much more I have to learn."

"Yes," I agree, and look back at her.

She smiles. "Actually—" (fingers over her lips) "I feel sorry for my guru!"

After all these days, Mr. Fu is able to get something on the radio. He flicks it on, gets a Chinese opera, punches it again, and strains of Western-sounding music come across the radio—a mandolin, an echo chamber. Dorje says it's a very popular song, a sad song, and she translates:

It is long time ago
You leave me and go far
I still waiting you
Coming back.
The outer world is wonderful
The outer world is no way …

Extraordinary, Noel Coward said, how potent cheap music is.

I had thought that I left my last *khata* scarf at the Khandro's altar, but as I search through my canvas bag thinking that the pendant or the coin might be there, I find that I have one last piece of *khata* silk crushed down in a corner of the bag, as wrinkled as the scarf Lama Mingme had tied about the handle of the bag at the airport—so long ago, it seems. This scarf touches in me something I cannot deny; the world of omens, portents, signs is not so easy to shake. Perhaps I have one more offering to make.

When we reach Chengdu, there is "P," come to help with further money-changing. Standing blandly in the hotel lobby for all China to see, he presses my farewell token, a portrait of the Dalai Lama, to his lips, then to his forehead, his eyes rolled upward toward the Pureland, partly mocking—what—the police who might see him paying tribute to the image of his God-King? His own traditional stylized kiss of the image? My role in our brief nonverbal exchange? Himself? I can't be sure, shouldn't be sure. Thank the gods for ambiguity.

Indefatigable Mum and Moon, taking Dorje along, go off on a sightseeing bus to the mountain of the sages, Emei Shan, and I head for the airport.

Where, together with my notebook, I have a long wait.

THE GOLDEN ROAD

Captain Bao came to his senses, and found himself alone in the yard behind the cyclone fence. In the distance he could see the departing jeep. He lifted his binoculars, and in the snowfall he could see the mountain path where a lone Tibetan was winding his way upward. What had passed might have been a dream, as if he had been caught in a time lapse since that morning—was it morning when he read the fax with his new orders? Was that the same Tibetan going on pilgrimage he had glimpsed only moments, hours, ago? Or yesterday? Yet, he was here in the worker's compound, and no one was about. He shouted for Orderly Wang. No reply. Helicopters were taking off. He heard the cargo plane on the runway.

"Sir, the men—they went on strike." It was Wang, with a bedazzled look, standing beside the elevator shaft.

"What!" Bao cried. A few of the miners scrambled out behind him, starting toward the airstrip. "Halt!" Bao called out.

"Please, sir." The orderly was trying to explain, and he spoke in the language of legend. "There was a spell cast on them," he explained, "a kind of dream. A beautiful woman came to them, who was clad in a transparent cloud and wore a coat of mail and whose eyes were crescent moons, and whose sword glinted red in the sun."

Bao stared at him.

"They believe she was Kuan Yin. She revealed to the men that their orders had arrived to remain at the base another year, and—she started a strike."

"A strike!" Bao's training surfaced. "This is no strike, it is treason."

Wang backed away from him. The last of the trucks was leaving, churning up dust on the other side of the cyclone fence; he didn't want to miss a ride. He wondered how he could break away from Bao.

Wang didn't expect the sudden collapse of his commander. But as the captain stared at the trucks, at the helicopters, he was considering the condition of the fleeing men and reflecting on his own part in their exposure to radon gas, to sulfur dioxide, to radiation poisoning. He was recalling the majestic figure before whom he had bowed, and who had somehow disappeared as swiftly as he had come. In a tense, muted voice, he asked Wang, "Was this Kuan Yin they claimed to see astride a horse? Riding a horse?"

The orderly nodded. Without a word, Captain Bao turned and left him. Wang rushed through the gate and hailed the last truck as it roared from around the cyclone fence, and he climbed aboard.

In his office, force of habit made Bao look at the telephone. Should he call? Should he fax? It was at that moment he realized his black notebook was missing.

His notebook! How could it be? He searched through the papers on his desk. He opened the files. Had it fallen down beside the folders? Was it on the floor? It had to be here. Everything was in the notebook! It contained all his thinking, all his great designs. His creativity! It was impossible. Something seemed to be cracking inside his skull, allowing strange seepage into his brain. He knew he was losing his mind. He could bear no more.

He unlocked the vault. Had he perhaps left the notebook there? But not finding it, he took up his U-Gun. In a frenzy of confusion, he went outside the building. His body reeled on the sandy terrain. He began to pray to Kuan Tí, muttering his chaotic thoughts. "You have given me a glimpse of your divine presence. Tell them in Beijing they are wrong. Show the way to them … In the distance, he glimpsed the figure and suddenly he knew it was Kuan Tí ascending the snow-streaked mountain. Through the haze of pink crystals falling, he screamed: "Kuan Tí, I must blast open their minds …"

Suddenly the people in the jeep were shaken by an explosion miles behind them in the desert. They turned back to see a vibrant fire spreading upward and into the snow, causing the incline to flare with hues of red, as if the mountain that had vanished had somehow burst into flames. Youngden lifted his binoculars, and passed them to Bodhi in stunned silence. The pathway where "A" had disappeared was a red inferno that engulfed the petal snowcaps of the mountain.

Captain Bao stood at the cyclone fence before the building, clutching his weapon. He gasped in a hushed exalted voice. "Kuan Tí!" Bao's face contorted in agony. In an instant of illumination that sometimes comes to the deranged, he knew that he had fired his weapon at his god. He ran back into the building. "Kuan Tí" he cried. "The nuclear fanatics have defeated us—divine destiny in the nuclear fire! Kuan Tí, My God, I have forsaken you!"

Once again, the jeep shook violently, its passengers hearing another explosion. The main building at the base blew up in an instant, dematerialized like "Mother's" cellophane garments. Only a vaporous cloud hovered where the offices of Captain Bao had been.

Mr. Fu stopped the jeep but did not turn around, for they had been told not to do so. Youngden called out once: "'A'!" The sound reverberated like a wail of grief across the desert. And then silence.

Then they saw the trucks roaring down the road after them to escape from the scene, the helicopters whirring overhead, the cargo plane.

They watched the cloud under which everything was disappearing, the burning flares in the snow, the rising fallout at Bao's headquarters, the multicolored mushroom cloud clustering in the sunset like a shattered rainbow.

Everything behind was vanishing.

Gone, gone, gone beyond.

Gate gate Parasamgate, bodhi svaha!

Scarcely able to hold his foot steady on the accelerator, Mr. Fu revved the motor and tore away across the plains. Everyone in the jeep was stunned, grief stricken, by what they had seen. But the terror of it lay heaviest in the heart of Mr. Fu, and repeated itself as if continuing explosions were destroying his brain cells again and again. Uppermost in his mind was his trophy, Captain Bao's black notebook. When Mr. Fu had picked up the notebook from Bao's desk, it was opened to the sketches and notes of a weapon, labeled "U-Gun," and as they drove away from the plant, Mr. Fu had imagined himself going to Hong Kong to seek out a fabricator, then an international patent attorney. Now he understood the drawings must be of the weapon that had created those blasts. And the words the monk had spoken to him came back to him now, striking him with awe. "You don't have much time." He felt the monk's touch on his forehead again, like the touch of destiny. To whom could he take the burden of this secret?

23

Look—we've come to the end of the Golden Road.
—Ciu Jian, Beijing rock star

The pitch of excitement among the Chengdu students had intensified. I glimpsed them only briefly as I left for the airport. A crowd of young men, angry and exuberant, stood chanting in the streets. But in Hong Kong, while I waited for a plane for San Francisco, thousands of outraged people were marching to the city's racetrack, the largest open space to be found in the concrete graveyard. A huge protest began. I learned that the PRC army had attacked the students in Beijing. Hong Kong people fear similar treatment when they return to China's control. I feared the worst for Lama Mingme.

In the airport, I bought a newspaper with a photograph on its front page of the styrofoam-and-plaster-of-Paris Goddess of Democracy the Chinese students had created, modeled after the iron-and-copper statue from Paris that stands in the New York harbor. And in the next days at home, I watched as a lone student Wang Wei Lin stood before a tank in the square called Tiananmen, the Gate of Heavenly Peace, and with all America saw more than many Tibetan or Chinese citizens may ever know of the events at the Square.

When I heard the Communist denials of the slaughter, I thought again of what Charles Bell had discerned decades ago, in a pre-Communist era, about the Chinese tactic of hedging around brazen lies to test how much the adversary will swallow.

On the plane back to the States, my notebook took up its task:

THE GOLDEN ROAD

Bodhi asked Mr. Fu to take them straight to the airport when they reached Chengdu, so they might buy or bribe or beg space on the afternoon flight to Hong Kong. All during the hard drive of five days, the travelers had sat stunned, with heavy hearts. Youngden repeated his vows as if they might escape him. Bodhi and "Mother" clicked their rosaries, crystals flashing in the light, Bodhi murmuring her mantra, *Om Tare Tam So Ha.* Sitting in the front next to Mr. Fu, "Mother" murmured again and again: "Mother Mary, pray for us," and "May God have mercy on our souls."

And Mr. Fu brooded over the trophy that had come into his possession. He thought with irony of that British attorney's curious question, "Can you keep a secret?" The moment when he prostrated himself at the feet of the monk, and the monk's response—"No one has the final say on who anybody is …"—that too tugged at him. Had he dreamed it all? Had this tiny old woman sitting next to him in the jeep really turned into a young woman warrior with a sword held above a company of military police? Was this little woman real? Was she even a living person?

At the airport, the three passengers insisted that Mr. Fu go on his way without waiting to see if they could get a flight. He was, they knew, exhausted after his many days of driving. Clearly the blisters on his heels were killing him. Their own exhaustion was immeasurable, yet their anxiety to leave outweighed any thought of rest. Before they waved him good-bye, "Mother" poked her head into the window, pulled Mr. Fu by the neck, and touched their foreheads together. He felt the bone of her forehead and it felt very real. Her gesture shook him. Only his own mother had ever touched him in that way, his neglected mother.

Bodhi, Youngden, and "Mother" entered the airport. They were on their way to the ticket counter when "Mother" reached for her companions' hands and said, "My friends, prepare for a miracle." They followed her gaze and gasped in shock.

Sitting there in the waiting room, with a small box of pastries on his lap, was "A," who set aside the bakery box, rose, and greeted them with palms pressed together. Youngden dropped his duffel bag, and Bodhi gave a shriek. The astonishment of his friends brought an amused smile to "A's" lips.

"None of you guessed that I would be here?" They stared at him, speechless. Their grief and fatigue soared away.

Bodhi and Youngden started speaking at once—Gesar's magical flying horse, Kyang Go Karkar, of course "A" could summon him. And *lung-gom,* of course. Sky walking! *Lung-gom!* It would be a simple thing for him to fly here. But there was more to it than that, they knew, and suddenly they understood "A's" disappearance, his true pilgrimage. Tears welled into Bodhi's eyes and Youngden pressed her hand. They gazed at one another and, remembering the lore of prophecy of a great battle for the souls of men—at the foot of a lotus-petaled mountain, that would signal the victory of justice over greed and fear—they whispered their realization to one another: "Shambhala."

Bodhi shook her head, amazed. "We were right there. We have all seen it, and we didn't even know it."

"Mother" smiled at them, understanding, and made the sign of the cross. She said, "Heaven lies about us."

"A" lifted his box of pastries from the bench. "I have our tickets and we have time for a delicious pastry before the flight." At a gesture from him, they sat down and he opened the box.

They knew they could not ask of the wonders he had passed through during his journey in the sacred mountain. Although he would tell them what they were capable of understanding, they would have to wait for understanding of the beneficience granted him, and when its effects would be felt. They understood that they would know in good time, as the world prepared itself for the reign of peace.

In the days that followed, Mr. Fu led a life of agony. He realized that if Captain Bao's weapon became available ordinary people in all the overcrowded, overbuilt cities throughout the globe could swiftly do one another in, before the great nations had time even to build up a sense of enmity. It might solve the world population problem, but it would leave behind only small elitist enclaves in the well-protected, secluded havens already built for the rich.

He was haunted incessantly by the events he had lived through. The monk's mysterious response to his sudden recognition of him repeated itself again and again in his mind. He felt he *was* no longer certain of anybody's identity, least of all his own. Flashbacks of the explosions he had witnessed on the high deserts of his mother country tore apart his nights. He knew they were no dream. Repeatedly he saw the bright flares, the presumed vaporization of "A" and Captain Bao. The sinister nature of his trophy troubled him profoundly. Wandering about the streets with his bandaged heels, he tried to find a solution to his dilemma—what should he do with his find? He smoked incessantly, and eventually sought help.

He visited dissident groups, but found no comfort in their heated argument; he saw into the innate tyranny in their plots. He went to temples, but neither was he solaced nor counseled; the priests were selling Thai lottery tickets and doing stick fortunes. He sought out easy women and his old male cronies, but there was none to whom he could confide his secret. He remembered the card given him by the British attorney and started to go to the international telephone, but an inbred xenophobia surfaced—the man was flawed with Colonial roots! He thought of going into exile, of going to New Zealand to work for Greenpeace, but he could make no move. Uncertainty piled upon uncertainty.

Tossing in his bed at night, he could not avoid a reiteration in his mind: The bomb going off there, in his own brain, shattering everything into a mushroom cloud of unknowing.

The last words the monk spoke at the jeep hounded him. "You don't have much time." It must mean that without karma he would soon die. He felt painfully confused about the monk's strange end. *Had* he died? And the monk's true identity, had he really recognized it? Was there a link between the monk's secret and the notebook? What was the secret? He thought of what the monk had said about his saint Padma Sambhava—secrets hidden away for the future until people were ready and able to make use of them. He was tormented by thoughts of right action. If he really had no karma now, how could he act upon it and how could he know what was right? Something was going on, perhaps had always been going on, that he just did not understand ...

He began to wonder if he would die with his questions unanswered, to imagine it might be best if he were to die, so difficult had life become, a responsibility he was unequal to. Over and over he asked himself: Suppose he had once possessed the only diagram for the first known atomic bomb in the world—what would he have done with it? Once he intentionally left the notebook outside in the rain, but the next day he found the formula was unaffected, and so he came to understand that knowledge is not easily cast off. What should he do? The question lodged like a weight in his heart, but somehow he knew it would not kill him, that it was something he must bear like a sack of salt rocks he had to carry up a mountain.

Back at home my son met my plane and took me to my mother, who still hung onto her life. And now I sit at her deathbed, with another notebook, looking at notes and fragments of another story, scenes from her life as she tries to hold onto it, tries to surrender it, as it disappears....

My dream of knocking at the door has not left me. It still comes in its stark simplicity of no presence. In a parable of Kafka's, a presence stands before the Gate of the Law, where a man begs admittance—this presence is a severe gatekeeper who warns that there are many other more frightening gatekeepers within and who forbids the man to pass through the first gate. Only at the end of his life does the man ask the gatekeeper why no others beg to enter, and the answer comes: "No one else could ever be admitted here since this gate was made only for you."

"Compassion is the first gate," "C" once said. The first and the last. But, he says, it is hidden. Perhaps that is what I await, at the door of my dream. The key to my gate is my notebook. As Lucille Clifton says in *The Making of Poems,* "though I fail and fail / ... these failures are my job ..." and they do involve searching for that which is hidden, knocking at its often terrifying door.

I hang in with my notebook, with its gleanings of presence, moments, sketches of people, thoughts about my diversionary, absurd, and yet somehow necessary journeys, promises of scenes, novel notes, fragments of memory that entice me to drag in like the kitchen sink everything of either fleeting interest or enduring necessity—don't forget that locus, that altar, of female devotional ablutions, where Tara in her twenty-one manifestations must surely comfort the faithful. Yet the notebook too is impermanent, may be lost for good in some other crevice, behind some other car seat—because after all it amounts to nothing. Especially when pieces of it are converted to electronic dots, so tentative and ephemeral, so dependent upon something discovered only a few decades ago, easily swept off in a surge, a blackout, moving flecks that are an infinitesimal ding-ding of time in the life span of words themselves, fleeting glimmers of light images that vanish into fumy or thinning air before they are fixed in place with narrative, like the life story of a dying person, slipping away in fragments almost with mere passing interest into a welcome emptiness. A way of carrying salt rocks pressed in yak skin up the mountain. . . .

24

> "The unleashed power of the atom has changed everything save our modes of thinking, and we thus drift toward unparalleled catastrophe."
>
> —Albert Einstein

Mingme returned alone after a month and, dressed in his lama robes, he came to tell me what had happened.

"Chinese question me," he said. "Took passport. Said I not allowed in Tibet. Why you bring foreigners here?" they ask me. "Foreign spies?" Eventually, however, they allowed the Khandro to travel to Chengdu with him so that she could attempt to come to the States to visit her brother. On the way they were not admitted to any of the Guest Houses. No Tibetans allowed. Even the monasteries would not take them. "Had to sleep in the open."

"Better if I had stayed to help you," I said.

He shook his head. He didn't think so. "It was Americans said *no* finally. Wouldn't give visa."

I see the Khandro at the American Consulate in Chengdu, where a black diplomat reads her application. On his face shows his doubt that this desperate woman, given the chance a visa might provide, would ever return to the desolate wilds that gave rise to her.

I imagine myself with her, a white ghost always experiencing a familiar anger that women are still not admitted the freedom of movement claimed by men who travel the rare corners of the globe, never allowed entry to the charmed circle of welcome, the firelit councils, the comforts of fellowship extended in all traditions to men in their wanderings. The white ghost has traveled alone in China, in Greece, in Spain, even in the wastelands of the Casbah and of Bourbon Street, always asserting a right of passage but always receiving the message: "You don't belong here, are not welcome." The Khandro has known for a long while what it is to be disempowered, but her face would have grown more and more fierce.

I conjure up the fury of outcasts, this rare bird and myself a contrary. Secret, black, and midnight hags—witches! The leathery-faced one—no civilized country could admit this weird sister, wild of eye, in filthy skins, who probably smells like fermented cheese. And the other—single white foreign female, wanton and immoral in youth, immodest and trouble-seeking in age. I have to speculate about this travel barrier as fear, to imagine in the unwelcoming world of men some threat in the woman on her own, some sense of a catalytic force that might be used against them to imperil their hold on the world. The Chinese had tried to kill the Khandro as a witch. Another way of killing witches is to keep them out of sight. Back to the blasted heath, back to the cauldron, crone!

I told Mingme that the Tiananmen Square massacre probably put the clamp on visas. Lama Mingme knew nothing about those events—even though at the same time he was visiting the consulate in Chengdu, students in that city too were being killed in the street. When I told him of this, he said, "I didn't know."

"You *must* know about such things," I cried. "Isn't ignorance one of the three causes of suffering?"

Even as I scolded him, the blameless faces of Tibetans rose in my mind—the hand of a child stops a page of a book we are looking at together, a monk asks me if the white mint I have given him is something sacred, an old woman with a seared but cheerful face offers me a cup of salty tea, two young monks point up to a cliff side, to show me foxes ... There is magic in Tibetans, their friendliness, warmth, and laughter surviving under all the duress they continue to endure, unlike people anywhere else on earth, their bodies grounded, their hearts light with the common air of their faith.

"You are too politic," Lama Mingme said to me once again.

I told him about the "Goddess of Democracy," of which he also had not heard. "A symbol of liberation," I underlined for him. "The Chinese students called her a goddess because freedom is a universal wish of the spirit, like a belief from the world we cannot see. She is their Bodhisattva."

It is Lama Mingme's belief in Bodhisattvas, to his mind far mightier than the strength of the ballot, that leads him to not "know" about the blood with which every law of human rights has been written, and I want to shake him until his teeth rattle, but I remember that his hands are already shaking from the damage done to him in infancy, and that it is up to me and others like me, whose aspirations fall short of the Bodhisattva way, to remember that ignorance breaks out everywhere. I remind myself how Mingme's nerves came to be shattered, and that despite the state of his nerves he has just returned from trying to liberate a Khandro. And so I say, "Welcome back to the land of the free," and we leave it there.

The Khandro went back alone, bearing more affront from men who hold temporal sway. But with her, I believe, went her fury, renewed by that passage in the outside world. It contains the original fire that first empowered her, that of the wrathful deities, who descend to trample upon the infamies of men. That fire of transformation, which changes the body, mind, and heart, is far from extinguished. On her own ground this woman, even in age, may rekindle her fire, just as the Goddess of Democracy is replicated all over the world in response to the world's crying need. There within the star streaks above her desert, which unlike our own concrete habitat invites unearthly intervention, she may again claim her right to dance the skies.

The Dalai Lama's proposal to the world for Tibet lies on my work table. Its simple language outlines a five-point plan that anyone brought up on the Bill of Rights can understand. It calls for China to respect fundamental human rights violated by the imprisonment and torture of Tibetans. It calls for a stop to the transfer of Chinese people into Tibet, which would allay the extinction of the Tibetan race and culture. It asks China to restore the forests and give up nuclear weapons production and the dumping of nuclear waste in Tibet. It asks for the transformation of Tibet into a zone of peace and nonviolence, which would mean the withdrawal of Chinese troops and an end to the border dispute at Ladak between India and China that was created by the occupation. In that nonviolent zone people of all nations would come to Tibet to study ecology, environmental problems, and world peace. And it asks for frank and honest talk between Tibetan and Chinese people to begin.

The unspoken message of this brief proposal is just as clear and direct—you have hurt us; we bear you no ill will for past injustices. We want only what every people wants, to govern ourselves as we wish. Talk to us, so that we all may learn what it is that you really want, let us find out together if it is strategic territory or some dominion of the spirit you have heedlessly sacrificed. Perhaps we can help you return to your true nature. We bear you no ill will, for we are alike in our common humanity, bonded as interdependent arisings on earth. You have hurt us, we have hurt ourselves.

The five-point plans sits there like a work of the imagination, a piece of fiction, a metaphor for both the possible and impossible. This secular text conjured up by a religious man invites us to go back to the imagination, which, after all, brought us to the terrifying state in which we find ourselves and which may also hold the potential to redeem us. Through the imagination we may come to grips with those appearances in our so-called real life that are so bewildering. The Dalai Lama's proposal for Tibet offers the world a mode of thinking so clear that it baffles diplomacy. We should not mistake the plan as solely intent upon rescuing Tibetan culture. Its message is of a global scale. It does not call for the restoration of old boundaries, for it acknowledges the impermanence of all boundaries. Rather, it suggests a tilt to our minds—even more, that our world believe the Einstein equation of our drift toward extinction, that we drop the bomb in our minds and imagine a new way of thinking that might give us some insight into our universal need to transform our seemingly innate cruelty and greed.

THE GOLDEN ROAD

Mr. Fu went at last to visit his old mother. He hadn't seen her since before his journey, but one day she too rose up in his conscience, and he went to the dark little room where she lived. He found her much the same, a sturdy, enduring old woman, with pieces of coral woven into her long braid, still living her fixation about her home near Lhasa—would she ever see it again before she died?

As he looked at her wrinkled cheeks, the image of the tiny old woman who had been called "Mother" on the journey imposed itself upon her face.

Suddenly he thought he ought to put an end to his mother's longing and take her home. The blisters on his feet were completely healed. He could drive again now, and the journey with the powerful visitors had proved to him that it was simple enough to get through checkpoints without being stopped. It would be easy to take her home.

No sooner had this thought come to him than the cloud under which he had been living became somehow transparent. He realized as he looked at his mother's seamed face that the notebook was a relic, that he should not destroy it but should somehow preserve it. Like the power of the bomb itself, it was everything, but it was also nothing. An idea, like other ideas people had found unworkable and turned away from in the past. He thought of the great libraries that had been burned or sacked, the libraries suppressed by China's ancient Emperors, and those ruined in Alexandria and Rome that he had learned about in school. He did not have to live by the invention in the notebook. And these thoughts liberated him, a little bomb going off in his mind. Captain Bao's notebook belonged in an archive, where it might perhaps gather dust for some years, decades, centuries. It was a relic for future generations to study, look back on, and wonder about.

He asked his mother if she knew of a library in Tibet, kept by a

Khenpo perhaps, who would take a valuable document and fold it inside brocade cloth, and put it in a safe place.

Her smile bathed him in Tibetan light. Of course she knew such a place. "Where they keep the innermost secrets," she said.

"Mother," he said, "I'm going to take you home."

He had not seen her so joyous since his childhood. Immediately she started to gather things for travel. She hastened about the city purchasing gifts for old friends she remembered at home. She asked him to tell her what things were in short supply, and she purchased brocades, toilet paper, tea. Mr. Fu marveled at her happiness. He couldn't bear to warn her that there might be a dark side to their journey. They might be stopped along the way. And perhaps the Khenpo's study was not greed-proof. Perhaps the formula would be uncovered in another outburst of persecution, a new Cultural Revolution. He didn't know. But placing his faith in his mother, he would keep imagining he was on the right path. He understood the great gift the monk had given him. In relieving him of karma, he had shown him the way to the only truth.